Chance of a Lifetime
(Chances Are #1)

By P.T. Dilloway

Copyright 2013 by P.T. Dilloway
ISBN-13: 978-1492149552
ISBN-10: 1492149551

Part 1:
The Fall

Chapter 1

Like most events in my life, this story begins in a bar. Squiggy's is my favorite watering hole, the kind of place where a man can get a drink without too much conversation. I motion to Big Al the bartender. "Fill 'er up?"

After seven shots of bourbon a nosier bartender might ask if I've had enough. Not Big Al. He knows the drill well enough after twelve years. He just waddles over and splashes more booze in my glass. Then he returns to his stool to watch a women's soccer game from England, the only game on at four in the afternoon.

I watch the screen for a few minutes, but I don't see the game. Instead I see Maddy at eight years old; she runs around the backyard with our golden retriever Max in pursuit of the soccer ball. "Daddy, watch!" she squealed before she kicked the ball into the refrigerator box she used as a goal.

I down another shot of bourbon. It doesn't erase the memory from my brain like I hope it would. "Could you put something else on?" I say. "I hate this fucking game."

My memory of Maddy turns to one of her face red, tears in her eyes. "How could you do that?" Debbie shouted. She poked me in the chest. "Do you have any idea how much she was looking forward to you being there?"

That was the last time Maddy asked me to go to one of her soccer games. It was the last time she asked me to do anything for her. Six months later I was in a tiny apartment, my stuff still in boxes. That was exactly twelve years ago.

It's my anniversary. Ironic that Debbie and I divorced on the same date as we got married. I plan to get plastered in this grubby bar to mark the anniversary as I usually do. Later I'll drag myself into a cab — or Al will carry me — and I'll pass out on my lumpy bed.

Jake used to be the one to drive me home. He would sit next to me and heroically stick to club soda while I gorged myself on booze. When I needed it, he would second my sentiments about Debbie and her lawyers and the whole cesspool that is the world. But after his daughter was diagnosed with cancer about five years ago, he had other priorities. I don't blame him for that.

Big Al's been here all along. Though tonight, when he thinks I've tortured myself enough, he says, "Why don't you call that daughter of yours? I'll even give you the quarters."

"I don't need your fucking quarters," I say. I reach into my pocket for a handful of change. There are probably a couple of quarters in there, though at the moment my vision is too blurry to know for sure. "Anyway, I don't know where she lives."

"I'm sure you can find out," Al says. "Don't you cops have computers like on TV?"

"Yeah, probably," I say with a snort. Then I wave my hand dismissively. "She don't want to talk to me."

I reach into my wallet and take out a picture of

Maddy in a cap and gown, both newsprint gray. Her face is yellowed because I never bothered to get the clipping laminated. It's the only recent photo I have of her. Debbie's lawyers made it clear that I was not to see Maddy. I can't blame Debbie for that; no sane mother wants her daughter to hang around with a broken-down wreck who smells like rum and lives in a roach-infested flophouse. She could have at least sent me some pictures so I could have something to remember Maddy by.

She's twenty-two now, old enough that I can call her if I want to. She can call me if she wants; I'm listed in the book. That she hasn't yet says everything. I'm not a part of her life anymore, if I ever was in the first place. And for me she's just a ghost that rises every year at this time.

"You better leave the bottle," I tell Big Al and slap down two twenties.

***

I'm not sure what time it is when I hear a familiar voice ask Big Al for some dollar bills. I'd know that whiny, high-pitched voice anywhere, even drunk and nearly passed out. My head is on the bar; I turn it to the right and open my eyes.

Carl Kovacs, aka the Worm in professional circles. The Worm's made a career out of squeezing his tiny body into all sorts of places: windows, air ducts, and even a garbage can once. We could have put him in jail for life about ten crimes ago, but the Worm's other talent is for snitching.

"Hey Worm," I say and give him a little wave. "Whatcha doing on this side of town?"

The Worm's face goes pale as he sees me—paler than usual since like a real worm he rarely sees the sunlight. He drops the money Big Al gives him on the counter. "Shit," he whispers.

I may be skunked, but I'm still fast enough to get off the stool and collar him before he can make it to the door. "Where you going? Can't I buy you a drink?"

"I don't want no drink."

I scoop his money off the counter. "How about a pack of smokes then? That's why you came here, isn't it?"

"I shoulda gone to that fucking chink grocery."

The Worm looks to Al for help. Big Al starts to wipe down a glass. "Try not to break anything, would you? I don't need the insurance on this dump going up."

"Look, I don't want no trouble. I got nothing to tell you," the Worm says.

From the way his mouth twitches, I bet he does have something to tell me. Something big. I drag him over to a stool and shove him onto it. I reach into my jacket for two cigarettes. I put one in his mouth and then catch it before it falls out. On the second try he holds on to it and keeps it steady enough for me to light it.

"You know how it is, Worm. You give me the goods and you keep your ass out of jail." I light my own cigarette and then blow smoke into his face. It's part of our ritual. If he doesn't break then the next step is for me to give him a peek at my gun. That usually makes the Worm think about self-preservation.

"I can't tell you nothing."

"Can't or won't?" I sweep aside my jacket on the left side so he can see my .45 in its holster. He knows it's loaded; he also knows I don't bother to bluff.

"Take your pick. I can't help you this time."

"Then I guess I won't be able to help you." I reach behind me for my cuffs. I give him a nice long look at these. "What's it going to be?"

"I'd rather go to jail. Better there than in the harbor."

I give him a grin, which is easy enough when I'm drunk. "You know what they do with guys like you in prison, Carl? They'll make you into a pincushion. In two months you're going to have to shit standing up."

The Worm takes a drag on his cigarette. He's doing the mental calculations, to weigh his options. I take the opportunity to down another shot of bourbon. The bourbon buzzes me a little, just enough that I can't feel the weight of so much guilt on my shoulders.

"Well?" I prompt him.

He tosses the cigarette on the counter. "All right, but you didn't hear this from me. There's something big going down at Lennox Pharmaceuticals."

"Big in what sense?"

"Big as in Lex is going to be there hisself."

Lex as in Artie Luther. He got the nickname Lex because of his bald head and also because he's a real son of a bitch. We all know he's behind most organized crime in the city. The problem is to prove it; people who try to testify against Lex usually wind up in the harbor with a pair of cement shoes.

"No shit?"

"No shit. Now, can I go?"

"Not yet. When's it going down?"

"Tonight. About midnight."

I check my watch; it's ten o'clock. Enough time to sober up with a few cups of coffee. "Good. Now get lost."

The Worm doesn't need me to ask again. Before he can slime out the door, I say, "You better not call in any anonymous tips. Otherwise you're going to piss me off."

He nods slightly before he leaves. I call Big Al over for a pot of coffee. It'll be a long night.

Chapter 2

The smart thing to do would be to call Captain Archer for some backup, preferably the SWAT team. The only problem with that is ninety percent of the force is in bed with Artie Luther; one of them is sure to give him a tip if I make a call. I ought to at least call my partner. I consider it for a minute before I shake my head. This is one of the few nights of the year when Jake gets to spend a whole night with his wife; one of the few nights when he knows he won't have to bail me out of a tight spot.

Besides, there's always a chance the Worm had lied. He could have given me a bum tip for fun or to keep me out of the way while Lex does his dirty business somewhere else. Might as well go in and then call for backup once the bullets start to fly.

Two pots of coffee and half a pack of cigarettes have cleared my head enough so I can get behind the wheel and not see double. I'm still moving a little sluggish, but by the time I get to Lennox Pharmaceuticals I'll be fine. All I need is the air conditioner on full blast and some Creedence on the stereo to get me the rest of the way to sober.

As "Fortunate Son" comes on, it reminds me of Maddy again. I remember her in the backseat when she was four. She whined, "Daddy, what is this?"

"This is music, honey."

"It's yucky." I popped the tape out and put on her *Beauty and the Beast* soundtrack. That was always her favorite movie; she pretty much wore out our VCR with it. What is her favorite movie now? I don't know. What kind of music does she listen to now? I don't know that either. I don't know a damned thing about her.

I pop the tape out. The radio is set to the local sports talk station. Listening to former or would-be jocks shout doesn't help sober me up, but it doesn't make me dredge up old memories either.

Along the way I try to think what Artie Luther would want with Lennox Pharmaceuticals. Sure there are a lot of chemicals there he could use to make crystal meth, crack, or other drugs. He might even be after some of the machinery. Doesn't explain why he would be there himself. A man with as much money as Lex doesn't need to stoop to grand larceny; he has people for that.

And why Lennox? There have to be a half-dozen drug companies in the area. Maybe he has an in with someone who works at the place, someone who can slip him in there without an alarm.

How did the Worm find out? A job this big has to be on a need-to-know basis and Lex isn't stupid enough to involve the Worm. Could be he overheard something he wasn't supposed to. Or maybe Lex fed him a bogus tip.

It's five minutes later when I get to Lennox Pharmaceuticals. The company made a big publicity splash five years earlier when they renovated an old factory by the waterfront to use as their new state-of-the-art labs. The old smokestacks no longer have any smoke coming from them, but I can see lights on inside. Again I wonder if it's a trap. Or maybe I'm on a wild goose chase.

Under other circumstances it would be easy enough to get inside. I could pull up to the front gate and hold out my badge. These aren't normal circumstances. If the security guard is still alive and conscious then he's in the employ of Artie Luther; to flash my badge would be a quick way to get six feet under.

I have to do it the old-fashioned way. I park the car across the street and hide it behind some old pallets. Before I get out, I make sure I have a couple of extra clips for my gun. I try to look as casual as possible as I walk around the fence. I keep my hands in my pockets and look down at the ground as if I'm just out for a little stroll.

The air still has the reek of rotten eggs leftover from when the factories down here still made transistor radios and car bumpers. The smell is enough to sober me up the rest of the way. The walk feels good too, a little exercise to limber me up before the big event.

As I walk, I steal a few glances at the fence, to look for a weakness. It's a pretty good system, with barbed wire on top of an electrified fence. No way to climb over that unless I want an impromptu appendectomy. It's too low and I'm too fat these days to crawl under it either.

But even the best systems have their holes. In this case it's a rickety wooden pier nobody bothered to fence off; they probably figured it would sink on its own soon enough. Or maybe they figure no one will be crazy enough to try to swim in this water to get on the pier. Usually they'd be right, but if it means I get to nab Lex then I'm game.

I don't have to swim, just wade through waist-deep water. The stuff smells even worse than the air, bad enough to make my eyes water. I hope there's nothing toxic in it to give me cancer or turn me radioactive.

I grab onto the rotten pier. It holds together well enough for me to lever myself onto it. While I lie there, I hear something slap against the surface of the water. A boat is on its way to the pier.

And on the bow, like George Washington in that old painting, is Artie Luther.

Chapter 3

I don't have time to think. I just roll off the dock, into the water. I slide beneath the dock as I hear Lex command his minions to tie the boat up. I claw at the rotten wood until I get a grip between a couple of slats.

While I try not to swallow any of the fetid water or mud around me, I hear footsteps on the dock. I slip one hand into my jacket to pull my gun from its holster. So long as I don't make any sounds, they shouldn't be able to see me down here, but it doesn't pay to take chances.

Between the cracks of the boards, I see a pair of combat boots. The boots step over me but no one calls attention to me. Once the boots take a couple of steps, I can see a pale, gangly man in a black overcoat. Will O'Neill, referred to as "the Tall Man" because of his height and no one could think of a better nickname. He's Lex's top assassin, responsible for at least two hundred deaths and probably a lot more than that.

Another pair of shoes step over where I lie, a pair of work boots. These go past to reveal Bobby Blades. No one's sure if he was born with the name "Blades" or if he gave it to himself; all we do know is that he uses knives like a surgeon. He's O'Neill's polar opposite: brown-skinned, short, and mouthy. "Hurry up, man. Let's get in there already."

"Patience, Robert," Lex says. He wears expensive loafers that would be ruined if someone were to push him off the dock. Someone like me. I'm tempted. The only problem is I don't have anything on him yet except for trespassing. Whatever he's up to, I've got to let it play out before I can intervene.

The last member of Lex's crew shows up a minute later. I know who it is long before I see him just by the way the pier creaks as if it will shatter at any moment. Thomas "Bruiser" Malloy looks like what you get if you shave a gorilla and then stuff it into a tank top and jeans. Malloy used to be a boxer, though never a good one. He's strong as an ox but dumb as a gnat. He can take orders and hurt people, which makes him useful to someone like Artie Luther.

I wait until the dock stops shaking from Bruiser's footsteps before I slide out from beneath the dock. I crawl to the bank and see the moonlight reflect off Lex's bald head. They're heading for the factory. Then that's where I'll go.

My overcoat is heavy with mud now, so I abandon it on the shore. I take off in pursuit of Lex and his boys; I try not to go too fast in case they look behind them. When I see a flash of light from the front gate, I flatten myself against the building.

I peek around the side of the building just in time to see someone lean out of the van that's pulled up to the gate and chat with the security guard. A couple of pops later and the security guard is down. Another tally for the Tall Man no doubt. The truck's tires squeal as it backs up. Soon it's gone. The driver might have got more than he bargained for when he signed on to be Lex's decoy.

I watch from around the corner as they split up. Lex swipes a card in front of a security reader—probably something he picked up from his decoy—and then disappears into the building with Bruiser. The Tall Man and Blades head for the front door. It's choose your own adventure moment. I can follow Lex and see what he's up to or Tall Man and Blades, who will probably take care of the rest of the building's security.

It's not much of a choice. As much as I want to get Lex, I don't want any more innocent people killed. So I get down into a crouch that makes my knees scream and then scurry as fast as I can towards the front doors.

Along the way I take my cell phone from my pocket. Now's the time to call for backup. There's no signal. Shit. Either Lex has jammed the signal or else he bribed the local carriers to "accidentally" lose coverage in this area for an hour or two. You can do stuff like that when you're the mob kingpin of a major city.

For now, I'm on my own.

***

By the time I reach the doors, I hear two soft pops. Another guard down, or else some poor schmuck working late. I peek through the doors to see a pair of feet sticking out from behind a reception desk.

I bolt inside and throw myself against the wall behind the desk. I get a better look at the dead man, a security guard about my age, with a beer gut that spills over his waist. Doesn't even have a gun on him, just a taser. Poor bastard.

I pick up the phone at his desk. The line's been cut. Maybe there's a phone somewhere else in the building that will work. That is if Lex didn't bribe the phone company to turn off those lines too. Only one way to find out.

I turn left and run past a bank of elevators. As I do, I catch sight of Blades and the Tall Man down the hall, at the stairs. I break into a run to catch up to them. I throw open the stairway door. I can hear footsteps below me. I look down and see Blades going downstairs, probably into the basement.

I try to line up a shot from the stairwell, but the angles are no good. I'll have to get in closer to take the bastard down. I descend the stairs as quietly as a guy who's six-three and two hundred thirty pounds can, which is to say not very. It probably sounds like a buffalo is charging down the steps after him.

I stop at the last landing before the bottom of the stairs; the hair on the back of my neck stands up. It's an instinct honed after thirty years as a cop. Turns out my instinct is right; a knife flies through where my head was a few seconds ago. Then I hear a door slam shut.

It's dark in the basement. I'm tempted to get out my cigarette lighter, but that will give Blades an easy way to home in on me. Instead I feel around with my hands like a blind man. It reminds me of when I had to go downstairs in the house I shared with Debbie whenever a fuse blew out.

I shuffle a few yards and then listen for any sounds. All I hear is the creak of machines and the hiss of pipes. I have no idea what Blades would want down here. Does Lex hope they keep some old treasures down here?

After a couple of minutes I see what he's up to. He stands in a wire mesh cage and faces a big metal box with a lot of wires. It's not unlike the fuse box in my basement, except that he's pulling out the fuses. That will take down power to the entire building, to deactivate whatever security they might have.

I get behind Blades, the barrel of my gun lined up with the center of his back. If the shot doesn't kill him, then it'll at least cripple him. I click off the safety. "Turn around slow, Blades. You're going to be sitting out the rest of this dance."

"You can't stop us, pig," he says.

"We'll see about that. Turn around, now. Unless you want to spend the rest of your life pissing into a catheter bag."

Blades starts to turn around. As he does, though, his left hand brushes against a switch. The light in the cage goes out. I pull the trigger; the flash from the barrel lets me see for a moment that Blades is already on the move.

I feel the blade slash across my left forearm. I grunt with pain while I thrash around with my right hand and hope to connect with something. All I get is air. The hair on the back of my neck stands up again. I pick my left foot up and sweep it around. This time I hit something. I hear Blades grunt and the clatter of something metal on the floor.

I reach into the pocket of my suit jacket and take out my lighter. Blades scrambles to his feet. I fire again, but he rolls to the right, his instincts almost as good as mine. He takes another knife out. He wastes little time to throw it at me. I've already dropped the lighter as I dive to the left. There's a sharp pain in my shoulder when I land; I'm not as young and flexible as I used to be.

"Give it up, pig," Blades says.

I'm sure by now Blades has another knife, or maybe the first one he dropped. I don't even have my lighter now to see him. Though unless he's part cat, he can't see me either. The best either of us can hope for is to stumble into the other first.

I do have one advantage, though: Blades likes to talk. "When I find you, I'm going to gut you like a fish. Then I'm going to cut you into little pieces to take home and feed to my dog."

His voice is like sonar I can use to track him down. While he goes on about all the things he's going to do to me, I crawl across the floor to home in on him. I turn my pistol around, to grip it by the barrel. "When I'm done, there won't be enough left of you—"

I silence him with a whack across the neck. It's a good thing I carry a big .45 and not some pansy gun. Though I'm pretty sure I've got him knocked out, I hit him again. I shake him a couple of times to make sure.

I feel around to locate my cigarette lighter. I flick it to life and see Blades passed out on the floor. I take out my handcuffs and attach one to his wrist. Then I drag him over to the edge of the cage. The mesh is wide enough that I can slip the cuff around it. That ought to keep him for a little while.

I make sure to take all of his knives off of him. Then I go over to the fuse box. I try to flick the switch he touched before the light went out, but it doesn't do any good. Something's blown out or else the system needs time to restart.

Either way, I've got to do the rest of this in the dark.

Chapter 4

It's not entirely dark on the second floor. There's a dim red glow in the corridors from the exit signs. That's better than nothing, I suppose.

I find a lunchroom on the second floor. With some help from my cigarette lighter, I see a phone on the wall. No signal there either. The lines are dead. Big surprise.

In the glow of the cigarette lighter, I see blood seep from the wound on my arm. I take off my suit jacket, followed by my shirt. The left sleeve of my shirt comes off easily enough. I tie it around the wound as a makeshift bandage. Then I put my suit jacket back on over my undershirt.

I climb up the stairs to the third floor. As I open the stairway door, I get another feeling. I flatten myself just as I hear the wheeze of a silencer. The Tall Man is up here. Not a surprise since he didn't go downstairs with Blades.

I lunge through the doorway and scurry behind a corner. I peek around the corner to try to catch a glimpse of him. There's only the flicker of a shadow against one wall. This is where I wish I had Jake to help me. With two of us we could use a pincer maneuver to corner him. By myself I'll have to hope I can get lucky.

I can't expect the Tall Man to give himself away by

talking smack either. That's not his style. He won't say a word even as he puts a bullet into me. I'll have to hope he makes some other mistake.

It would be suicide to go around the corner, so I trot down the corridor as fast as I can. There's another corner here. I peek around it to look for any sign of the Tall Man. I can't see anything. That doesn't mean he isn't there.

I start down the corridor and hope for the best. If I'm lucky he'll still be watching over by the stairway, to wait for me to come out. Then maybe I can sneak up on him.

No such luck. I hear the cough of the silencer. I throw myself to the floor just in time. Before he can fire again, I roll to my right. There's a door there. I flatten myself against it and try the knob with one hand. It's locked.

I count to three before I run back into the corridor. Before the Tall Man can get a bead on me, I run back towards the door and barrel into it as hard as I can. The door gives way. I tumble through the doorway and land on my face in someone's office. There's a desk, file cabinets, and a shelf of books with scientific names. A degree on the wall identifies the office as that of Dr. Gita Nath.

I roll over to beside the doorway and then get into a crouch. I count to three before I stick my head around the corner. A second later a bullet almost gives me an impromptu facelift. I jerk my head back before the Tall Man can adjust his aim.

I decide I'd better adjust my position. I make a break for the other side of the doorway. Another bullet hits the tile floor just behind my left foot. That's twice I've gotten lucky. Especially lucky because in the darkness of the hallway, the only way for the Tall Man to have seen me so easily is that he must have a pair of fancy goggles on to let him see in the dark. Since his shots were a little bit off, they're probably infrared goggles that let him see my heat signature.

    I look around the office for anything else that might be of use to end the standoff. Unfortunately Nath isn't the kind of doctor who has a bazooka or flamethrower in her office. The thought of a flamethrower gives me an idea.

    If the Tall Man really does have infrared goggles, then maybe I can give him something else to shoot at. I reach into my jacket for my cigarette lighter. Now all I need is something flammable to light on fire.

    I search through Dr. Nath's drawers, at least those that aren't locked. It turns out the doctor is a bit of a germaphobe, which isn't a surprise given her line of work. In a bottom drawer I find an industrial-sized bottle of hand sanitizer. That should work well enough.

    I dump out the entire bottle of sanitizer on Nath's office chair. Lucky for me it's a cloth one, not leather. Then I wheel it over by the doorway. I'm not religious by any means, but I still say a prayer as I strike my cigarette lighter.

    It takes a moment for the sanitizer to light. When it does there's a whoosh, followed by a burst of blue flame. I drop to my hands and knees behind the chair. Now it's time to put my ruse into action.

    I stay behind the chair as I wheel it into the hallway. Once I get it into the center of the hallway, I drop to the floor. My hope is he'll hit the chair and not me. I get my wish; three shots go through the back of the chair, over my head. Though it doesn't matter, I hold my breath and wait for the Tall Man to check out his handiwork.

    I hear his boots on the tile. I wait for a couple more

seconds before I jump to my feet. He stands in the center of the hallway, the gun still aimed at the flaming chair as I take the safety off my pistol. "Drop it!" I shout. He does so.

I kick the chair out of the way, followed by his pistol. Then I rip the red-lensed goggles from his eyes. He grunts, which for him is like a scream. Maybe I should keep the goggles, but I don't have any idea how they work and there isn't time to learn. So I toss them down the hallway. Then I motion for him to step into Dr. Nath's office.

"Time for you and I to have a little chat."

***

I use the power cord from a lamp in Dr. Nath's office to tie the Tall Man to a chair. His eyes are watery, but they follow me as I pace in front of him. "What's Lex doing here?" I ask him.

When the Tall Man doesn't say anything, I pick up Dr. Nath's stapler. I use it like a brass knuckle to hit the Tall Man across his pale horse face. He grunts with pain, but still doesn't say anything. Jake's not here to play good cop, so I hit the bastard again. "You want to have any teeth left, you better start talking," I say.

The Tall Man still doesn't say anything. I hit him a couple more times. A gash opens up on his cheek. "What's he doing here?" I ask.

When he still doesn't talk, I decide on another approach. I stick the barrel of my pistol between his legs. Even the Tall Man isn't immune to this form of persuasion. "Don't," he says.

"So you can talk. It's a fucking miracle." I take the safety off my pistol. "What does Lex want here?"

"Some drug they're working on."

"Why?" When I don't get an answer right away, I push my gun harder into his crotch.

"I don't know."

"The hell you don't. Unless you want your friends to start calling you the Tall Woman, you better start being cooperative."

"He wants to sell it."

"To who?"

"I don't know." For the first time I see real panic on the Tall Man's face. "He hasn't said anything!"

"I believe you." I pull the gun back a little. "Where is he?"

"Fifth floor."

"Thanks." I take the thickest book off the shelf. I hit him across the jaw with it. There's a snap of bone and a scream. I've probably broken his jaw. He's still conscious, though. Another whack from the book takes care of that.

I leave the book on the desk and the Tall Man tied to the chair. It's time to go find Luther.

Chapter 5

There's no one to welcome me to the fifth floor with knives or bullets. I keep my pistol ready anyway, just in case. I'm not sure where Lex is on this floor or if he's still here. Why he wants to steal and sell a drug is beyond me. Seems a bit penny ante for Lex, given how much he makes off one shipment of coke or heroin or whatever else he's into.

Before I have any more time to consider this, a door beside me flies open. A beefy hand reaches out to grab me by the collar. A moment later I'm airborne. Another moment later, I hit the wall hard enough that my pistol flies out of my hand.

I collapse forward, onto a table. Unluckily for me, the table is covered in all sorts of beakers, tubes, and vials. It's like one of those old Westerns as Bruiser sweeps me along the table; shattered glass cuts my face and chest. I run headfirst into another wall.

Bruiser turns me over so I can look up at him. "Boss says to get rid of you, pig," he says. I'd say something witty, but I haven't caught my breath yet.

He grabs me by the lapels of my jacket and then flings me across the room as if I'm a football. I'm somewhat lucky to land on the floor, instead of on the edge of a counter or anything that could knock me out or break my neck. It still doesn't feel good as I lie there and bleed from dozens of tiny cuts.

Before Bruiser can get me again, I scramble to my knees. Discretion being the better part of valor, I run. Bruiser is big and strong, but he isn't fast. I'm old, slow, and dinged up, but it's still easy enough for me to put some distance between us. I'm not sure where to go; I just know I need a moment to think things over.

I bash through another door; my shoulder screams with pain. I shut the door behind me, although I know it won't do a damned bit of good. Then I turn and nearly give myself a heart attack.

I'm in a zoo. Or maybe a pound would be a better description. There are rows of metal cages all around me. In them I see mice, rats, rabbits, and on up to a couple of chimps. The animals start to get fussy when they see me; the smaller ones hide in the corners of their cages while the bigger ones slam at the bars. Each cage is tagged with a number and a basic description of their purpose. I see a couple with Dr. Nath's name on them.

I don't take any more time to read the labels. Bruiser is dumb, but it won't take him long to find me. I look around for a weapon. I'm about to grab a chair to use like a lion tamer when I see something else, something much more fitting: a tranquilizer gun. No doubt it's so the animals in here can't rebel against their owners.

I use my elbow to bash open the case for the tranquilizer gun. The animals start to go nuts as they watch me load the thing. They say animals can sense when natural disasters are going to happen; maybe that extends to manmade ones too. The door bursts open with a thunderous crack that knocks it off its lower hinges.

"You can't hide, copper," Bruiser says. He takes a couple of steps towards me. I see that he has a length of pipe he probably tore out of a wall.

I kick the cage nearest to me. It's not enough to open the thing, but the lock is weakened enough for the chimp inside to break out. It's a fifty-fifty proposition on whether he'll come after me or Bruiser. Maybe the monkey is smart enough to remember who helped release it, because it goes after Bruiser.

The chimp moves faster than I think possible and then throws itself into the air, towards Bruiser. He swings the length of pipe like a baseball bat and connects with the chimp's skull. The chimp goes down in a heap on the floor. But his sacrifice is not in vain. I use the distraction to pump three darts into Bruiser's back.

He turns to me; he still clutches the now-bloody pipe. He stomps towards me, ready to finish me off. Before he can, his knees wobble. He collapses to the floor, the boxer KO'd by animal tranquilizers. I drop the tranquilizer gun to the floor and then sigh with relief.

I drag Bruiser into an empty monkey cage. It seems a fitting place to leave him.

Then it's off to find Lex.

***

In the lab I find my .45 on the floor. I change out the magazine to put in a fresh one in case the old clip got damaged. I wish I had time to strip down the weapon to make sure it still works, but there's no time. I have to find Lex before he takes off.

As I turn a corner, I hear Artie Luther's voice. "I'm losing patience, Doctor. I want the formula for the serum."

"I don't have it here," a woman's voice says. "It's in my office."

"We'll see about that." There's a hiss of static following this. "Thomas? Thomas, come in." There's nothing but more static. "William? Robert?"

By the time he's done, I'm at the door. "It appears we're about to have company," Lex says.

I spin into the middle of the doorway to pull off a shot that will get Lex in his big, bald head. Instead I see him facing the doorway, an Indian woman in a lab coat pressed against him. Lex has the barrel of a nickel-plated pistol against the Indian woman's temple.

The nametag on her lab coat reads, "Dr. G. Nath." She's the one whose office I broke into on the third floor, where I left the Tall Man. Lex gives me a smug grin as he sees me. "Hello, Detective Fischer. So good to see you again."

"It'll be better to see you at your funeral," I say. Maybe not the best comeback, but I've lost a pint or two of blood. I tighten my grip on my pistol. "Let the girl go."

Dr. Nath's eyes narrow in a way that indicates she doesn't like to be referred to as a girl. Tough shit. This isn't the time for political correctness. "I will do no such thing," Lex says. "You, however, will lower your weapon and let us walk out of here."

"Why would I do that?"

"Because otherwise you'll be responsible for this dear woman's death."

"You shoot her and I shoot you."

"Perhaps." Lex grins wider. "This is what they mean by a Mexican standoff. I trust you neutralized my associates?"

"If you mean that I knocked out your thugs, yeah. All three of them are sleeping like babies right now." I motion to him with my gun. "You might as well join them."

Lex stares back at me. Sweat starts to form on his forehead. "I know all about you, Detective," he says. "You're a brave and honorable police officer. All those commendations and medals. A man like you isn't going to let an innocent woman die."

"Yeah? You want to bet your life on it?"

"Are you ready to bet her life on it?" Lex says. He cocks his pistol. Nath's eyes go wide. She stares at me; her eyes plead with me to do something.

I take a step away from the door. "Go on, you son of a bitch."

"Thank you, Detective," Lex says and I'd like to punch myself for it. He steps out of the room with his human shield turned to face me. He's not stupid enough to give me an opening to shoot him, not unless I want to hit Dr. Nath.

At the end of the hallway, in front of the door for the stairs, she screams, "Help me!"

To walk down five flights of stairs with a human shield is an awkward and slow proposition. So Lex pushes the doctor to the floor to get rid of her. He could shoot her, but in the time that would take, I'd line up a shot on him.

I race down to the end of the hall and kneel down in front of her. She sobs and shivers despite the lab coat. I take off my suit jacket to put around her shoulders. "Thank you," she says.

"You've got to get out of here. Run down to the nearest place that's open and call for the police. Got it?"

"Can't you stay with me?"

"'Fraid not." I take off down the stairs then and hope Nath won't go into shock or blubber until Lex's thugs escape captivity. In the meantime, there's still a chance I can catch Luther.

Chapter 6

I hope to catch Lex on the stairs or at least in the building, but the weasel can run fast when he wants to. I open the stairway to the ground floor in time to see him run through the front doors. I plunge on after him.

There's no getaway car in the driveway, which is a relief. Instead, he heads back towards the pier and the boat he came here on. I'm not quite to the pier when he reaches the end of it. As he unties his boat, I try to line up a shot. It goes wide and hits nothing at all. Jake always says I couldn't hit an elephant unless it stood on me.

The shot does at least get his attention. He fires back at me. His bullet might be closer, but still misses. It does get me to break my stride for a few seconds. By the time I can get a head of steam up again, he's got the boat untied.

He jumps on board as I get halfway down the pier. I try another shot that hits the boat and makes a hole in its hull. He looks up at me and then squeezes off four shots in quick succession. I flatten myself on the rotten pier, which is what he wants.

I hear the boat's engine start up. I'm almost out of time. I push myself to my feet. I run faster than I have in twenty years to the end of the pier. As I reach the end, I hurl myself into the air.

I'm lucky Luther has a small boat, the back of its hull low enough that I manage to land on top of it, next to the motor. I hear something crack—probably a couple of ribs—and groan with pain. The impact also shakes the gun from my hand. I see it on the bottom of the boat as I start to push myself on board.

My ungraceful landing has drawn Lex's attention. He comes back from the front of the boat, his gun aimed at my head. He squeezes the trigger. Nothing happens.

As I reach for the pistol at my feet, Lex lets out an animal snarl. He grabs the nearest thing handy—an oar—and then hits me in the face with it. I groan in pain again and drop to my knees. The oar's shattered in the middle, which leaves a few sharp edges at the end still in Lex's hands.

Before he can use that to slit my throat, I punch him in the midsection. It's his turn to groan with pain this time. I hit him again in the face and the oar falls from his hands. Another punch and he's down on the floor of the boat.

I grab him by the lapels of his suit. "It's over for you, Lex."

"Not yet," he says. He raises his right hand and I see a syringe filled with something pink. Before I can react, he stabs me in the neck with the syringe. He pushes down on the plunger to bury the needle deeper into my neck.

There's a tingle in my neck and then my entire body goes numb. My hands release Lex. I fall backwards, onto the floor of the boat. I stare up at the orange-brown sky that represents night in the city. I desperately want to move, but every muscle in my body is frozen.

Lex's face appears over me. A moment later, so does the barrel of my pistol. "Goodnight, Detective," he says.

I have just enough time to see Maddy's face in my

mind. Then there's a boom and a flash of light.

***

I have the strangest dream. When it begins I'm underwater. It's one of those out-of-body experiences they talk about on television, where I can see myself.

It shouldn't come as a surprise that I've got an anchor chained to my leg. Lex probably chopped off the anchor from the boat so he could weigh down my body to make sure it stays at the bottom of the harbor.

From my vantage I can see I'll have a lot of company. It's already a graveyard down here. I can see one skeleton in a zoot suit, another in a leisure suit, and still another in a tracksuit. I'm a lot more casually dressed in my undershirt and pants.

There's something else I can see from where I hover: the red hole in the center of my forehead, made by my own gun. Makes me wonder why I'm still here if I'm dead. Maybe I'm a ghost. Or maybe this is just a dream. The latter would be preferable; I don't want to rattle around chains for all eternity or whatever ghosts are supposed to do.

I'm not weighted well enough to land on my feet. When I hit bottom I come down on my left side. That was always the side I slept on when I shared a bed with Debbie. Now I just share the bottom of the harbor with a bunch of corpses. I suppose that's an appropriate end to the life of Detective Steve Fischer, world-class screw-up.

It's too bad I'll never get to see Maddy again. I call to mind the clipping I took from the newspaper and try to imagine her face. If I'm a ghost, will I get to haunt her? At least that way I might be able to check up on her, see how she's doing. The only problem is I have no idea where she lives. By now she could be across the country in LA or

Seattle or she might be on another continent, in Paris or London.

As I think about this, a funny thing happens: the wound in my head starts to close. At first I think I must be seeing things, but within a few seconds the hole is gone; only a pink mark remains. Even that is gone after a few more seconds. The rest of the cuts and scratches on my body from the broken glass Bruiser ran me through disappear as well.

My eyes don't open. I don't return to my body. I still lay there on the bottom of the harbor, only now my wounds are gone. Not that it will matter in a few months when I'm a bunch of bones.

Then I notice something else: my hair is growing. Not just growing, but turning from gray back to its natural brown. It gets shaggy like when I was a kid, but then it continues to grow. It grows to my shoulders, far longer than I ever wore it. It just keeps on going until it's halfway down my back.

The hair isn't the only thing about my head that's changing. My face thins, my jaw narrows, and my nose shrinks to lose that gin blossom look. The stubble on my jaw and cheeks turns brown, then to white peach fuzz, and then disappears entirely.

The changes don't stop there. My arms turn thinner as the flab melts away, along with most of the muscle. My hands get thinner too; my fingers narrow until they seem *dainty*. The fingernails get longer, much longer than I ever kept them.

My middle age spread gets smaller and smaller until it's gone entirely. At the same time my waist gets narrower. With this change, my pants and boxer shorts slip off to collect down around my ankles. What the hell is going on?

The answer becomes clearer once my chest changes. Beneath my undershirt, my breasts inflate and become rounder—like a woman's. The wet fabric of my shirt presses against them tight enough that I can see nipples stand out at full attention. From my vantage I get a good look at my ample cleavage.

That all might have been a turn-on if it were happening to someone else's body. But this sick joke is happening to my body. It gets even sicker when my manhood disappears. My penis pulls back like a scared turtle; it crawls back farther and farther until it's retracted inside of me. Skin and hair cover the hole, until there's no trace of it.

My legs are the last things to change. Like my arms, they become thinner, all the fat and most of the muscle stripped away. Even my feet get thinner; they shrink and taper at the same time until they seem as small as my feet when I was ten.

The advantage of these last changes is that the anchor attached to my leg slips right off. My pants and boxer shorts go along for the ride, so that from the waist down I'm naked. Just like that, this new female version of me is free. She floats right towards me. I want to move back, but I can't.

When we merge it's like an electric shock runs through me. The next thing I know, I'm looking up towards the surface of the water. I try to kick, but something heavy restricts me. I realize it's my undershirt, which is now about five sizes too big. I waste precious air grappling with it, until it too sinks to the bottom with the rest of my clothes.

These arms and legs aren't as strong, so it's hard to

see if I'm making any progress at all as I kick and paddle. I keep at it though, desperate to live. My lungs begin to burn; they demand fresh air in them. I think of Maddy again; that helps to spur me along. I keep her face in the front of my mind as I break through the surface of the water—

Part 2:
Reborn

Chapter 7

I wake up to something wet and slimy in my face. I wipe at it with one hand, to push it away from my face. As I do, I feel it all around my head, down my back. I give it a good tug only to feel a sharp pain in my scalp.

I open my eyes at the pain. When I see two full, round breasts, I scream. I've heard enough screams in my time on the force to know a woman's scream when I hear it. I clap a hand over my mouth to try to silence the sound.

It wasn't a dream! What I saw in the harbor actually happened. I hold out my hand and note it's just as thin—as *dainty*—as what I remember from the dream. I touch one hand to my forehead, where the bullet wound was. It's gone.

I should scream again and perhaps run around in circles out of panic. But despite everything else, my instincts are still the same. Instincts honed by thirty years as a cop kick in. I think back to what happened and try to piece a timeline together.

I went to Lennox Pharmaceuticals on a tip. I found Artie Luther there with some of his goons. I got Luther alone. We struggled. He stabbed me with a syringe. My whole body went limp. I passed out. Then that crazy dream. And now—

Now I'm a woman. It seems implausible, but I only need to look down again to know it's true. That syringe. What the hell was in it? Some kind of toxic chemical? Something radioactive?

No, that's stupid. This isn't a *Spider-Man* comic. There's a logical explanation for everything—or as logical as an explanation can get under the circumstances. I need to go back to Lennox and ask what the hell was in that syringe.

Just a couple of problems: first, I'm naked and second, no one will believe me. If I show up there naked and scream about an instant sex change, I'll wind up in the loony bin. That is if I make it that far. It doesn't take long for something bad to happen to a naked woman on these streets.

I take a deep breath to relax, and then try to figure out where I am. I'm on a metal pier. I must have grabbed it when I surfaced and then pulled myself up. The city's skyline looms over me, the skyscrapers still lit up for night. How long until morning? I'd better find some clothes before then. That's my first priority.

The pier I've beached on is actually part of a private marina. In front of me are a dozen small boats. None of them seem to have any people aboard at the moment. Still, maybe I can find something to cover myself with on board one of the boats.

I get to my feet too fast; my head spins. I almost topple back into the water, but at the last moment I grab a metal pole with a reflector on it. I take a couple more breaths to try to collect my strength, such as it is. It doesn't work; I double over and puke into the water. Apparently this girl can't hold her liquor. The gallon of bourbon I drank at Squiggy's tastes three times worse as it comes back up.

I kneel on the pier; a trickle of puke dangles from one corner of my mouth and my entire body shakes. I have to use the pole like a cane to lever myself up. My legs are still wobbly when I take a step, but this time I keep my balance.

My first steps as a woman are hesitant. I still have two legs and ten toes, but my feet are a lot smaller now. These breasts sticking out also shift my balance. The wobbly pier doesn't help either.

I need five steps before I start to get the hang of it. The important thing is not to take too big of steps, to remember that these legs are shorter. Baby steps, I tell myself.

With these baby steps I make it to the end of the pier. Now comes the most difficult part: I have to jump from the metal pier to a cement wall that runs on the side of the marina. It's difficult not only because my body is different, but also because I'm naked. I have to be careful not to cut my bare feet on the cement.

After I size up the situation, I know it's too far to jump. Instead I get up next to the cement wall and then try to pull myself up. I almost fall back onto the pier, but barely manage to keep my balance. With a surge of effort I make it onto the wall.

From there it's easy enough to get onto the wooden docks that run between the boats. I decide to try one of the yachts first; its owners are richer and thus more likely to leave spare clothes around. I can't turn on any lights, so I have to go by the dim lights of the marina and the moonlight.

I feel my way through the galley; my tiny new stomach gives a queasy groan to signal it doesn't want to think about food right now. There's a stateroom past the galley. The bed's made up, which means no one should be aboard.

I search through the drawers beneath the bed and against one wall. Nothing. Not even a sock left behind. The closet yields the same result. Damn it! My face turns warm. Something tickles my cheek. I put a finger to my cheek and realize I'm crying. I haven't cried in thirty years.

"Oh shit," I say, but it's not the gruff voice roughened by years of cigarettes and booze. This voice is high and sweet, like a little songbird. "Shit," I say again.

Out of morbid curiosity I go to the head. I forget about subtlety and turn on the light. In the mirror is a woman's face, her cheeks red and eyes wet. At least those eyes are the same color. They're still my eyes. What's strange is there aren't any wrinkles around them. No crow's feet or laugh lines anywhere. Not even any creases on the forehead. I look as young as Maddy in the picture I kept in my wallet. I wonder again what the hell was in that syringe that could make me not only a woman, but also thirty years younger.

I hold up my left hand; the woman in the mirror does the same. I force myself to smile and so does she. Good Christ, this is real! I brush soggy brown tresses forward to cover up my breasts, like how they paint Eve in images from the Bible. The hair doesn't cover everything, but it's less indecent now. Too bad there aren't any fig leaves for my bottom half.

I click off the light; the woman's image disappears. I wipe at my eyes and sniffle a couple of times. After another deep breath, I go out the way I came in. Then I move on to another boat.

The best I can find after I search five boats is a dark blue windbreaker left on the back of a captain's chair. The man who left it there is the same size as I used to be. From the way the coat fits, I'm at least nine inches shorter than that now. The sleeves dangle as if I'm a child, but the hem of the coat covers up my naughty bits.

I zip up the coat all the way to my chin, relieved that I can't see my breasts anymore. It's ironic that after all the time I looked at nudie magazines I can't stand to see *myself* as a naked woman. I shiver as I think of what any man who finds me like this will do to me; he'll do a lot more than look, that's for sure.

There are some galoshes next to the seat. Like the coat they're much too big for me; they look like clown shoes on my tiny feet. Still, they should protect my feet well enough from splinters, stones, broken glass, and other hazards.

I hurry off the boat. I hear the creak of a gate nearby. I crouch down and try to make myself as small as possible. A man with fishing poles and a tackle box is on the dock. Why anyone would want to fish in this harbor I have no idea. There's probably enough mercury in each fish to fill ten thermometers.

The man whistles a jaunty tune as he boards one of the sailboats. As he gets his boat ready, he doesn't seem to notice me. I wait until he bends down to sprint for the gate he came in from. "Hey!" he calls out, but I don't stop.

Chapter 8

I'm lucky to be on the streets in that rare golden hour when most of the criminals have passed out and the good people haven't woke up yet. The few people around are drunk enough or smart enough to mind their own business. I manage to walk—run really—the forty blocks to my apartment building without any serious trouble. I do hear a couple of belated catcalls, but no one's quick enough to stop me.

Now that I've got my land legs under me, it's easy enough to run in this body. I'm not carrying around thirty pounds of fat anymore. In fact I'm so healthy that by the time I get to the building I'm not winded.

That's just as well because the elevator is broken again, which means I have to climb five flights of stairs. Usually when this happens it takes me the better part of an hour to get up to my apartment after breaks to catch my breath and then lose it again when I smoke a cigarette on the landing. So far I haven't felt any nicotine cravings, though that might change in a day or two.

The obvious problem is my keys are gone along with everything else. I don't really have a plan on how to get inside. It's not like I can ask one of my neighbors to help me out. We weren't on the best of terms before tonight and there's no way they'll believe me now. As I trot up the stairs I just hope to figure out a way inside when I get there.

It turns out someone's already taken care of that problem for me. I see the door open from down the hallway. I instinctively reach to my shoulder, where my gun should be, but only get a handful of jacket over my breast. I flatten myself against the wall so I can approach slowly. That's tough to do in rubber boots several sizes too big.

As I close in, I can see whoever opened the door did an amateur job of it; the lock is busted open with a crowbar. This is intentional, so the police will know it's an amateur robbery and not the work of organized crime. Luther wants to pin my disappearance on a robbery gone wrong so he doesn't take any heat from it.

I stick my head in the doorway. I don't own a lot of stuff, but what I do have is either on the floor or vanished. The TV, VCR, and radio are gone from in front of the couch, which is turned over on the floor. I don't hear anyone inside; whoever did the job has probably left by now. When someone comes to look for me—or Luther plants an anonymous tip—they'll see the evidence of the crime.

And where will I be when that happens? I can sit in here and wait. I could even call the police myself. Then what will I tell them? That Artie Luther shot me up with some weird drug and now I'm a young girl? No one will buy that. If I plead loud enough maybe I can get them to do a DNA test. Would that prove I'm who I say I am? Did the drug change my DNA too? That's much too scientific for me to know.

I need to go somewhere and think things over. Get

some rest, maybe even a shower. First I need some clothes. I step over the pieces of broken glass from pictures of little Maddy on the floor. The bedroom isn't much better than the living room. My entire wardrobe is laid out on the floor, along with the mattress, which has been slashed open. Whoever did this is a real pro; even I start to believe it was a random burglary.

I mount the nightstand so I can see the top shelf of the closet. Damn, he got my spare pistol. That would have come in handy. Nothing I can do now but get some clothes and leave.

There's never been a woman in this apartment longer than a couple of hours, so there aren't any women's clothes around. I find a pair of sweatpants; I have to cinch them so that the string hangs down almost to my knees. I put on a gray T-shirt that looks more like a nightshirt on me. At least it covers me up.

I hear a creak behind me. I turn around just in time to see a gloved fist. All I see after that is a man in a black ski mask before I pass out again.

***

I don't expect to wake up this time. Or if I do, I figure I'll be back at the bottom of the harbor. When I open my eyes, I see it's still my apartment. There are just two differences: it's gotten a lot hotter and the stench of gasoline makes my eyes water.

I roll over and see that whoever knocked me out has covered the living room in gasoline. There's probably more of it throughout the rest of the apartment. He probably thought that knock to the head would keep me out long enough for the fire to do the job. When the fire department gets here they'll just find a charred corpse. Forensics might be able to identify it as a woman's body, but so what? They'll just think it was a vagrant or a hooker or some random girl in the wrong place at the wrong time. No one will give it a second thought. The real me will be a pile of bones while my old pals at the precinct will think I've been cut up and fed to an incinerator.

Except that even as a woman I've got a hard head. Hard enough that I wake up before he figured I would. He didn't even bother to tie me up. Sloppy on his part. And he'd done so well up to that point.

I push myself up; the fire motivates me not to waste any more time. I rush out the door. "Fire!" I scream. I have a pretty good set of lungs on me, enough that the old woman two doors down sticks her head out. "The building's on fire!"

"It is?"

"Yes. You have to get out of here."

She studies me for a moment; she wonders if it's some kind of scam. Then her nostrils twitch and she nods. "I'll get my sweater."

"Forget your sweater. Just go!" I grab the old woman's arm to yank her through the doorway. While she still complains, I run inside to find her phone. I dial 911 and tell the operator about the fire; I give her the address for my building.

The old woman has made it to the stairs when I get there. Along the way I've banged on doors and shouted. Those who don't answer their doors will hopefully do so once they get a whiff of the smoke. If not there's not much I can do about it now.

I let the old woman use me as a cane all the way down the steps. A herd of people passes us by; one gives me an elbow in the face as a reward for my good deed. I keep going; the old woman's fingernails dig into my neck as we round a corner. I want to pick her up and carry her out, but I'm too small for that now. So we have to limp the rest of the way down the stairs.

Firemen meet us on the ground floor. The one who takes the old lady is as big as I used to be. The one who grabs my arm is a bit shorter. "Thank you, sweetheart!" the old woman calls out.

The fireman takes me down to an ambulance for a paramedic to check me out. There's nothing wrong with me except a little smoke inhalation—and a nasty bruise around my left eye. "Boyfriend do that to you?" the paramedic asks.

"No. He wasn't a friend."

"Who was he?"

"I don't know."

"Stay here for a minute, honey," the paramedic says. I know he's going to find a cop. They'll want to ask me a lot of hard questions, questions I don't want to answer. So as soon as the paramedic is out of sight I gallop away on my galoshes.

Chapter 9

I spend the next three hours on a train. It was easy enough in this body to jump a turnstile. Then I found a seat on the half-empty car and closed my eyes. When I wake up we're halfway across the city and the car is packed nose-to-asshole.

From the way people try not to look at me—even in these tight confines—I brush some long hair forward to cover most of the bruise around my eye. Like the paramedic they probably think I took a punch from an abusive boyfriend. Most people don't get involved in those situations if they can help it.

I ride the train until it starts to empty out. As we go along, I try to work out a plan. Now that I've got clothes, I need to get some money. There's an easy way a girl like me can make some quick money, but I don't want to resort to prostitution yet. I can try some old-fashioned begging. The black eye should make me look especially pathetic at the moment.

I get off at the next stop. There's already some longhaired guy with a guitar at one corner of the station. I dig into the trash for an empty coffee cup. Once I sit down at an opposite corner from the folksinger, I put the cup between my legs. I brush the hair back from my eye so it's fully visible again.

When a man in a suit comes near—the first one who isn't on his cell phone—I reach out for the hem of his coat. I hold up the cup to him. "Please, sir, help me. I need money to escape my boyfriend. He's a maniac." I manage to push out a few tears.

The man reaches into his pocket. "Here you go, little girl," he says. I look down to see a five-dollar bill in the cup. That's a start.

"Thank you so much, sir."

I beg for a couple of hours, until I've got about sixty bucks. That's more than enough to get train fare back across town, a hot meal, and maybe a cheap pair of shoes. I never realized the people of this city could be so generous. With my loot shoved into my stolen jacket, I go to buy a ticket that will take me uptown.

***

My next stop is a thrift store. It's in an old department store; I'm faced with what seems like an acre of clothes. The majority of these clothes are for women. I stare at the racks that stretch as long as a football field. A pink football field.

I hold up a shirt only to realize it's a pink tube top. I wince and let it drop from my fingers, onto the floor. I scurry over to the men's clothes, where I feel more at home. I start to browse through the jeans and wonder what size will fit me now. Maybe I should go to the boy's section.

"Buying something for your boyfriend?" a woman asks.

I turn and see a girl a few years older than I look. Her hair is the same color, parted unfashionably in the middle too. We could probably pass for sisters. This thought turns my cheeks warm. The jeans I was looking at fall from my hands.

She picks them up. She looks inside them and then shakes her head. "Your boyfriend must be a big guy."

"Excuse me?"

"A size forty-two? That's big and tall."

"Oh, right," I say and try to laugh. "He is kind of big."

"He always have you do his clothes shopping?"

"Um, no. This is a surprise."

"Right." Like everyone else, the woman looks at my black eye. Then she looks down at my outfit. Before I can protest, she takes my arm and steers me back towards the women's clothes.

"I don't need any help. I'm fine." I yank my arm away from her and then start to stumble towards the rear of the store. "Leave me alone."

The woman puts up her hands. "I'm sorry. You just look as if you could use a little help."

"Well I don't. I'm fine. Just fine." I turn my back on her. I've wandered into the shoe section. I grab a pair of men's sneakers at random.

The woman chuckles at this. "When was the last time you bought yourself clothes?"

"A couple months ago," I say, which is true. I bought some new underwear two months ago—boxer shorts. I see how big the shoes are that I've pulled out and grab another pair that are even bigger.

"You don't have a boyfriend, do you?"

"What?"

"I've seen it before. Your parents bought all your clothes for you. They did just about everything for you, didn't they?"

"I don't know what you're talking about."

"Daddy was a real control freak, wasn't he? Or maybe Mommy had some issue that she liked to dress you up like a boy."

"You're sick, lady, you know that?"

She only smiles at this insult. "Sorry. It's part of what I do. I'm a psychologist. Or I'm studying to be. Haven't finished my dissertation yet."

"Well go analyze someone else, would you?"

She puts up her hands again. "I'm sorry. I didn't mean to insult you. Maybe your parents are very nice people. Maybe you're just doped up or something. Escaped from the loony bin."

"What? I'm not a dope head. Or a nut."

"OK, have it your way. Can I at least help you find some clothes?"

"You work here?"

"No." She reaches into her pocket and produces a business card. It's a powder blue card with the title "Second Chances Boutique" at the top, followed by an address in the garment district, and then her name "Grace Meredith" in smaller print. "That's my store. I come here sometimes to look for bargains. They don't have much that's any good, but sometimes I get lucky."

"Then you mark it up to resell?"

"I know, but that's capitalism for you." She holds out the card until I take it. "We could go back to my shop—"

"No! I'm fine right here," I say. I know all too well what happens to girls in this city who go off with strangers. "I don't need any help."

"Sure, you're a big girl. But maybe I could make a couple of suggestions?"

I think about it for a moment. As embarrassing as

this is, I do need some help. And she'll probably bother me until I give in. "Sure," I say. "But I get final approval."

She finds a pair of sneakers that are dingy white with green trim. The insoles are worn, but the shoes fit perfectly. "How did you know?" I ask.

"Magic," she says with a laugh. Then she pats my back. "It's what I do."

Grace leads me to the women's section. I brace for her to pull out another pink tube top or something girly. She doesn't. Instead, she holds up a black T-shirt. She examines it with a jeweler's eye, as she studies it for flaws. "This looks good." I'm surprised when she presses her nose to the fabric. "Smells fine too."

I take the shirt from her. It does smell all right, though an odor of sweat still lingers. At least it will fit better than what I've got on. "Thanks," I say.

She stops at a pair of pink sweatpants with the word 'PINK' helpfully written on the ass. Grace glances at me and then shakes her head. "That's not really your style, is it?"

"Um, no."

She nods and then keeps going. She pauses at another rack. I brace myself for what she'll find next. What she shows me is perfect. It's a white tracksuit with green piping that matches my sneakers. She gives it as close of an examination as the T-shirt before she hands it to me.

"That looks about your style. I had something like this, only it was an official tracksuit of the '84 Olympic team. That was the year I was born, so it seemed like a great coincidence."

"It's very nice," I say.

"You should go try those on."

Grace points me to the little booths at the back of the store. She waits outside while I try on the clothes; I start with the T-shirt. Everything fits perfectly, as if it were made for me. I do a little turn in the mirror for myself. I don't look too bad—for a girl. At least I don't look like a refugee anymore.

I step out of the changing room to show Grace. She gives me a thumbs-up. "You look great," she says. "Now, we should probably get some other things—"

"No, that's fine," I say too quickly. These clothes will cost forty bucks and I don't want to use up all my money just yet. I still have other things I need to do. "But thank you so much for helping me."

"It was no problem," Grace says. "If you are in the market for anything else, stop by my store. I'll even give you a discount." She winks at me before she walks away and leaves me to check out. I bring my old clothes with me in case I'll need them later. I hope I'll need them later, if someone can find a way to make me myself again. But first things first.

It's time to find my partner.

Chapter 10

When I get to Rosie's, I stop to peer in the window. Jake isn't in our usual booth over in the corner. That makes sense since it's going on noon and by now he's probably figured out my apartment burned to the ground. Does he think I'm dead or just missing? He might think I burned the place down myself after a heavy night of drinking.

Rosie is at the counter; she chews on a piece of gum since she can't smoke anymore. Her husband named the place for her, but ever since he died in a botched robbery ten years ago she's run it herself. It was cheaper and easier to keep the name than to change it.

I sit down on a stool and stare at her for a moment. I've been a customer of Rosie's for twenty-five years, back when Rosie looked about the way I do now. I hope she'll see something in me that's familiar, to recognize me for who I am.

Instead she spits the gum out and smiles a nearly toothless grin. "What'll it be, darling?"

"A cup of coffee, black, with a plate of scrambled eggs and bacon with whole wheat toast." That's my usual when I come to Rosie's. I hope she'll pick up on this, but she doesn't. She just calls the order back to the kitchen and then hobbles off to fetch the coffee pot.

As she pours the coffee, I get more daring. "Have you seen Jake Madigan today?"

She stops pouring to give me a dirty look, like I'm a snitch who wants to get something on her. "You a friend of his?"

"My dad is. I just got into town. I was hoping to see him."

She gives me a hard stare, hard enough that it takes every ounce of courage in my body not to look away. "He stopped in for a cup of coffee. That was about it."

"What about Steve Fischer?"

"He a friend of your dad's too?"

"I know he hangs out with Mr. Madigan a lot."

"Yeah, those two are like an old married couple. Never seen two people so made for each other. Too bad they got the same parts below the waist."

I'm glad she finishes pouring my coffee as she says this so I can use the cup to hide my grimace. I chug the coffee in one gulp before I signal for another. "You shouldn't drink too much of this stuff. It'll stunt your growth."

"I'm already grown."

"Yeah? How old are you? Sixteen?"

"What? No! I'm twenty-one," I say. If I'm going to make up an age for myself I might as well at least make myself old enough to drink legally.

"Huh. Guess that young face will come in handy when you get to be as old as me, right?"

"I guess so." I reach into my pocket for a dollar bill. "Could I get some quarters? I need to make a phone call."

"Sure thing, sweetheart."

I take the quarters Rosie gives me over to the pay

phone in the corner. It's time to try the direct approach. I call Jake's cell phone; I figure he's probably not at his desk right now. The phone rings six times before he answers it. "Madigan here."

I try to deepen my voice to sound mysterious; the end result sounds like I'm gagging. "Detective Madigan, we need to talk."

"About what?"

"I know where Steve Fischer is."

"Who is this?"

"That's not important," I say. The truth—such as it is—isn't the kind of thing I can explain over the phone. It'll be easier to get him here to explain. "Meet me at Rosie's as soon as you can. I'll be in your booth."

I hang up the phone before Jake can say anything. I'm sure he'll show up; he won't write me off yet. Not after being partners all this time.

I take my plate and another cup of coffee over to the booth in the corner. Over the years my ass has worn a groove into the vinyl of the seat; that groove isn't nearly so comfortable now. It feels like I'm sitting in a crater. I try to adjust myself to make it more comfortable, but it doesn't help. The only thing that would help is for me to get my old body back. I'll need Jake's help to see about that.

I've finished the eggs and bacon and am on a second plate when Jake opens the door. He looks around the place, no doubt to search for any of Luther's goons. Then he turns and sees me in the booth. His face turns red around the edges and a vein shows on his forehead, always a good indication that he's pissed off. I can't tell you how many times I've seen that vein throb as he berated me when I worked over a suspect too hard.

"You're the one who called about Steve?" he asks but

doesn't sit down. "I could have you arrested for interfering with an official investigation."

"I'm not interfering. I'm solving the case for you."

"That a fact, Nancy Drew? Then why don't you tell me where he is?"

"Sit down, would you? I'm not one of your perps in the interrogation room."

"You got a real smart mouth on you," he says, but he sits down with a huff. Once he's settled into his groove, he glares at me. "Well, you little punk, where is Steve?"

"I'm right here."

Chapter 11

I've imagined the various ways Jake might respond to my announcement. My first scenario was that he would punch me. Jake didn't ordinarily hit girls, but that might not matter in this case. Or he might simply laugh it off as a practical joke.

What I don't expect is for him to have no reaction at all. He stares at me for a moment and then reaches into his jacket for a stick of Juicy Fruit gum. He offers the pack to me. "No thanks," I say. "I'm still eating."

"Yeah, I guess you are." He chomps on the gum for a minute, his face more impassive than when we play poker. "So what's the gag, kid? You want me to buy some candy bars for your band or something?"

"It's me, Jake. I know it's hard to believe."

"It's not that hard to believe. Let me guess, you were sleeping and some magic fairy came in through the window to sprinkle pixie dust on you?"

"Jake, please, you have to believe me. You're my partner. Partners believe each other without question. Remember the Mackenzie case?"

The Sherry Mackenzie case was one we worked fifteen years ago. It started as a missing persons case when Sherry's mom reported she had been kidnapped. It was the kind of case the media feeds on and thus everyone in the department gets involved in.

Jake and I followed a lead from one of our snitches to a house on the south side. We didn't give a damn about probable cause as we busted inside. We split up to search the house for any clues about Sherry. I took the upstairs, Jake the downstairs. He found what remained of Sherry in the basement.

The owner of the house chose that unfortunate moment to come back from the hardware store with some supplies to help him dispose of the body. I was still upstairs when I heard the shots fired. I ran downstairs to find the man dead in his driveway, garbage bags and a hacksaw in a pile to one side.

Jake knelt over the man; his hands pressed something into those of the dead man. "Christ, Jake, what happened?"

"Son of a bitch came at me. Had to put him down."

I looked down at the dead man. There was a pistol in his hand. Just one problem: I'd seen that gun on the kitchen table when we came in. I knew Jake had shot the man on sight. But I nodded and said, "Right. You didn't have any choice."

That's how we wrote it up too. If anyone had run any tests on the weapon they might have noticed the dead man hadn't fired it. No one goes to that much trouble with a dead child murderer, so Jake got away with it and I never mentioned it until this moment.

His eyes narrow so much that they about disappear from his face. He reaches across the table to grab my arm. His grip is like iron; I can't shake him loose. "He tell you that at the bar last night, you little shit? Or maybe in bed?"

"Jake, stop it! It's me!"

"You the one who burned down his apartment?"

"No! One of Luther's men did it. He's the one who gave me this shiner." He twists my arm until tears come to my eyes. I squeal, "You're hurting me!"

Jake's a tough cop, but he's got a soft heart. That's why he always plays the good cop for interrogations. He lets me go, and settles back into his seat. "Sorry, kid. Steve's my partner. My best friend. Tell me what happened to him or so help me I'm going to put your pretty face through this window."

"How many times do I have to tell you? I'm Steve."

"Stop that bullshit right now. I don't believe in fairy tales."

"You pigheaded son of a bitch. Listen: I was at the bar getting skunked like usual when I saw the Worm. He looked nervous, more so than usual. I collared him and he said something was going down at Lennox Pharmaceuticals. Something big enough that Lex himself would be there.

"I didn't want to tip anyone off, so I went alone to give it a look. He had his whole crew there: Blades, Tall Man, and Bruiser. The Tall Man said Lex wanted a drug they made there to sell it to someone. He didn't know who. I caught up to Lex, we struggled, and then he stabbed me with a syringe.

"I'm not sure what was in the damned thing, some kind of pink stuff. Soon as he pushed down on the plunger I went limp. Lex shot me and then dumped me in the harbor with an anchor around my leg."

"So Steve's at the bottom of the harbor?"

"No, you idiot! I was at the bottom of the harbor. Then the hole he put in me closed up. I started changing. I became, you know, a girl. When I woke up I was on the docks. I made my way back home, where one of Luther's guys was ransacking the place. He knocked me out and then burned the place down. I got out just in time.

"Once I got some clothes and stuff, I called you. I thought you might believe me." I hate myself when I begin to sob. It's the female hormones I bet. "You're the only one I can talk to about this. You have to believe me."

Jake shakes his head. "That's the dumbest story I've ever heard. You got anything to back it up before I take you to the psych ward?"

"There was a scientist there, a Dr. Nath. Talk to her."

"Great idea, except we found her with two slit wrists this morning."

"Well isn't that convenient?" Neither of us says anything for about a minute. "Look, Jake, you're not a dummy. Someone raids Lennox, Dr. Nath winds up dead, I go missing, and my apartment burns down—you really want to tell me it's not connected?"

"It's a long way from that being connected to some mystery drug turning my partner into a little girl."

"Damn it, I'm not a little girl!" I shriek this loud enough that everyone turns to look. If I could see my face I'm sure it would be beet red—except my bruised eye.

Jake reaches across the table to grab my hand, although this time he's not so rough. "Come on, kid. Let's go talk somewhere private."

Chapter 12

Jake's '57 Fairlane 500 is his pride and joy. I never cared about cars, but Jake is different. Jake came here from suburban Detroit; his father worked on the assembly line at Ford for thirty years. That gave Jake a much different perspective on automobiles, so that he spent most of his off time in the garage with the car. It's pretty much his second kid—his only kid now.

He guides me roughly onto the passenger seat; he just about bangs my head on the doorframe in the process. I've spent plenty of time in the car during stakeouts and whatnot; it always felt so cramped before, as if my head would pop through the roof or my legs start to cramp at any minute. Now my head has a few inches to spare and I can stretch my legs out if I want.

Jake gets behind the wheel, but he doesn't put his keys in the ignition. He reaches into his jacket for a cigarette. It's still legal to light up in your own car, so he does. "You smoke?" he asks.

"I quit," I say.

"There's strike one, kid. Steve smokes two packs a day."

"Yeah, well, *this* Steve quit this morning."

He blows a little smoke my way on purpose. I cough

at it; I don't miss the stuff in the slightest. After a couple of drags, he says, "You like game shows?"

"You know I don't watch those."

"That's a point for you. Let's see how much else you know about Steve. Where did he go to college?"

"Trick question. I didn't go to college."

"Right. Where did we first meet?"

"The 17th Precinct. Back when it was still in the old colonial building. I'd been there two months already when you showed up. Our lockers were next to each other."

"Right again. What's my wife's name?"

"She goes by Tess, but her real name is Teresa Marie Madigan nee Nagel."

"The judges will accept that." I can see the vein on his forehead start to pulse. He's going to start asking some harder ones. Bring it on. "All right, kid, time for the lightning round. What was the stripper's name at my bachelor party?"

"Carlita. She had a little surprise hiding in her piñata too."

"Which was?"

"Her real name was Carlos." It's no surprise Jake would think of that after the story I told him. But where Carlita was just a man in drag, I'm all woman, except in my brain.

"Who found that out?"

"Captain Kinsey. He got a little more than he bargained for with his lap dance."

The vein on Jake's forehead beats like crazy now. "Where does my daughter go to school?"

"Another trick question. She doesn't go to school anymore."

"Why not?"

"She's dead."

"How?"

"Leukemia. She died two years ago—August 19. The doctors gave her six months, but she fought like a little hellcat. She lasted three years."

Jake's eyes begin to water as I'm sure he thinks of those awful days, when his daughter, once a talented softball player and gymnast, became little more than a pale sack of bones. "What were her last words?"

"Jake, stop this—"

"If you really are Steve then you'll know."

"She asked you to close the window because she was cold." But the window wasn't open and she had three blankets and a quilt on her. I had slipped out of the room then; I knew she was leaving us and unlike the other times she wouldn't come back.

Jake wipes at his eyes. "You're good. Real good. But he could have told you all that."

"I'd never tell anyone about Jenny, no matter how drunk I got. You know that." I put a hand on Jake's shoulder; he doesn't brush it away. "Look, I'll be the first to admit it's a crazy ass story. If things were reversed I wouldn't believe it either. But it is happening."

Jake stares at me for a moment. Then he nods. "Yeah, that or you've done a hell of a lot of homework on the bastard." Jake snuffs out his cigarette. He reaches for another one, to buy time while he thinks. "What I don't get is why you look so young. Shouldn't you have changed into a woman the same age?"

"I don't get it either. Maybe someone at Lennox does."

"I already told you Nath is dead."

"So? She must have assistants, or at least some notes that might help explain what that stuff was Lex put in me. There has to be something there we can use."

"Maybe not. The captain's got Woods and Jefferson down there with the forensics people. They've probably pulled the place apart by now. Even if they haven't, I can't bring a civilian in there, especially not a kid."

"I'm not a kid!" I give Jake a punch in the arm, like we used to do in the locker room. We took pride in giving each other bruises. I doubt he would get a bruise from that punch.

"You're a kid to me." He lights up his cigarette. "You look about the same age Jenny would be now."

"About the same age as Maddy too," I say. Unwelcome thoughts creep into my head about what to tell my daughter and ex-wife about this situation. "Have you told her or Debbie anything yet?"

"Not yet. They're bound to hear about it eventually."

"Unless we can figure out how to get me back to normal."

"Yeah." Jake sticks his key into the ignition. "Better buckle up, kid."

Chapter 13

Lennox Pharmaceuticals looks a lot different in the daylight. Mostly because it's surrounded by police vehicles. There's a uniformed officer at the gate who waves us through once Jake shows his badge. I look around for my car, but it's probably already in the river or scattered around a dozen chop shops.

Terry Woods stands outside to smoke a cigarette and talk on his cell phone. In a black suit with a silk purple shirt he looks like he just got out of a nightclub. He holds up a hand to stop us before we can sneak inside the building. "Nothing so far, Captain. Place has been wiped clean. We'll keep looking." Woods lowers his hand once he turns off the phone. "We got this under control Madigan. What's with the kid?"

"My niece St—Stacey," Jake says and just like that I've got a new name. "She's studying criminology in college so I thought she might like to see how real cops do business."

"Yeah, well, the first lesson for her is we don't allow civilians on crime scenes."

"Come on, she's not going to touch anything."

"This is my scene and I say who sees it and who doesn't."

Any other time I'd rear up to my full height like a

grizzly bear and then intimidate Woods until the little prick backs down. I can't do that in this body and Jake doesn't have the heart to back down a fellow detective.

Or usually he doesn't. This time, maybe sensing the gravity of the situation, he gets so close to Woods that their noses almost touch. He pokes Woods in the chest with an index finger. "I'm the senior detective here and I'm saying she can go inside." He pulls his finger back and adds in a friendlier voice, "I'll take responsibility for her with the captain."

I worry that Woods will hold out, but he's never liked the rough stuff. He wouldn't know what to do with a snitch like the Worm unless it were written in some fancy journal. "Fine, but if she contaminates anything it's your ass."

"You've probably contaminated everything already," Jake grumbles as we walk away. He puts a protective arm around my shoulder to steer me past the other cops around the building.

"Stacey?" I whisper to him.

"I used to have an aunt named Stacey. You got something better in mind?"

I catch my reflection in the elevator doors as we approach them. Do I look like a Stacey? I sure as hell don't look like a Steve. "No, I guess not."

***

We start on the third floor, in Dr. Nath's office. Most everything has been taken already, the file cabinets and drawers emptied of papers that might prove useful. The chair where I tied up the Tall Man lies in one corner, along with the slashed remains of the electrical cord I tied him up with. There are cards left on the carpet and desk to mark the spots of the Tall Man's blood.

"Doesn't look like much left here," Jake says.

"There might still be something that would help," I say. I'm about to go over to the desk when Jake puts out a hand; he inadvertently cops a feel of my right breast. Our faces turn red at the same time.

"Sorry," he says, "but you can't touch anything. We don't want your prints getting all over."

"My prints are already all over." As soon as I say this, I get an idea of how I can prove to Jake I am who I say I am. All I need to do is to find some of my old prints so I can compare them to my new ones.

I see the perfect device for this on the floor, next to a potted plant. It's the book I clubbed the Tall Man with, some of his blood still on the gilded edges. Before Jake can stop me, I bend down and pick it up by the sides. I leave it on the desk for later.

There's a box in the corner with the mundane office supplies from Dr. Nath's desk. This includes her tape dispenser. I roll out a few pieces to use for my test. The first one I press against my left index finger. The next three I press against the cover of the book.

The third piece of tape is the charm. I hold it up triumphantly to Jake. "Here's the proof."

"A piece of tape?"

"No, my fingerprints. Look." I lay the strip with my old print on the desk, next to the one I took off my hand. Since my finger is smaller and skinnier, they aren't the same size. The whorls of the print are the same, though. "You see?"

Jake studies both pieces of tape. After a long moment of deliberation, he nods and then sighs. "Yeah, I see it," he says.

"Now do you believe me?"

"Not yet."

"Why not? You think I could fake that? You were standing right here the whole time."

"They might look the same to me, but I'm not one of those forensics nerds with a microscope," Jake says.

I shake my head. What's it going to take to convince him? "Can I look around here now?"

"Knock yourself out," he says.

We search the office, but there's nothing of value, just like I thought. I can feel the tears start to come back, but I manage to repress them. There's still plenty of building left to search. "Come on," I say. "Let's go upstairs."

***

There's no one in the lab on the fifth floor where Bruiser used me to play squash. The doorway is barred by yellow tape that we duck under. No one's cleaned up the broken glass yet, so we have to watch our steps.

I tell Jake about what happened in here. "He shoved me along that counter, into that wall," I say.

"Jesus," Jake says. He bends down to study the counter. "Is that your blood?"

"Probably."

He picks up a piece of glass not stained with my blood. "Hold out your finger."

"Why?"

"Just do it."

I hold out my right index finger to him. A moment later, Jake slashes the glass across the end of it. "What the hell did you do that for?" I shout at him as drops of blood trickle onto the counter.

"Watch this," Jake says. He dips a piece of glass into the blood. Meanwhile I stick my finger in my mouth. Girl blood tastes the same as boy blood as far as I'm concerned.

So much for that rhyme about sugar and spice. "Looks like we found some evidence."

I smile at this and see what Jake's doing. To ask the forensics people to take a sample of my blood would raise a lot of questions. This way forensics will think it's part of the crime scene. If my blood is the same as both Steve and Stacey then there won't be any note. If my girl blood is different from my boy blood, then forensics will make a note of an unidentified person at the scene.

"Let's hope you're who you say you are," Jake says.

"Yeah, let's hope."

***

Our last stop is Dr. Nath's lab, where Lex used her as a human shield. Jefferson munches on a donut in there—there's a reason for that old cliché. With his other hand he checks something on his phone. He must have been woken up for this; the buttons of his shirt are misaligned, so that I can see some of the pale flab of his stomach through the gaps.

"Woods said you were coming up here with someone." His beady eyes narrow as he stares at me. "I didn't realize it was Take Your Niece to Work Day."

"Yeah, well, I thought it'd be nice to have someone with brains at the crime scene," Jake says.

When Jefferson snorts, it makes him seem more piggish than he already is. "Brains, huh? She even out of diapers yet?"

"I'm twenty-one, asshole," I snap.

"She's got a real mouth on her."

"She gets that from her uncle," Jake says. "You mind if we have a look around?"

"Yeah, I mind. This is my scene."

"We're just borrowing it for a couple of minutes."

"Why? You and Nancy Drew planning to crack the case?"

"There might be something you missed," Jake says.

Jefferson sneers at this. "I forgot you and Steve are the real hotshots around here. Or *were*, I should say. Looks like Steve finally got in too far over his head."

"Listen you son of a bitch, that's my partner you're talking about," Jake says. The vein on his forehead begins to pulse while his fists clench.

I put a hand on his midsection. Much as I'd like to see him clean Jefferson's clock, I don't need Jake getting suspended right now. "Don't fight, Uncle Jake. Please?" I say in my sweetest girl voice.

He puts an arm around my shoulder. "We're not going to fight, honey. Are we?"

Jefferson stares back at Jake for a moment. "Yeah, that's right, kid. We aren't going to fight. I was just going to make a call anyway."

"Probably to call for a pizza, the fat bastard," Jake growls after Jefferson's gone. He lets go of me so I can look around Nath's lab.

Like her office, there isn't much to find. The stuff Jefferson's deemed important has already been taken. What little remains is written with so much jargon that it might as well be in Chinese. I toss a few pages to the floor. The tears finally start to flow. "It's hopeless," I say. "There isn't anything here. Even if there is, I can't understand it."

Jake pats me on the back in fatherly fashion. "Don't give up yet. Nath had to have some people working for her, some assistants. One of them might be able to help us."

"Maybe," I say with a sniffle.

"We'll check out the files. OK?"

"OK."

Jefferson waits in the hallway for us. "So you crack the case?"

"Not yet," Jake says. "What happened to all the files?"

"They're down in the truck."

"Great. See you around, Stu."

Before I can leave, Jefferson holds out a business card smeared with chocolate frosting from his donut. "You think of anything else, kid, you call me."

"Yeah, I'll do that." I stick the card in a pocket, but drop it in a trash bin as soon as we're out of his sight.

***

"Jesus Christ," I hiss as we come out on the first floor. "Can you believe the nerve of that guy checking me out? If you weren't there he'd probably have tried to fuck me in a closet."

"You know how hard it is for Stu to meet women," Jake says with a grin. "Not every day he gets to talk to a pretty young woman who still has a pulse."

"You think I'm pretty?"

"If you cleaned up a little. And once you get rid of that bruise."

"Gee, thanks."

"You'd rather I said you're ugly?"

"I might."

"Fine. You're so ugly we ought to put a bag over your head."

"Thanks."

Woods has moved all of ten feet since the last time we saw him. "Stu said you want to look at the files?"

"Yeah. We need to know about a Dr. Nath. She

turned up dead in her tub this morning. There might be a connection."

Woods shrugs. "Look at 'em if you want. Just keep the kid from touching them. I don't want her prints all over everything."

"It'll be like she's invisible," Jake says.

The files are in a delivery truck, packed into boxes. Poor uniformed bastards probably spent all morning on that. Most of the information is on the computers anyway, but you can't take chances when it comes to crimes like this.

I ignore what Woods said and help Jake rifle through the files. It takes us a good hour to find one with Nath's name on it. The file is for a project of something with the memorable designation FY-1978. There's only one slip of paper left in the file, a memo from four years ago that indicates the drug is about to undergo animal trials. Included in the memo is a list of the personnel involved, with Dr. Nath's name at the top. Below it is Dr. Clarita Palmer, the assistant project coordinator. Jake scribbles down the names so we can look them up later.

After he returns the file and says goodbye to Woods, Jake and I head back to the car. "We should probably find this Dr. Palmer before Luther does," I say.

"You think he's going to go after everyone who worked with Nath?"

"He might if he thinks they have something that could help us."

Jake turns to look me in the eye. "Does Lex know what happened to you?"

"No. I was in the water when it happened. He hasn't seen me since."

"Then Palmer will keep."

"You think."

"He's already bumped you and Nath off; any more is going to look suspicious."

"More suspicious."

"Yeah. He's drawing enough attention to himself already with that little crime spree."

"So what are we going to do?"

"I'm going to take you home."

"My home burned down, remember?"

"My house. Tess can look after you while I check out these names."

"I don't need looking after."

"Yeah, well, you need a shower. And some sleep. You look like hell."

"I thought you said I look pretty."

Jake shrugs. "Even pretty girls can look like hell."

I try to fold my arms over my chest, but my breasts get in the way. I have to fold my arms under them. "You just want me out of the way."

"Yeah, I do. We're lucky we got away with what we did back there. I can't take you into the station and try to run that bullshit past the captain."

"So what do you want me to do: sit around and play with my dollies?"

"I want you to get some rest. Maybe you'll remember something helpful." Jake flashes a tired smile. "Please, Steve. I'm just trying to look out for you."

"Yeah, maybe." I reach out to poke his arm. "As long as I'm there when you talk to Palmer or anyone else, OK?"

"Deal." Jake makes a left turn and we head to my new home.

Part 3:
Growing Pains

Chapter 14

Jake's house is a split-level ranch, the kind en vogue with the parents of the Baby Boomers. I had one like it, only with black trim instead of blue, but Debbie got it in the divorce. She turned right around to sell it for a trendy condo closer to downtown.

Jake puts an arm around my shoulders as he walks me to the door. His wife opens it before Jake can. Tess always did have a good set of ears on her. That came in handy whenever Maddy came over for a play date with Jenny.

Tess looks a lot older than back in those days. Her hair went gray during Jenny's cancer treatments and she began to cut it short out of solidarity with her daughter. The wrinkles that settled in on her face back then have only deepened. The sweater and pants she wears add to her grandmotherly appearance.

"Who's this?" she asks. She sounds as if I'm three years old and she's about to pinch one of my cheeks.

"This is Stacey—" Jake looks around and sees an ad in the mailbox that proclaims, "Last Chance to Save!" "Chance. Stacey Chance. She's a witness in a case. I thought she could stay here for a few days. Just until we can find somewhere more permanent."

She gives Jake a look to indicate she's not happy to be put on the spot like this. But Tess is a good Christian woman; she won't turn away a young girl who's obviously in trouble. "Of course she can," Tess says. She offers me a hand that's as wrinkled as an eighty-year-old's and dotted with liver spots. I take the hand to give it a brief, polite shake. "It's good to meet you, Stacey."

"You too," I say. I've spent literally months around Tess over the last thirty years, so it's tough to act as if we're strangers. "This is a lovely house."

"Yes, it is." Tess puts a hand on my shoulder to pry me away from Jake. She takes me down the hall to show me the living room. It doesn't look any different than it did three years ago, after Jenny died. The only difference is the magazines on the coffee table are updated, *Redbook* instead of *Seventeen*. Tess sits me down on the couch. "Would you like anything to drink? Maybe a snack?"

"I'm fine."

Jake clears his throat. "I thought she could use Jenny's room while she's here. She'll need to borrow some clothes too."

Tess's wrinkles shift as she frowns. She still dusts Jenny's room every day and keeps everything the same, as if she expects her daughter to come through the door at any moment. The way her mouth twitches, I know she's torn between her duty a good hostess and her love for her daughter. The former wins out. She smiles and says, "Yes, of course. Our home will be your home for as long as you're here."

"Thank you so much, Mrs. Madigan," I say.

"Call me Tess, please."

"I'll try not to be too much of a burden."

"I'm sure you won't be, dear." Tess pats my knee

gently. Then she leaves me alone in the living room while she goes to talk with Jake privately. I can imagine their discussion is far less cordial. I wish I could hear it so I know what sort of story Jake is feeding her about me.

When they come back a few minutes later, Jake's face is red. Tess's eyes still burn with anger, but she forces herself to smile at me. "Why don't I show you upstairs?" she suggests.

"I'll see you later," Jake says. "After I check out a few things down at the station."

"Thanks," I say. I want to linger a bit longer, but Tess has already started to drag me up the stairs to lead me to Jenny's room.

***

The walls of Jenny's room are pink, but the posters are for bands called Fallout Boy and My Chemical Romance, bands of boys dressed in black who wear more mascara than a cheap whore. It's hard not to notice how neat and tidy everything is; all of Jenny's softball and gymnastics trophies shine as if new. "Will your daughter mind me using her room?" I ask. I hate to do it, but I need to sell my cover.

"Jennifer died two years ago," Tess says.

"I'm sorry."

"It's all right. You didn't know." I did know, but I can't say anything or else I'll give myself away.

"What happened to her?"

"She had leukemia. She fought as hard as she could, but in the end—" Tess begins to cry, which makes me want to give my other eye a nasty bruise for hurting her like this.

"I'm sorry," I say again.

"It's not your fault." Tess turns away to go over to

the closet. She pulls open the doors so I can see dresses, blouses, and jackets hanging up with rows of shoes on the floor. "You can borrow whatever you want. I think Jennifer was about your size."

"That's very kind of you, Tess."

"The bathroom is two doors down the hall, on the left. The hot water sometimes takes a few seconds to get started. Are you allergic to anything? Jennifer was terribly allergic to peanuts; just touching one shell would make her break out."

"I'm not allergic to anything," I say. I hope this is still true. I guess we'll have to find out the old-fashioned way, by trial and error. "Whatever you make will be fine. I'm not picky."

"I don't suppose you would be after such a rough life," Tess says. She touches the bruise on my eye. "I think we have a steak in the freezer I could put on that—"

"It's fine. I can't even feel it."

"You poor dear. Why don't you get a shower and then take a little nap? I'll wake you for dinner."

"That sounds great."

"Towels are in the closet next to the bathroom."

"Thanks."

I watch Tess limp out the door and wonder if anything at Lennox Pharmaceuticals might bring back the vibrant young woman Tess used to be.

***

It's a new adventure to shower as a woman. For one thing there's a lot more hair I need to wash. I ought to get it cut as short as Tess's to make it easier. As it is now, I scrub at it for a good five minutes before I decide I've got everything. I never bothered with anything like conditioner back then either. From the commercials on TV

I know you're supposed to use it if you don't want split ends and whatnot.

More worrisome than my hair are my new private parts. I run the loofah over my breasts and wonder how hard I'm supposed to scrub them. I decide not to bother too much with them for now. As for between my legs, I give the area one halfhearted swipe.

When I step out of the shower I catch my reflection in the mirror. I look about the same as when I woke up on the dock, with my hair a dark, wet mess. I'd try to put it up in a towel the way Debbie used to do, but I don't have any idea how. I push the hair back from my face and then try to smile. It's still hard to believe that this is me—will be me for the foreseeable future, unless that drug wears off. I wonder what Jake is up to, if he went to talk to Dr. Palmer without me. He wouldn't do that, not after I made him promise.

I wrap a towel around my midsection to keep my breasts covered. There's no one to see me as I run down the hall from the bathroom to Jenny's room. I slam the door shut before Tess can see me.

Jenny's brush, comb, and other accessories are on the vanity. I don't want to touch them. I don't want to wear her clothes either, so I get back into the ones I bought from the thrift store. I suppose at some point I'll have to break down and do it, just not tonight.

I do allow myself to slither beneath Jenny's blankets and put my wet head on her pillow. I lie there in the darkness and think of Maddy. I wonder what's become of her. Not anything as serious as cancer I'm sure. Debbie would have told me that if nothing else. Wherever she is, whatever she's doing, I hope she's happy.

I don't remember when I fall asleep. When I wake

up, Tess is gently shaking my shoulder. "Stacey, dinner is ready," she says. "If you're not feeling up to it—"

"I could eat," I say.

From the clock I see I've been asleep for five hours. My head is still damp; I guess this much hair takes a while to dry. "Oh my," Tess says. My pulse quickens as I wonder if there's been some kind of side effect from the drug, if maybe I'm starting to change back to good old Steve Fischer. No such luck. She adds, "Such a pretty girl."

We stand in front of the mirror; I look like her granddaughter by comparison. Tess smoothes wet tendrils of hair away from my face. "There now," she says.

"Thanks," I say. I've still got the black eye to mar the scene.

Jake waits for us downstairs in the dining room. "You clean up nice, kid."

"I guess so," I mumble. I'd like to talk to Jake about the case, but Tess steers me over to a chair between them at the table. She begins to ladle mashed potatoes onto my plate before I can say anything. Brown gravy follows; it drenches the mountain of potatoes. The slab of meat loaf she puts in front of me is as big as a brick.

For a girl I have a good appetite, so that I've polished off half the mashed potatoes on my plate before Tess has touched hers. From the corner of my eye I can see Jake watching me to find a sign of his partner and not some runaway girl.

"How did it go at the station?" I ask.

Tess clears her throat. "We don't talk about business at the table," she says.

"Oh. Sorry."

We eat in silence for a couple of minutes. From the looks Jake and Tess give each other, I wonder how silent their dinners usually are. Jennifer's death had changed a lot, especially with Tess. When Debbie, Maddy, and I used to come over, Tess would always have some new joke or funny anecdote. Since Jenny got sick, more than Tess's hair had turned gray; her whole outlook on life had become muted as well.

"So what did you two do while I was gone?" Jake asks.

"I took a shower and then fell asleep," I say, not much in the mood for conversation either, at least concerning non-business-related subjects.

"Good," Jake says. "I bet that bed is a lot nicer than your old one."

"I didn't have much of a bed before," I say. "Most of the time I slept on benches or in boxes. Sometimes just on the ground if it wasn't too muddy."

"You poor dear," Tess says. "I can't believe anyone would abuse such a beautiful child. Especially not one who's so well-mannered and sweet."

This is the first time anyone—even Debbie—has referred to me as "sweet" before. My cheeks turn warm at the compliment. "They weren't very nice people."

"I'll say," Jake grumbles. "Of course we see all kinds in the precinct. Had a mother who tried to—"

Tess clears her throat to cut Jake off. "I don't think she needs to hear about that."

"I'm not some naïve innocent," I say. "I've seen some pretty rough stuff since I left home." I touch my bruised eye for emphasis.

"Yes, of course. I didn't mean to say you were, dear. I just don't think you need to hear Jake's horror stories.

Let's talk about something happier. I was reading an article in *Redbook* about a mother and daughter who were reunited after fifty years. Can you believe it?"

Something of the old Tess—the young Tess really—comes back to her as she describes the article she read. "This mother and daughter had been separated during a flood in Mississippi when the child was three years old. Fifty years later, she started working at a nursing home and there was her mother! It's amazing how these things can happen. So much more than coincidence, don't you think?"

"I guess so," I say. I had given up on religion after Debbie and I split up. Jake lost his passion for it after Jenny died. Tess still believes though. I suppose it's because she wants to believe Jenny is up there in Heaven.

"Of all the nursing homes in all the world and she walks into mine," Jake says. "It's unbelievable."

Jake and I could tell Tess an even more unbelievable story, but we don't. We finish our meals in silence. I've polished off everything Tess gave me, plus seconds on all of it. If I continue to eat like that, I'll lose my girlish figure in no time. That might not be such a bad thing.

Jake stands up first. "Let's let Tess take care of the dishes while we talk in the study."

"Sure. Where is the study?" I ask, to play to my cover.

"I'll show you."

He takes my arm and leads me to his study, where he locks the door so we can have some privacy. "I found Dr. Palmer," he says.

"Is she dead?"

"Not so far. She'll meet us tomorrow at her place."

"Great. What else?"

"I leaned on the boys at the lab about those blood samples." He pauses dramatically; I'd like to punch him in the arm for that. "They're the same type."

"Now do you believe me?"

"It's not definite," he says. "There are still more tests. But I'm closer to believing you."

"Thanks. You find out anything else?"

"Sure did." He opens up some files he took from the precinct and we get to work.

Chapter 15

I'm about to turn out the bedroom light when I hear a knock at the door. "Are you decent?" Tess asks through the door.

I open the door for her. Right away she clucks her tongue and then shuffles past me, over to the dresser. I watch as she rifles through a drawer and finally takes out something pink. She shakes out a nightgown with a lacy collar, the kind of thing I wouldn't wear if someone put a gun to my head.

"Here you are, dear. This should fit you just fine."

"I'm OK like this," I tell her. I still have on the pants of the tracksuit and the black T-shirt. That's more than I usually wore in my apartment. As a man I would strip down to my boxers unless I was too tired or drunk, in which case I'd crash face-first onto the bed until I woke up in a puddle of drool the next morning.

Tess clucks her tongue again. She seizes my hand, her grip even stronger than her husband's. She drags me over to the vanity. "Sit," she says as if I'm a dog. Like an obedient dog I sit on the stool and face the vanity.

"What—?" I start to ask until she grabs a brush and starts to run it through my hair.

"I know things have been very difficult for you," she

says as she works, "but it's time you start to take care of yourself. You're not a street urchin anymore."

It's amazing the change she works on my hair with the brush. Where it had been snarled and dull before, now it's smooth and shiny, like one of those models in shampoo ads on TV. I'm not sure how she did it; she must be a miracle worker. "Yes, ma'am," I say.

"I want you to change out of those clothes. I'll put them in the wash for you to get out some of that smell."

"That's kind of you, Mrs. Madigan—"

"I don't want to hear any arguing about it. If you ever want to make something of yourself, you have to stop looking and acting like a street person." Tess brushes a tress of my hair forward to cover up part of my eye. "We'll see what we can do about that. I think with a bit of makeup we can cover most of it up, let the world see just how pretty you really are."

"Thank you, Tess."

"You're welcome, dear. Now go on and change. You can leave your old clothes outside."

"Yes, ma'am."

As Tess leaves the room, I stare at the mirror. I think of Jenny, who used to sit on this stool and brush her hair. Maybe that's why Tess is so insistent I turn my life around, so I don't end up in a hole in the ground like Jenny.

It's after I take off my clothes that I remember I don't have any underpants. To wear a nightgown without something covering my privates seems grossly inappropriate. I take a deep breath and then look through the drawers to find a pair of panties. I can see my face turn red in the mirror; I feel like a pervert as I go through another girl's underpants. I grab a pair of white cotton ones, the least racy of the bunch. It's amazing how comfortable they feel.

The nightgown is a bit too big for me, so that the hem covers up my feet to make me look like a cartoon ghost. Any bit of denial I might have clung to earlier falls away when I turn back to the vanity. There's not a trace of manliness left to me, not in a pink nightgown with lace around the collar. I look like I should be at a slumber party giggling about cute boys. To think last night I had gotten drunk in a bar, interrogated the Worm, and then busted heads at Lennox Pharmaceuticals.

I leave my thrift store clothes in the hallway for Tess to take. Then I turn off the light and slip into bed. I stare up at the ceiling, not really tired after my lengthy nap earlier. I think about what Tess said. If no one can find a way to change me back, then I'm going to have to start a new life. A new life as Stacey Chance, a twenty-one-year-old woman. What kind of job can I get? Where am I going to live? I can't stay with Jake and Tess forever.

More importantly, what about Maddy? I stayed away from her before because of Debbie's lawyers, but there was always the chance I could see her again someday. Now even if I do see her, she won't recognize me. I'll never get a chance to talk to her again, to find a way to make up for the pain I had caused her.

I fall asleep with tears in my eyes.

***

In my dreams I'm back in the water. I'm still a woman at the bottom of the harbor. Again I watch myself from the outside. Even though it's a dream, I hope it will work in reverse and when I wake I'll be myself again.

Something does happen, but not what I hope. A hole begins to open in my forehead, just like the bullet hole Lex left me with. I always thought they said you woke up before you die in dreams. Maybe that doesn't count if you already died.

A drop of blood emerges from the hole, followed by another. Soon the drops become a thin trickle. The trickle gains momentum, until it's a river of blood that colors the water all around me red.

Then my eyes flash open—

I awaken with a scream. That's followed by a sharp pain in my midsection. I look around frantically, but can't see anything in the darkness. I can't remember where I am or who I am. All I know is I'm not in the water.

I grapple with the blankets for a few seconds before I free myself. Still in a panic, I roll right off the bed and land with a thud on the floor. I scramble to my feet and then flail around to find a light switch.

The light flicks on to reveal Jenny's old room in Jake's house. I'm still clad in the pink nightgown Tess gave to me. I put a trembling hand to my forehead, but there's no bullet hole, only sweat.

I let out a sigh of relief. It was just a dream. I think that for about two more seconds. That's when I see the drops of blood on the carpet. I follow the drops back to the bed, where there's a vibrant red stain on the pink sheets.

I manage to put a hand over my mouth to muffle another scream. I pull up the hem of my nightgown to see fresh blood dripping onto the carpet. Oh, shit.

I remember what Tess told me and run down the hallway to the bathroom as fast as I can. God, this can't be happening. I suppose it was inevitable, but why now? My first night as a woman and I'm having my period.

I throw open the medicine cabinet to look for something to plug up the bloody hole. There are bandages and aspirin, but no tampons or maxi pads. Tess must keep those in the master bedroom's bathroom. That makes sense; she wouldn't want some guest to find her feminine hygiene products.

I decide to forget modesty and strip off the nightgown, followed closely by my bloodstained underpants. With nothing else at hand, I unroll a handful of toilet paper. I do what I can to shove the wad of paper between my legs. It seems to work, at least for the moment. Long enough I hope to get to Tess's bathroom.

I have to go much slower down the hall to keep the paper in. With each step I look down to make sure I haven't started to leak. I pray I'm still asleep, that at any moment I'll wake up in my apartment and find myself a fat old man again.

I'm lucky Jake and Tess don't have their door locked. I ease the door open and then peek inside. They're both asleep, backs to each other. I wonder when was the last time they made love. Probably not for a while.

I see a shiny drop of blood on the wooden floor at my feet and then burst into the bedroom. The knob of the door glints in the moonlight. I rush over to it; I don't care anymore if the paper falls out. God, how much blood have I lost? The rate it's going, I'll need a transfusion for breakfast.

I fling open the medicine cabinet and want to scream again. Still nothing. Is she out? Maybe she keeps some in her purse—

I do scream again when I feel a hand on my shoulder. I spin around and see Tess in the doorway with a sad look on her face. "They're under the sink," she says. I'm about to ask how she knows, but then I think of the trail of blood I've left.

I open the cabinets beneath the sink and there's a pink plastic bag of maxi pads. I hold up the bag and then stare at it uncertainly. What am I supposed to do now? Tess stares at me expectantly. A woman my age should know what to do; whoever heard of getting your first period at twenty-one?

I drop the package to the floor. I follow after it and dissolve into a sobbing heap on the floor. It's a good thing Tess is there and that I can't see any sharp objects or I would slit my wrists to be done with this nightmare.

She bends down to put a hand on my shoulder. "What's wrong, sweetheart? You can trust me. I won't hurt you."

"I don't know how," I say between sobs.

"Surely this can't be your first time. Is it?"

I still have enough rationality left to shake my head. Tess tilts my chin up to look me in the eye. "Didn't your mother teach you?"

"No."

"An aunt? A grandmother? A teacher? Anyone?"

"No!" I shout and then continue to sob. "No one taught me anything."

"You poor, poor girl." She puts her arm around my back to help me up to my feet. "Don't worry, dear. I'll show you how. All right?"

I nod my head, the only coherent response I can make at this point. She sits me down on the toilet and then fetches the package of maxi pads. While I cry into a towel, Tess gives me a lecture on the female anatomy. "They aren't usually this heavy. When you get to be an old woman like me you won't have to worry about it anymore."

"Lucky you," I say before I can think better of it. Tess

has been anything but lucky in recent years. "I'm sorry about the mess I made. I've ruined Jennifer's bed."

"I doubt that, dear. We can wash the sheets. And your underpants as well."

"Thanks."

When we finally emerge from the bedroom, Jake is still asleep. It's amazing the racket I made didn't wake him up. He's a hell of a heavy sleeper. Or maybe he knew better than to get involved with this situation.

Back in Jennifer's bedroom I put on another nightgown and fresh panties to go over the pad. I sit quietly in the corner while Tess changes the sheets. As she said, the mess isn't too bad on the bed; nothing soaked through to the mattress. The carpet will need a good cleaning.

In lieu of a sheet, Tess puts down a towel for me to lie on. She pulls up the covers to my chin as if I'm a child who needs tucked in. She even smoothes hair away from my face to kiss me on the forehead. "Goodnight, sweetheart."

"Goodnight, Tess," I whisper.

Though Tess closes the door behind her, I know she won't go very far. She's outside in case I need her. A part of me would like her to stay, to lie on the bed with me to keep me company for the rest of the night. Despite the blankets, I shiver.

Chapter 16

I wake up the next morning to Tess shaking my shoulder. "Time to get up, dear," she whispers. "You have a big day ahead."

I groan at this. I know I need to get up, but my body feels as if it's made of wet sand. Tess throws back the covers to help motivate me. I shiver on the mattress for a few moments before I drag myself off the bed.

She pats my back and smiles at me. "It's all right," she says. "What you're feeling is perfectly normal."

"I know."

I stumble down the hallway to the bathroom. After the night I had, a nice hot shower will feel good. I don't wash for a couple of minutes; I prefer to stand under the water and let it flow over me. None of my many hangovers ever prepared me for this; it's as if every part of my body has some complaint: my head aches, my stomach is queasy, and my legs are swollen. On top of that I'm so tired I almost fall asleep in the shower.

The only thing that keeps me going is the thought of meeting with Dr. Palmer. She has to know about this FY-1978 drug; she has to know some way to cure me. If not, I don't know what I'll do. I can't go on like this. It's too much.

After a half-assed attempt to wash my hair and scrub my sore body, I step out of the shower. Tess must have slipped in at some point to leave my clothes—freshly pressed—and another maxi pad. This time I know what to do with the pad, not that it's any more pleasant.

I remember what Tess said last night about taking care of myself, so I grab a comb and start to work on my hair. I'm not nearly as good at it as she is, so that soon it becomes a mess. With a sigh and tears in my eyes I throw the comb down. I ought to find a pair of scissors and cut the shit off.

Of course Tess notices when I step out of the bedroom. She puts a hand on my shoulder. "Here, let me help you," she says.

"You don't have to treat me like a baby. I can take care of myself."

"I'm sure you can on the street, but this is a whole new world for you." That's an understatement. She guides me back to Jenny's bedroom to sit me down at the vanity again. There are some cosmetics open on the counter, probably for my eye. "Just sit very still."

I watch with awe in the mirror as again she transforms my tangled mass of hair into a silky masterpiece. This time she pulls it back tightly and wraps a scunci around it to keep it in a ponytail. That keeps it out of the way while she works on the bruise around my eye. When she finishes, there's just a bit of discoloration still visible. She balances out the other eye with some mascara so that someone would have to look really close to notice the difference. After a little blush and lipstick I look like a grown up.

"Wow," I say. "You should have a salon."

"It's just practice, dear," she says. "I had a lot of it

during Jennifer's illness. She didn't want people to know she was sick, at least not until we couldn't hide the effects anymore."

"I'm sorry."

"Don't worry about it. You just go downstairs and have some breakfast."

"I'm not very hungry."

"I know, but try to eat something anyway. You'll feel better."

"I guess." Tess has been right about everything else, so I go downstairs to the dining room. Jake is already there with the morning paper. "Anything interesting?"

"Nothing about Steve Fischer. A couple paragraphs about Dr. Nath in the back."

"Oh. So are they still looking for—him?"

"I suppose they are."

Tess has laid out scrambled eggs, bacon, toast, and cereal—a real balanced breakfast—but my stomach is only up to nibbling on the toast. That is until Tess comes downstairs. "Go on, eat," she says. After the kindness she's shown me, I force myself to down the whole meal. By the time I finish, I feel ready to throw up.

"You feeling all right?" Jake asks. "You look a little green around the gills."

"I'm fine," I snap.

"Maybe you should stay here. I can handle Palmer—"

"No! I have to go."

Tess reaches out to pat my hand. "Maybe it would be for the best—"

"I have to see her. I have to!"

"Stacey—"

"Shut up! Both of you, just shut up and leave me

alone. I can make my own decisions." I stomp out to the Fairlane in the driveway. It's locked, so I sit on the trunk and wait for Jake to come out. Tess is probably telling him what happened last night, about how my Aunt Flo came for a little visit. When will this nightmare end?

I know I'm right when Jake forces a smile as he walks out to the car. "Hey, kid," he says, "it's all right. We're just worried about you. You've been through a lot."

"I'm sorry," I say. "It's just everything's different now, you know? I don't know who I am or what I am." I start to blubber again. It's become a nasty habit.

Jake does something I never expect: he pulls me in for a hug. He pats my back and says, "It's all right. Just let it out."

We stay there for a long time as I cry on Jake's shoulder. The strangest part about it is that I don't feel embarrassed to cry in front of Jake. All those years we were partners and we never shared a moment like this. Now I wonder why.

***

After I buckle up, I ask Jake, "So you believe me now?"

He shrugs as he reaches into his jacket for a cigarette. "If you're faking it then you're the best con artist I've ever seen."

"Thanks."

Once we get started, I put my head against the window. I'd really like to go back to sleep, but I can't. I don't want Jake to leave me in the car while he goes in to visit Dr. Palmer. This is much too important for me to miss.

"You mind if I ask you something?" Jake says.

"What?"

"How does it feel?"

"You mean having a period or the whole thing?"

"The whole thing. Is it really weird?"

"Sometimes." I turn to Jake and smile a little. "Sometimes I feel almost normal. But then I see myself in the mirror or wake up with blood squirting out between my legs and I remember I'm not really me anymore."

"I don't think I could stand it."

"What other choice do I have? Finish what Lex started?" When I feel a surge of anger, then I feel like my old self again. It's the first time I've really thought about Artie Luther since what happened; I've been so busy just trying to survive. More than anything I'd like to make him pay for what he did to me, Dr. Nath, and scores of other people in this city. "Not until he's finished."

"We'll get him. After we see about getting you fixed up." A few moments go by in silence. Then Jake says, "If they can't do anything right away, you can stay with us for as long as you need."

"Thanks, but I don't want to be a bother."

"You're not. I think it does Tess good having you around. With Jenny gone, she doesn't have anyone to take care of. I've tried to get her to go back to work, at least part-time, but she doesn't want to. She tried once. Lasted about two hours. Her first clients were this family with a kid about Jenny's age. Soon as she showed them the kid's bedroom she broke down. I had to go and pick her up."

"I can't replace Jenny."

"I know that," he snaps, "but it's been hard on her with Jenny and all that menopause shit. She just needs someone to help her feel normal again."

"What about you?"

"We've kind of been on the outs since Jenny died. I

think she blames me for it."

"You didn't give Jenny cancer."

"I know. Try telling her that." Jake leans against the window to blow out a cloud of smoke. "I guess she thinks if I'd loved Jenny more, she would have beaten it."

"I'm sure you loved Jenny enough. It's just one of those things you can't do anything about." I catch my reflection in the mirror and hope this isn't one of those things. I hope it's not a death sentence for Steve Fischer.

Chapter 17

Lennox Pharmaceuticals must pay pretty well because Dr. Clarita Palmer lives in one of the sleek buildings put up about ten years ago along the northern rim of the harbor. There's a security guard at the front desk, a fat middle-aged guy who carries only a flashlight in his belt. His job is mostly to keep the bums and petty thieves out of the building. Real scumbags like Artie Luther's henchmen won't be intimidated by a flashlight and walkie-talkie.

Jake holds up his badge before the security guard can say anything. "We're going up to have a chat with Dr. Palmer. Anyone else been in here to visit her today?"

"Not that I know about," the guard says. "I can check the book."

"Don't bother. We'll ask her ourselves."

With that Jake starts for the elevators with me behind by a few steps. My stomach is still queasy, now with nerves as well as nausea. My legs have gone from lead to nonexistent, so that I have to force myself ahead with each step, my eyes down on my battered sneakers.

As we wait for an elevator, Jake says, "You still want to do this?"

"Why wouldn't I?"

"If you're still feeling sick—"

"I'll be fine. I'm not going to bleed all over her carpet or anything."

"I just mean if you're not feeling up to it—"

"I'm not scared," I say, though I'm sure Jake can hear the quiver in my voice.

"All right. Just let me do the talking. And no rough stuff."

I snort at this; I can't do more than hurt her feelings at the moment. "I guess the good cop-bad cop is out, then?"

"Let's hope we won't need it."

The elevator doors finally open. We have to wait for a man in a tight biker outfit to get off along with his bike. I'm not sure if it's because I'm not fully a woman yet or because of my period that I don't feel anything at the sight of his well-toned rear in those spandex shorts. I sigh with relief at that thought.

According to the Lennox personnel file, Dr. Palmer lives on the seventh floor. Her place is at the end of the hallway. Jake and I walk slow and keep our eyes open for any signs of a body being dragged down the hallway or any evidence of a struggle. There's nothing to indicate that Lex's goons have paid the doctor a visit.

I stand back almost to the opposite door as Jake knocks on Dr. Palmer's door. It takes a minute before the door opens a crack, the chain lock still in place. All I can see is a sliver of bronze skin and a brown eye. "Are you Detective Madigan?" she asks.

"Yes, ma'am."

"Where's your badge?"

Jake reaches into his pocket for his identification. She studies this for a moment. The door closes. Before I can groan with disappointment, I hear the chain lock come off.

The door opens to reveal a Hispanic woman in her late thirties. She wears a T-shirt and sweatpants and has her hair pulled back into a sloppy ponytail, which probably means she woke up not long before we arrived.

I didn't feel anything at the sight of the biker in his tight shorts and I don't feel anything for Dr. Palmer either. At least not in that way. Instead I cringe with jealousy because even in this rumpled state, Dr. Palmer still looks better put together than me. Her eyes are clear and free of bruises and even though she's nervous, she still has an air of confidence as she shows Jake inside.

"Who's this?" she asks when I step towards the door.

"That is Stacey Chance. She's a civilian observer," Jake says. He lies so smoothly that even I would believe it. "Making sure we're in compliance with Federal laws and all that."

"She looks a little young for that."

"I just have a young face," I say. "It's hell when I go to the liquor store."

Dr. Palmer stands aside so I can follow Jake into the apartment. The furniture is tasteful and not cheap, what there is of it. There's only a couch in the living room; Jake has to fetch a chair from the dining room table—which only has room for two—to sit on while us two ladies take the couch.

The doctor brings her purse with her from the kitchen. She rummages inside to retrieve a pack of cigarettes. "You mind if I smoke?" she asks.

"Only if you give me one," Jake says.

"What about you?" the doctor asks me.

"No thanks. Those things will kill you."

"So will a lot of other things in this city," the doctor observes. "And much faster."

"Like slitting your wrists?" Jake says.

"Having someone slit them for you is more like it," Dr. Palmer says. She lights two cigarettes and then hands one to Jake. I lean back into the plush white back of the couch to avoid smoke in my face.

"You don't think it was a suicide?"

"Gita wouldn't commit suicide. Not when the drug was ready for human trials."

"That would be the FY-1978 serum?"

"You've done your homework."

"It's part of the job." Jake gives me a look before he asks, "So what does that drug do?"

"It's supposed to be an anti-aging drug. Like the next generation of Botox. But Gita had bigger plans for it. She envisioned it as a cure to degenerative diseases: Alzheimer's, Parkinson's, AIDS, and even cancer by letting us turn back the body's clock to a younger, healthier state. Like the Fountain of Youth in a syringe."

"Sounds pretty ambitious."

"Gita always was ambitious."

"You think that's why someone killed her?"

"Maybe. If it had worked, FY-1978 would have been a game changer for the health care industry. It would make dozens—maybe even hundreds—of drugs obsolete. And once Lennox got it patented, you'd have a lot of big drug companies hurting real bad."

I could have fallen off the couch with shock at that point. I knew from the Tall Man that Lex wanted to sell the formula, but I hadn't imagined it could be that valuable. He could make hundreds of millions, maybe even a billion to a desperate company.

"Sounds like plenty of motivation for someone to kill Dr. Nath," Jake says. "Any idea who it might be? Did she have any enemies?"

"Not that I know of. She didn't have any friends either. All she did was work. She had the maintenance guys bring up a cot so she could sleep in there too. That's how dedicated she was."

"Did you two get along?"

Dr. Palmer shrugs. "About as well as anyone could get along with her. Like I said, she wasn't exactly a people person." The doctor blows out a cloud of smoke. "She wasn't mean or anything like that. She just didn't know how to relate to people."

"So you wouldn't say she was very well liked by her staff?"

She shrugs again. "Maybe we didn't like her, but we all respected the hell out of her. She was brilliant. FY-1978 was her baby. She did just about everything on it herself. Me and the others were mostly there to push a few buttons and help hold down the test subjects."

I jump in to ask, "What's going to happen to the project now?"

"There is no project now. Our notes are gone and Dr. Nath was the only one who could hope to replicate it. Too bad; we were making real progress with it."

"What kind of progress?" Jake asks while I put a hand to my stomach; I feel sick again, though not from the period anymore. If Dr. Nath was the only one who knew how to make it and she's dead, who will find a way to cure me?

"We tried it in mice then rats and then chimps. We had a ninety percent success rate."

"Success?"

The doctor pauses to take out a fresh cigarette and light it. "In those ninety percent of cases, the animals got younger. In our last case study, an elderly chimp reverted back to almost a pubescent state. The arthritis and dementia she had been suffering from were all gone. She was just as healthy and active as any young chimp."

I think of the animals in their cages on the fifth floor. Some of those cages had had Dr. Nath's name on them. Her test subjects? The chimp that Bruiser killed might even have been the one Dr. Nath had experimented on.

"Sounds impressive. But you didn't get to try it on humans?"

"No. Dr. Nath was working on the sample. I was trying to find a volunteer. That's why I wasn't at the lab when it was robbed. I was here, going over records from local nursing homes. They're on the table if you want to look."

"So you were here alone?" Jake asks while I get up and go over to the table. There's a pile of manila folders there just as Dr. Palmer said.

"Yeah, that's right. Should I get a lawyer?"

"I don't think that will be necessary. We have information suggesting organized crime was responsible for the break-in and probably Dr. Nath's death."

As I go through the folders, I notice a pattern: all of the potential volunteers are women. Women in their sixties or seventies with degenerative conditions like Alzheimer's, Parkinson's, and arthritis. I clear my throat to get Jake and Dr. Palmer's attention. "Are these all the files? Didn't you have any male subjects?"

"Not for this trial. The drug has to be specially tailored for an individual's physiology." When Jake and I both give her a blank look, she explains, "The drug utilizes a combination of hormone treatments, gene therapy, and stem cells to reverse the aging process. Some of that is unisex, but some of it—like the hormones—vary according to gender. So our first batch of FY-1978 was designed for female patients."

Jake asks the obvious question before I can, "What if the drug were used on a male instead?"

Dr. Palmer shrugs again. "Not sure. We never tried that, not even on the animals."

Jake gets up and comes over to the table where I'm still standing. He puts an arm around my shoulder. "Dr. Palmer, meet your first human subject: Detective Steve Fischer."

Chapter 18

I wait for Dr. Palmer's reaction. Will she laugh us out of the apartment? Will she scream for help? Maybe like Jake she'll have no reaction at all.

Her reaction is to get off the couch and walk over to us. She bends down a little to look me in the eye. I back away when she touches my hair. "You're saying you were a man?"

"Until the night of the robbery," I say.

"Huh." I'm glad when she takes a couple of steps back, though less glad when I notice her eyes going from my face down to between my legs. "Maybe you should give me the whole story."

Jake and I take the couch this time while Dr. Palmer sits on the dining room chair to study me as I tell her what happened. She smokes a couple more cigarettes while I tell her everything from the night of the robbery to this morning—I leave out my period. I can tell that like Jake she won't believe it.

"You said the syringe was filled with something pink?" she asks when I finish.

"Yes."

She nods. "The serum is actually clear. Dr. Nath added the pink coloring so we'd know which batch it belonged to. The male version would have been blue."

"So you believe me?"

"Not by a long shot."

"But—"

"If you want to prove it, then we'll have to run some tests."

"I have our boys in the lab comparing blood samples," Jake says. "So far they're a match. Her prints match Steve's too."

"We'll need more than that. A full work-up on her. Do you mind if I call you that?"

"It's fine," I say. "I'm getting used to it."

"Since it's only been about thirty-six hours, the drug is probably still in your system. We should be able to find traces of it in the blood work."

This gives me a queasier feeling than before. I remember what she said before about the chimp they used that drug on that had turned almost pubescent. "Does that mean it's still working? Could I get even younger?"

"Probably not. There's no way to be sure without getting a peek inside you. I do some consulting work for St. Vincent's; they'll let us use their equipment."

"When?"

"Just as soon as we can get over there," she says. "And after I throw on some clothes. You got room in your car for me?"

"Stacey can squeeze into the back," Jake says.

***

Of everything I've experienced so far, perhaps the strangest moment is to be naked in front of a relative stranger. It's of slight comfort that Dr. Palmer is covered as much as a woman in Saudi Arabia. "Do you think I'm contagious?" I ask and think of Jake's house with my blood all over the sheets and floor. Tess has probably come into contact with a fair amount of it; could my blood give her a dose of the FY-1978, make her years younger?

"I don't know what you are," she says. "Hop up on the table and we'll find out."

The table is so cold that I cry out. "Why can't I wear one of those paper gowns at least?"

"I want to get a look at everything. Saves time this way."

I never asked Debbie about any of her gynecological appointments; I'm sure they aren't like this. Dr. Palmer turns on a tape recorder on a tray. Then she starts to look over my entire body; she pays special attention to my most sensitive parts. She actually uses a magnifying glass to study my breasts. "I don't usually let someone do that until the second date," I joke.

"These are perfectly formed. No abnormalities that I can see."

"Thanks."

Even with most of her face covered, I can still see the annoyance in her eyes. "This is being recorded, so could you pipe down until we're finished?"

"Sure."

The doctor rewinds the tape. She presses a button. "Patient's name is Stacey Chance. Caucasian female, roughly eighteen years old."

"Twenty-one," I interrupt.

"*Eighteen*—and that's pushing it."

And just like that I'm three years younger. I can't drink legally, but at least I can still buy cigarettes, vote, or play the lottery, not that any of those hold much interest for me.

"Patient weighs 49.89 kilos. Height: 1.67 meters. No

irregularities or deformities visible except for a bruise around the right eye. Patient says that occurred after the incident at Lennox Pharmaceuticals.

"Patient's breasts are fully formed. Areola and nipples are consistent with those of a normal female. No scars or other evidence of surgery performed."

"You think I did this to myself?"

"Shut. Up," Dr. Palmer hisses. As revenge she goes down to the end of the table to stare at my private parts. "Put your feet in the stirrups, please."

"Do you have to do that?"

She turns the recorder off again. "Is there something you don't want me to see?"

"No. It might be a little messy though," I say. I tell her about what happened this morning, when I woke up to my first period.

She turns the recorder back on. "Special note: patient reports menstruating began this morning. This began with abdominal cramping, followed by heavy bleeding and nausea." The doctor goes over to the garbage can. With her plastic gloves she fishes through the trash until she finds my stained maxi pad. "Feminine undergarment supports patient's claims. Will have to have bloodstains analyzed to make sure they match samples taken from the patient."

Like Jake and I do at crime scenes, she stuffs the maxi pad into a little baggie so she can preserve it for later. So far Dr. Palmer seems thorough enough that I'd want her on any of my crime scenes. Maybe Jake should ask her to take a peek at Dr. Nath's lab to search for anything we might have missed.

Now we get down to the most awkward part of the exam. After she snaps on a fresh pair of gloves, Dr. Palmer brushes a hand against my pubic hair. I squeal for a moment as she yanks one out. "Patient has fully-developed pubic hair." She gets out the magnifying glass again to study between my legs. "Labia appear normal."

What comes next is even less pleasant. Dr. Palmer wheels over what looks like a computer with a console and flat screen. She holds up what looks like an electric toothbrush, except it's got a cord to connect it to the computer. "This is an ultrasound transducer," she says. "To verify you really are a woman, I need to insert this into your vagina. That way we can make sure everything is where it's supposed to be."

"Can't you do that from the outside?"

"I'm afraid not. It is a pretty common procedure. There's really no risk of anything bad happening to you." The doctor gives me a hard stare. "Unless there's something you don't want me to see in there?"

"No, it's not that," I say, my eyes focused on the transducer. It's hard to believe she plans to stick that thing *inside* of me. I remember when my old doctor gave me a prostate exam; this will be like that times a thousand. But if I don't do it, then she'll think I'm faking. "Go ahead."

"This shouldn't hurt at all," she says. "It might just be a little cold." She motions to the computer screen. "You can see what I'm doing on that."

"Great," I mumble. I close my eyes as she inserts the transducer inside of me. She's right that it doesn't really hurt; it's more like when I had to put a suppository up my rear for a nasty case of hemorrhoids.

About a minute goes by. There's a bunch of white and black noise on the computer screen. I remember when Debbie's obstetrician showed us an ultrasound of Madison. Despite my keen detection skills, I couldn't see a baby amongst all that chaos.

This time there's no baby to find. Dr. Palmer taps the screen with one finger. "There's your left ovary," she says. "Looks perfectly healthy."

"An ovary? So you mean I can have babies?"

"As many as you want," she says. "There's your uterus. No little Staceys in it right now."

"That's a relief," I say, and put a hand to my stomach. "So I guess I really am a woman, huh?"

"You are a woman. There's no denying that," she says as she pulls the transducer out of me. "It doesn't prove the rest of your story."

"How do we do that?"

She holds up a metal tray; on it is a very nasty-looking syringe and a half-dozen clear containers. "We'll start by taking some blood. If the drug is still in your system we should be able to see it."

"Are you going to leave a little blood in me?" I can see her smile beneath her mask. "What?"

"I remember why I like working with animals better than humans. They complain a lot less. Now, close your eyes and it'll be over soon enough."

I do as she suggests; I close my eyes and turn my head towards the door. I've never liked needles, especially needles that suck out my blood like little vampires. Still, if that's the only way to convince Dr. Palmer I'm telling the truth, then I'll let her take my last drop of blood.

A couple minutes go by before the doctor says, "All finished. I'd give you a lollypop if I had one."

"So now what do we do?"

"You can get dressed. Then we'll go upstairs for an MRI and some X-rays."

"Lucky me," I grumble.

Chapter 19

The rest of the exam is easy enough. For most of it I lie on a table; I occasionally move as they take pictures of the inside of my body. By the time I've changed out of my paper hospital gown, used the bathroom, and drank a bottle of Gatorade from the vending machine, Dr. Palmer has the X-rays back.

"That was some fast work," I say.

"Just had to lean on them a little. Helps when I can say it's for a police investigation."

We stand in a little room lit with blue-white light for the X-rays. She puts one against the lights. I see a ribcage and spine—*my* ribcage and spine. There must be something wrong with the film, because there are a lot of lines on the film that look almost like spider webs. "That isn't how it's supposed to look, is it?"

"No, there shouldn't be any of those squiggly lines. Not for a normal person."

"Meaning what?"

"The serum contains low dose radioactive isotopes—"

"It's *radioactive*?" Saying the word brings to mind monster movies I saw as a kid that featured giant ants, lizards, or turtles. Maybe before long I'll grow to fifty-feet-tall and rampage through the city.

"About as much as the average carrot from the grocery store. I said it's a low dose. Not enough to do any damage, but enough to show up on an X-ray."

I'm not a scientist by any stretch, but even I can put the pieces together. "So that means there is some FY-1978 in me yet?"

"That's the best possible answer. Not the only one. We'll have to wait until we get the blood work back to know for sure."

"But still, you know I'm telling the truth now. I wasn't born like this and I didn't have any sex change surgeries either."

Dr. Palmer nods and then turns to me. "I think you are telling the truth. And that scares the hell out of me. No drug should be able to work that kind of change, not in the amount of time you described. It should take days or even weeks if at all. Our test subjects in the lab took ninety-six hours on average to show signs of a change."

"But there has to be some way to reverse it, doesn't there? Or maybe it'll wear off. Once all this FY-1978 is out of my system."

"It doesn't work that way. The FY-1978 will eventually break down, but the changes to your cells—to your DNA—are permanent."

"But you have to be able to do *something*. You're a scientist." Tears bubble up in my eyes as much as I don't want them to. In the back of my mind I always knew a cure wouldn't be easy to find, but the opinion of a scientist like Dr. Palmer carries a lot more weight.

"I'm not as good of a scientist as Dr. Nath. Few people are. She was the best in her field." As I begin to sob, Dr. Palmer puts a hand on my shoulder. "I'll do what I can. I know some people who might be able to help.

After we get everything together, I'll show them and maybe they can find a way."

"But you still don't think it'll work."

"I have to be honest here, Stacey. I don't know why it worked the first time. It's incredible. Until about two hours ago I would have said it was impossible."

"So what am I supposed to do now?"

She pulls me in closer, to hug me to her body and stroke my hair. After a day of being prodded and poked like a steer going to market, this kind of intimacy feels good. "You have to stay positive. You've been given a second chance. You can start a whole new life. You're young and pretty and you're not dumb either. Find yourself a job. Go back to school. Is there something you always wanted to do before you became a police officer?"

I shake my head. Being a cop was all I ever wanted to do. Ever since I began to play cops and robbers with my toys as a toddler. "I don't want to be anything else."

"Well, you could always try rejoining the police force."

I sniffle but don't say anything. I could try to go back to the academy. Maybe I could make it through and become a beat cop again. In another five or ten years I might even make detective again. That hardly seems fair.

"I'm sure you can think of something. Give it some time. In the meantime try to relax. Get some rest. I'm sure Detective Madigan can help you get through it."

"Maybe." She gives me a couple of minutes to cry myself out before we go down to the cafeteria, where Jake nurses a cup of coffee while he checks something on his phone. The moment he looks up, he winces.

"Didn't go so well, did it?" he asks.

"Let's talk in the car," I say.

***

I give Jake a PG-rated version of Dr. Palmer's examination. "She says with Dr. Nath dead there's probably not much they can do." I look in the mirror to see my face. I'm about as much of a wreck as I was this morning. I run a hand through my hair to try to smooth it down. If I'll see this face for the rest of my life, I ought to try to take care of it. "I'm probably going to be stuck like this forever."

"Jesus," Jake says and takes a puff on his cigarette. "I'm sorry."

"I know." We go a couple of blocks in silence. Finally I say, "Dr. Palmer says I should look on the bright side. I'm getting a second chance and whatnot."

"I guess so." Jake flicks his cigarette out the window. I'm sure he hoped I'd get back to normal too. "Any idea what you want to do?"

"Yeah. I want to kill Artie Luther."

"Steve—"

"Look what he did to me! He took everything away from me: my job, my home, my family." I choke up. The tears start to flow again. There doesn't seem to be anything I can do about it. Maybe it's because I'm too inexperienced to handle all these hormones. "I know things weren't good with Debbie and Maddy before, but now I can't ever see them. Maddy's never going to call me 'Daddy' again. And it's his fault! He took all of that from me."

"That doesn't mean I can let you kill him."

"Jake, please. We've been partners for twenty-five years. Doesn't that mean anything to you?"

"Yeah, it means I don't want to let you do something stupid."

"It's not stupid!"

"Are you looking in the mirror at yourself? You think you can go up against Lex's thugs like that? What are you going to do, scratch their eyes out?"

I look down at my ropy arms and legs. He's got me there. "Just get me a gun," I say, though it sounds ludicrous in my little songbird voice. "All I want is to put a hole in his head when the time comes. Like he did to me. Is that too much to ask?"

"Yeah, it is too much to ask."

"Then what am I supposed to do? Go learn to bake brownies? Find some husband to take care of me and pump out his babies? Is that what you want?"

"What I want is for you to have some fucking common sense. You're not a cop anymore. You're not Steve Fischer. You're a cute little girl. You should be hanging out at the mall, giggling about boys."

"Is that how you see me? As some empty-headed bimbo?" I reach across the seat to poke him in the chest. "Whatever I look like on the outside, I'm still me on the inside. I'm still the guy who's pulled your ass out of the fire more times than either of us can count. Got it?"

He seizes my hand and begins to bend it back until I hear something pop. Though I don't want to, I whimper; fresh tears come to my eyes. "Stop it!" I shout like a little girl with a boo-boo.

"You see my point? You aren't Steve anymore."

He lets my arm go. I hold it against my chest as if it's broken. It's not; it'll just need a couple of hours to feel better. "I get it. Can't I help you track him down?"

"How are you going to help?"

"I don't know," I whine. "I can do something."

"What you can do is stay home with Tess. I'll feel a

lot better if I know you've got someone looking after you."

"I don't need looking after. I'm still an adult."

"You don't have money, a job, a place to live. You don't even have any ID. No one knows Stacey Chance exists except for me, Tess, and Dr. Palmer. For now you are my child."

I sulk for a few minutes. The silence lets both of us cool off a little. I'm sure Jake knows how important it is for me to nab that bastard Luther; he wants to protect me from myself. "I can at least help you go through some of the files. I can still read."

Jake sighs heavily. "All right, you can help with some of the legwork. But when it comes time for the muscle, you're going to be at home with Tess. Deal?"

I reach across the seat with my good arm to shake his hand. "Deal."

Chapter 20

My second night in the Madigan household goes a lot more smoothly than the first. Though I insist I'm fine, Tess tucks me in again. She's changed the sheets, to a set of dark blue ones that won't show any stains. At least she hasn't put garbage bags under the sheets like I'm a bed wetter.

This night I sleep like a baby. When I wake up it's still dark in the room, but the clock says it's almost eleven in the morning. Tess didn't wake me up. She probably wants me to get some rest after how bad I've felt the last couple of days.

Before I go downstairs or even to the bathroom I go over to the vanity. As I start to brush my hair out, to replicate what Tess did, I notice something: the bruise is gone! There's a little bit of a dark circle left, but otherwise my eye looks normal. The arm Jake put into his kung-fu death grip feels normal as well.

There's only one explanation: FY-1978. Dr. Palmer said the drug was still in my system. It probably still is working its magic on my boo-boos. I lean forward until my nose almost touches the mirror to see if anything else is different. Can I still call myself eighteen or am I seventeen now? Maybe even sixteen? I can't see that much of a difference other than with the shiner. I'll have to see if Tess notices anything.

She of course notices that my bruise is gone. "Such a wonderful job with the makeup," she says.

"It's not makeup," I say.

She frowns at this; she does the math like I did. "That's remarkable. I've never seen a bruise heal so quickly."

"Guess I'm a quick healer."

For the moment it seems my period is gone too. It might be lying dormant, but there's no fresh blood on my maxi pad and my stomach feels just fine as I wolf down the eggs and bacon Tess puts in front of me. She doesn't eat anything herself; she probably ate hours ago when Jake left. I slow down a little when I see the way her lip is curled, a rebuke on the tip of her tongue. I'm supposed to be a young lady now, not a street urchin.

"Are you feeling up to going out?" she asks after I finish breakfast.

"Sure. What about Jake—Mr. Madigan? What's he doing today?"

"He said he's going to work on a case. He promises to be home for dinner."

Jake's the kind of guy who usually keeps his promises too. He's probably going to do a little work on the Lennox Pharmaceuticals case, the kind of work he doesn't want me around for. Maybe lean on a few snitches like the Worm. Someone out there has to know where Artie Luther is holed up. Someone might even know where to find some more FY-1978; if there's any more to be found.

In the meantime there's nothing I can do but get dressed and go shopping with Tess. I'd rather shop for men's clothes, but whatever we get will be better than this stinky old tracksuit or a dead girl's clothes. Tess spreads ads across the table. All of these are for suburban stores: department stores, outlet shops, and supercenters. I stare at the models in their T-shirts and jeans. When I see a girl in sweatpants with "PINK" written on them I remember the thrift store and that nice woman Grace.

"What do you think, dear?" Tess asks.

"Um, actually, this stuff isn't really my style," I say. "I thought maybe we could go to the garment district."

"Of course, dear. Whatever you want," Tess says, though I can see disappointment on her face.

***

The garment district got its name because it used to be populated by textile mills and seamstresses, though most of those have gone in the last fifty years. The garment district doesn't have all the trendy stores like downtown or the suburbs, but it does have plenty of boutiques that charge reasonable prices. At least that's what Tess says as we make our way there.

"When I was a girl it was still a lot of hippies and drugs," she says. "It's been cleaned up a bit since then."

Cleaned up means taken over by the hipsters. They're the ones in the "vintage" clothes with too many piercings and look as if they haven't bathed in a month. I could probably fit right in with them.

We leave the car in a lot so we can get out on foot and explore. I haven't spent a lot of time in this part of town as a cop. I only came a few times on a tip or to find a snitch. Those were always in the dark; in the light the place looks worn and dirty and claustrophobic. The buildings are all squeezed together; most of them date from the 1910s or 20s, back when everyone still believed in progress.

I feel around in my pocket for Grace's business card,

but Tess must have taken the card or else it got destroyed by the washer. If there were still phone books we could go look it up. The garment district isn't that big; we'll probably run across it eventually.

The first shop we stop at smells like meat. Old, salty meat. In its past life the store must have been a butcher shop. Now some woman almost Tess's age who dresses like she's still my age runs the place. "My niece needs some new clothes," Tess says. "What do you have that would look good on her?"

The woman's judgment runs contrary to what I want. She shows me a lot of peasant blouses and flowing skirts, the kind of outfits where I'd just need to put some flowers in my hair to look like someone from Woodstock. After the fourth such outfit Tess says, "Thank you so much, dear. We'll think about it."

The next shop features a girl with a pink Mohawk. There's a lot of leather in the place, not all of it clothes to wear in public. Tess and I beat a quick retreat from there. From the way Tess's face has paled, I know she's having second thoughts. We probably should have gone out to the suburbs, to the mall or Wal-Mart.

Then I see the sign for the Second Chances Boutique, which is hand-painted and matches the font on the business card. "Let's try in here," I say to Tess. I hope I don't sound too eager.

The boutique isn't much to look at, just a space about as big as my old apartment with racks of mismatched clothes on the walls and scattered throughout the store. There's a wooden counter with an old brass cash register. Grace sits behind it on a stool and reads a psychology textbook as large as the phone book. She marks her place and then looks up at me.

A smile comes to her face as she recognizes me. "I remember you. The thrift store, right? You were looking around at the men's clothes."

"That was me," I say. My face flushes with embarrassment.

"That outfit looks like it's working out for you."

"It is, thanks."

"And now you've come for more?"

"Yes." I motion with my head to Tess. "My aunt and I are doing some shopping."

"Oh, this is your aunt? It's nice to meet you. My name's Grace Meredith. I run this place, such as it is."

"It's a lovely shop," Tess says, her voice dry. I'm not sure if she just doesn't like Grace or if she's annoyed I kept from her that Grace and I already met.

Grace hops off her stool and then comes around the counter. She takes my arm to show me rows of T-shirts. Most of them are for bands I've never heard of or elections I never voted in. "Everyone nowadays is selling ironic T-shirts, but these are the real deal. See how faded some of these are? That's not because I sit around here washing them for hours like some of these shysters."

I go through the racks, but don't see anything that catches my eye. "Don't you have any plain ones?"

"I should have known. You're not the ironic type, are you?"

"No."

"You're a functional girl."

"That sounds right."

"That's fine with me. I think I got some things that will be up your alley." She shows me another rack of ordinary T-shirts and blouses. I find a few in my size. I try to stick with neutral colors: dark green, dark blue, black, and white. Nothing pink. Maybe I'll be stuck as a girl for the rest of my life, but that doesn't mean I have to dress girly just yet.

There are some jeans too. I pick out a pair of bellbottoms that along with the dark blue T-shirt remind me of Debbie when we first met. All I'd need to do was get my hair feathered and dyed blond like a wanna-be Farah Fawcett. I feel myself edge closer to a breakdown at the thought of Debbie, which always leads me back to Maddy.

Grace pats me on the shoulder to snap me out of my daydreams. "That looks really sharp," she says. "You've got a great sense of style."

"Or lack of style," I say.

"Style is supposed to suit the individual. This look you've got really fits your personality. It's straightforward, no-nonsense—"

"Functional?"

"Right. You don't mess around, do you?"

"Not if I can help it."

Tess joins us and nods in approval. "You look very nice, dear." She insists I buy at least one dress. "You need something for church," she says.

I consent to let Grace show me some dresses fit for church. I settle on a white one with a floral print; the skirt goes down to almost my ankles. "That will do nicely," Tess says. Then she clears her throat and turns to Grace. "She's going to need some…unmentionables as well."

Grace smiles and nods. "I know what you mean. We keep that stuff in the back. And don't worry, they're not vintage."

The panties come in a plastic bag, six to a pack. Without me saying anything, Grace picks out the least lacy ones—*functional* underwear. I take these without a word. Then I catch her staring at my chest. My face turns warm. Is she checking me out?

She is, but not the way I think. "You look like you're a C-cup," she says. "A thirty-four-C I'd say." She rummages through a rack of bras until she finds a plain white one. "This looks about right. You should go try it on to make sure."

"Oh. Right." I start to feel queasy again, but not from my period. This is just old-fashioned nervousness. I've never put a bra on before. I couldn't even take them off when I was with Debbie. The first couple dates in the backseat of my car, I had to let her take the damned thing off after my fingers couldn't get the knack of it.

I take a deep breath and then go into the little changing room. It's about as big as a phone booth, with barely enough room for me to turn around. Grace guesses right about the size of it; it fits securely to my chest without constricting me. The problem as always is to hook it in the back. I try three times without success. In the mirror I see my face reddening.

There's a knock on the door. "Do you need any help, sweetheart?" Tess asks.

"I'm fine," I squeak. The tears I held back before start to come now. I want my old body back! My nice, simple man's body, where the hardest thing was to tie my necktie. Being a woman is so complicated. Complicated and annoying. I think of what Dr. Palmer said and once more the terrible reality hits me that I might be like this forever.

The hormonal storm passes after a couple of minutes. "Stacey? Are you all right?" Tess calls out. "Are you feeling ill?"

"I'm fine," I mumble. "I'll be out in a minute."

I look myself in the eye and try to stare myself down. I can do this. I've caught hundreds of criminals; I can put on a fucking bra. With renewed determination I reach back. This time I hook it together securely. Then I put my T-shirt on over it.

I make sure to wipe my eyes before I step out. I'm sure Tess and Grace can still see how red they are. "How'd it fit?" Grace asks.

"Great," I say. "Just great."

"We'll need six more in the same size," Tess says.

"Not a problem."

The bill comes to nearly three hundred dollars. I put a hand on my pocket before I realize I don't have any money. I don't have anything, not so much as a bus pass. I remember what Jake said, that I'm no one except to him, Tess, and Dr. Palmer. I'm just a plain young woman in a city with millions of them.

"I'll pay you back," I whisper to Tess.

"Nonsense, dear. It's my treat."

Grace clears her throat. "If you're looking for a job, I could use another hand around here."

"Really?"

"Sure. I can't pay more than minimum wage, but you get a discount on the clothes too."

"We'll have to think it over," Tess says. "I'm not sure Stacey is ready for that yet."

Grace nods. She reaches beneath the cash register for a business card like the one she gave me before. "You can call me anytime. If I don't pick up, just leave a message on the machine."

"OK," I say and pocket the card.

"At the very least, tell me how the clothes are working out for you, all right?"

"I will."

With that we leave the store, armed with four shopping bags. I look back; something tells me I'll return soon enough.

***

We don't go very far. Just down a block to a greasy spoon like Rosie's. The woman who waits on us is about as old as Rosie, though not so sunny. "Specials are on the board," she says. "See anything you want?"

"I'll just have a coffee," Tess says. "Two sugars and one cream."

"I'll have the same," I say.

With a huff the waitress saunters off to eventually fetch our coffee. Tess lets out a weary sigh. She looks ready to curl up on the booth seat and go to sleep. "Are you all right?" I ask.

"I'm a bit tired."

"Looking after a kid is a lot of work."

"It's not your fault, dear. I'm worried about Jacob. I know he's hiding something from me. I can always tell when he's keeping a secret."

I know what secret Jake is keeping: my *real* name. So I guess it is my fault after all. "Don't policemen keep lots of secrets from their wives?" God knows I kept plenty of secrets from Debbie. Then again she wasn't all that interested to hear my stories about fighting crime in the city after Maddy was born. By then my job no longer sounded like a television show and just another *job*, same as a window washer or garbage man.

"Yes, but there's something different about this. He's been acting very evasive."

"He probably has a good reason."

"I'm sure he thinks he does."

"But you don't agree?"

"There's no way I can know without knowing what it is," she says and yawns. "Did she go all the way to Colombia for the coffee?"

"Maybe she's unloading it from the burro."

We laugh more than is deserved at this crummy joke. The waitress picks that moment to return. From the way she glares at us, she knows we were talking about her. "Here's your coffee," she says and slams down both cups. "You want anything else?"

"Not now. Thank you," Tess says. She takes a sip of the coffee and then makes a face. I sip mine and make an identical face. The coffee tastes like motor oil that's been burned for a couple thousand miles. There's not enough cream and sugar in the world to erase that taste.

Tess drinks hers anyway. "Those are some nice clothes you bought," she says to change the subject from her husband. "That dress is really pretty. Did your parents ever take you to church?"

"They weren't very religious."

"Did they at least get you baptized?"

"I'm not sure. I don't remember much from back then."

"I'll talk to Reverend Crane on Sunday. I'm sure we can arrange a baptism if you want one."

"I don't know," I say. If I do get baptized then in the eyes of the Lord I'd be Stacey Chance for all eternity. I shiver at that thought. "I'll think about it."

"Of course, dear. It's not something to take lightly."

I take another sip of coffee—or try to. I turn away so Tess can't see my reaction. Out the window I see a coffeehouse across the street, a grungier version of Starbucks called Kozee Koffee. It can't be any worse than this shit. "I'll be back in a minute," I say.

"Where are you going?"

"To get some real coffee." Then I remember I don't have any money. "Can I borrow a couple of bucks?"

"Here you go, sweetheart," Tess says. She hands me a ten.

To get across the street I have to weave around a lot of slow cars. I get honked at once and cussed at in three different languages. I flip them off as I wind my way over to the coffeehouse; I hope Tess didn't see me.

The place smells about as bad as the coffee across the street tastes. It's dark inside; only a pair of dim overhead lamps provide any light. I don't see anyone behind the counter at first. With my luck I caught them on a break.

"Anyone here?" I call out.

"Just a moment!" a woman's voice says back. From the sound of it, she's on the floor behind the counter. I get confirmation of this when she pops up like a whack-a-mole a moment later.

The girl is about my age with hair the color of pink cotton candy. There's a ring in her nose, another in her left eyebrow, and a half-dozen more in each ear. Despite all of this, I know the girl's face.

It's Maddy.

Chapter 21

Maddy doesn't recognize me. Why should she? The last time she saw me I was a thirty-eight-year-old man. I had a beard back then, until it became so gray I had to either dye it or shave it; I chose the latter. There's no reason at all she should recognize me as an eighteen-year-old girl. No reason at all—except that I'm her father. Shouldn't there be some special bond that tells her who I am?

"What can I get you?" she asks.

I trip over my own tongue until I spit out, "Coffee."

"What kind? We have lattes, cappuccinos, espressos, frappes, or just plain old boring coffee. We also have tea—hot and cold—and juice."

I can tell there's going to be no tearful reunion here. If there are any tears it'll just be me because my own daughter doesn't recognize me. I force myself to take a deep breath and then say, "Cappuccino. Two. To go."

"Coming right up."

I can't help but stare at Maddy as she works. She's so different than she was at ten years old. So different even than her high school picture. What's happened to her in the last couple of years? The father in me wants to grab her by the collar and drag her back home so she can get that shit out of her hair and all those rings off of her face. Nose rings are for steer, not little girls.

But she's not a little girl anymore. She's older than I am. She's free to do whatever she wants, pierce whatever she wants. Even if I were still a man I couldn't force her to do anything.

When she bends down for something, I see a tattoo on the small of her back. One of those Chinese characters. A "tramp stamp" as they're less-affectionately known. Is my daughter a tramp? Is she sleeping around with someone? Does she have a child? Am I a grandfather?

A hundred other questions flit through my head while she makes two cappuccinos. I can't ask any of them. How can I? I'm just a stranger to her. Maybe I always was.

"Here you go," she says. "Two cappuccinos. Just be careful, they're hot."

"I will," I mumble.

"Do you want a carrier for them?"

"No. I'm fine."

I'm about to turn and walk away, defeated. Then she throws me a lifeline. "Did you buy those clothes from Grace's?"

"Yeah. How did you know?"

"I shop there all the time. She's got such great taste."

"She does. She picked this out for me." I think of what Grace said before I left. "She offered me a job there."

"No way! Are you going to take it?"

"I might."

"Well if you do, maybe you could share your employee discount with me."

I smile at this. "I guess I could. If she lets me."

"She doesn't have to know," Maddy says. She leans

forward as if someone might hear us. "It could be our secret."

"And maybe you could give me a discount on coffee."

"I could." Maddy extends her hand over the counter. "My name's Maddy Griffith."

Griffith? That's Debbie's maiden name. She must have changed it after the divorce. Whose idea was that? "Stacey Chance."

"It's good to meet you, Stace. You mind if I call you that?"

"No, it's fine," I say, though I really want her to call me Daddy like she did when she was little. For now this will have to do.

***

I return to the diner, where Tess dozes in the booth. Her eyes shoot open when I set the cappuccino in front of her. "Oh, how sweet of you."

"Just thought you might like a decent coffee."

"That's so thoughtful. Thank you." She takes a sip of the coffee and nods. "That's wonderful. Just what I need."

We leave our used motor oil on the table and set out for the car. I ask Tess to wait outside Grace's store. Grace sits behind the counter and reads her enormous textbook. "Back so soon?" she asks. "Clothes not working out for you?"

"They're fine," I say. "I decided to take the job. If you're still offering it."

"That's great." She snaps the book shut and then drops it on the counter with a thud. "So when can you start?"

"Tomorrow, I guess. Unless you need me sooner."

"Tomorrow works for me." She reaches beneath the counter for something. It's a couple sheets of paper.

"You'll have to fill this out to make it all nice and legal."

I take the papers from her. It's a job application. The first line is easy enough; all I need is my name. The next box stops me cold. I need a Social Security Number. I could probably use my old one, at least for now. The Feds might have a problem with it in a couple of months, especially if Steve Fischer is declared dead by then, which he certainly will be unless Dr. Palmer comes up with a cure for me.

"Could I take these home? My aunt is waiting outside and she's kind of tired."

"Sure. Just bring them back tomorrow. Be here at nine if you can make it. I should be up by then. If not, knock really loud. OK?"

"OK." I fold the papers up. "Thanks a lot for this. You don't know how much it means to me."

"It's no problem." Before I can leave, Grace comes around the counter to give me a hug. "You're not my employee yet so that doesn't count as sexual harassment."

I laugh at this. It might be fun to work for Grace. And it'll allow me to see Maddy every day. At least whenever she works. That's a lot more than I've seen her for the last twelve years.

Chapter 22

Jake is less than supportive of my decision when I tell him in his study. "What the fuck do you think you're doing?" he hisses. "You can't tell Maddy. She'll never believe you."

"I'm not going to tell her. I just want to be around her more."

"She's not your daughter, *Stacey*."

"She'll always be my daughter. No matter what I look like."

"Jesus Christ," he says with a groan. "Yesterday you were so hot to go and kill Artie Luther and now you're taking a job at a dress shop?"

"It's not a dress shop. It's a clothes store."

"A women's clothes store."

"Well I am a woman in case you hadn't noticed. You'd rather I were working at the S&M store down the road?"

"I'd just like to know what the fuck you're doing. Is this the hormones again? All that estrogen got you going batty?"

"I'm not going batty." It doesn't help my case when I start to cry again. Eventually I have to get a handle on these damned hormones. Maybe after all this FY-1978 leaves my system it'll even me out. Or maybe I just need more practice at being a woman. "What if things were reversed? What if you were the one turned into a woman and it were Jenny working at the coffee shop?"

"We're not dealing with hypotheticals here. We're dealing with reality."

"None of this is reality. It's all crazy."

"True." Jake puts a hand on my knee. "This isn't a good idea. I know you love Maddy, but this is only going to hurt you in the end."

"I don't care! This may be my only chance to get close to her. I'm not going to let it slip away. If you don't understand that, then the hell with you."

Jake lets out a weary sigh reminiscent of his wife's. "Fine. Take the stupid job. You'll figure out I'm right."

"I will take the job." But then I look down sheepishly at my feet as I remember the job application. "There's just one problem."

"Only one?"

"I don't have a Social Security number. Or any ID. I need it for the application."

"Well, you're in luck on that score." Jake takes a manila envelope off his desk. He shakes it open and out pops a Social Security card, state ID card, and a birth certificate. "I had one of our mutual friends make these up."

I pick up the ID card. There's my name: Stacey Lynn Chance. Eighteen years old. The height is a little shorter and the weight a little higher than what Dr. Palmer said. The picture isn't of me, but the girl is a close enough match that no one will notice. I hold the ID card up to the light: the laminate is legit. "Must have gone to Sampson?"

Ricky Sampson is the best forger not currently behind

bars. He would be except that he cut a deal with the DA. He works as a forensics consultant for the city, and the city keeps him out of jail.

"Yeah. He hasn't forgotten anything."

"Must have cost a pretty penny."

"He did it pro bono."

"Oh yeah?"

"We exchanged favors."

"What did you do for him?"

"I didn't blow his fucking head off."

I laugh at this. For a moment at least it's like old times. Makes me wish we could go down to Squiggy's and tie one on. But we can't do that, not anymore. "You couldn't have got him to make me twenty-one?"

"You go up to some bartender and say you're twenty-one and they'll know it's a fake ID. Probably cut it up in front of you and then you'll be screwed."

"Yeah, I guess."

"Hey, come on, it'll be all right. Why don't you fill out your application? I need to go out and get a smoke."

"Sure." As Jake starts to go, I add, "And thanks."

***

When I finish with my paperwork, Tess waits for me with a black purse about the size of a toaster oven. "Here you go, dear. You'll need this."

"I don't need a purse."

"Every girl needs a purse. You can't go around with everything sticking out of your pockets, can you?"

That had worked well enough for me before, but that was when I had a wallet. "I guess not." I take it from her. From the weight I realize it's already got some stuff inside. I open it up and see lipstick, a compact, eyeliner—none of which I know how to use—as well as a hairbrush and three maxi pads. "That's so thoughtful of you."

"Now you'll look like a woman," Tess says.

"Yeah, great."

"Just make sure you take good care of it. There are a lot of people with sticky fingers in this city."

"I'll be careful." I'd die of embarrassment if I let myself get victimized by a purse-snatcher like some little old lady.

Tess wraps me in a hug. "I'm so proud of you, sweetheart. You've been here just three days and look at you! You're all cleaned up with some nice new clothes and now you've got a job."

"I've come a long way." And it's true. When I woke up that first morning I was naked, with nothing, not even a name. In three days I have what amounts to nearly a normal life.

Maybe Dr. Palmer was right about that second chance.

Part 4:
Stacey Rising

Chapter 23

I'm so excited I can hardly sleep. It isn't as much about the job as the job's proximity to Maddy. I hope she works tomorrow so I can go over for a coffee and have a little chat with her. If I play my cards right, I might be able to find out a few things about her, about what she's done since her mom and I divorced.

I lie on Jenny's bed and think of hundreds of different conversations between Maddy and I. Most of them go badly, with her realizing her old dad has become a young girl. In those conversations she screams and sobs while I lurch away into the night like the Frankenstein monster. There are a couple that end better, where she hugs me and I promise things will be different now. I don't put much stock into those.

I know Jake is right that I can't tell Maddy who I am. She'd never believe me. Maybe after Dr. Palmer's tests are done I could show her the results. But then what? She probably hates me not only for the divorce, but also because I didn't contact her the last twelve years. That my lack of involvement was her mother's idea wouldn't be of any help.

I toss and turn for a few hours, until I'm sure Jake and Tess are asleep. Then I sneak downstairs and turn on the

TV. Mostly it's infomercials at this hour, so I lie on the couch and watch two beautiful people hawk skin care products. I snort as I remember what Dr. Palmer said. FY-1978 would have made products like this obsolete. It would have made just about the entire beauty industry obsolete. That was a lot of money; no wonder Lex wanted to get his hand in that pie.

Does he have any of the FY-1978? Or any of Dr. Nath's notes? Something that might help Dr. Palmer find a way to cure me? Wouldn't that be a great universal irony if the only person who could save me was the one who did this to me to start with?

I sigh and try to think of happier thoughts. Maddy looks a lot different than how I had envisioned, but it doesn't matter. I love her anyway. As I told Jake, she'll always be my daughter. I remember the moment the doctor handed little Maddy to me, how perfect she looked. She still had some blood on her, but I didn't care. She was my little angel.

The tears start to flow again. I do what I can to wipe them away. I try to focus on the present: Maddy with her pink hair and nose rings. Is she on drugs? It didn't seem like it from what I'd seen. That doesn't mean she can't toke a doobie every now and then. What if she is on something? I can't turn in my own daughter.

I'm not sure when I fall asleep, but when I wake up, Tess stands over me. She has a look of concern on her face. "Are you feeling all right?" she asks.

"I couldn't sleep," I say. "Nerves."

"Oh, I see. I could call that woman—"

"No!" I say, harsher than I mean to. "I'll be fine."

I don't eat a lot for breakfast, just some toast with jam and a cup of coffee. The coffee I need most of all since I got almost no sleep. I shamble through breakfast and a shower like a zombie.

The biggest decision of the morning is what to wear. I go through my drawers—where Tess put most of my new clothes—to find something that will look presentable for Maddy. I settle on a black T-shirt and a pair of jeans with a hole in the left leg Grace assured me was made naturally. I try to smile in the mirror, though my face still looks tired. I suppose it's too late to dye my hair pink and get a few piercings. Not that Tess would ever let me do that. I make sure to grab my new purse before I head downstairs.

Tess takes me as far as the nearest subway station. I can't escape before she wraps me in a hug. "Have a good day, sweetheart. If you need anything at all, you call me right away."

"I will."

"And be very careful. This city isn't safe for a young girl all by herself."

"I'll be careful." I want to tell her I've been a cop for thirty years, but I can't. The look on her face as I leave is like a mom as she sends her kid to school for the first time. I'm sure Tess would have liked to look after me a little longer, to have me all to herself so she wouldn't be alone. Jake and I really need to talk about that at some point; there has to be something we can do to cheer Tess up.

I can't think of anything right now, so I leave her to her loneliness and board the train.

***

I feel normal again as I ride the train. I get a seat next to a young woman in a business suit who's too busy with her phone to notice me. A middle-aged guy stands next to us. He tries to be subtle, but I can see him peek at the girl next to me. I feel a little jealous he doesn't notice me. Am

I that plain?

The girl and her admirer get off at the next stop. A woman with a baby carriage gets on. I shift over so she can sit closer to the door. She nods her thanks to me before she reaches into the carriage for her baby.

It feels oddly good that no one talks to me. I'm just an anonymous face, one among millions. I'm not any different from any of the other women here. I feel a lot better than the last time I was alone on a train, when I wore clothes much too big for me and felt everyone could see through them. I suppose after a few days I've started to settle into my new skin a bit, to feel at home in my own body again.

I get off in the garment district and start towards the stairs. Along the way I see a girl with a cup. She doesn't look too different than me that first day, her hair disheveled and clothes baggy. I give her some of the money Tess loaned me for lunch. "God bless you," she whispers.

I wish I could do more for her, but I can hardly take care of myself at the moment. I climb up the steps and then join the great crush of people on the sidewalks. Again the anonymity feels good. I'm elbow-to-elbow with people of every size, age, and color and yet no one pays any attention to me. No one screams that I'm a freak.

That gives me hope for Maddy. She didn't notice anything yesterday, so as long as I don't come on too strong, she shouldn't notice anything today. How long can we go on like this? Years if it takes that long.

***

I get to Grace's right at nine o'clock. The door is still locked, so I do as she suggested and rap on the glass with my left hand. The knock sounds timid to my ears. I take a deep breath before I try again, hard enough to rattle the glass.

"I'm coming!" Grace shouts from inside. "Keep your panties on."

Her face turns a little red when she sees it's me. "Oh, sorry about that," she says. "I thought you were someone wanting to use the bathroom."

"I didn't mean—"

"I'm joking!" she puts an arm around my shoulder. "You aren't going to last long here if you take things too seriously."

"Oh. I'll try to do better."

"Hey, come on, don't be nervous. I don't want to be your boss. I want us to be friends. Except I get to tell you what to do. OK?"

"That sounds fine." I unzip my purse to take out the papers she gave me yesterday. "I filled these out. Do you need a copy of my ID or anything?"

"These should be fine." Grace skims the application I sweated over so much last night. "To be honest, you're my first employee."

"I am?"

"My mom used to run the place. She started it about fifteen years ago, after she split with my dad. Then she got sick and I came back to run it for her."

"That's too bad," I say. "Is she—?"

"She died four years ago. Pancreatic cancer."

"I'm sorry."

"Don't be. You didn't know her. She was a really interesting lady. A little crazy. Kind of like me, huh?"

"Um—"

"I'm just kidding. I can see it's going to take some time to crack that shell of yours. That's all right. I like a challenge."

"So what am I supposed to do?"

Grace leads me over to the old brass cash register. The black buttons are so big they look like you need a hammer to make them work. "Mostly you just run this old monstrosity. Mom got it from a flea market because she thought it looked neat. It's kind of a pain to use, but I've gotten used to it. You will too after a couple of months. If I'm not such an ogre that I drive you away, right?"

"You're not an ogre."

"You just don't know me well enough." Grace gives me a lesson on how to use the cash register. As I suspected, I have to slap the buttons hard for them to go down all the way. The "No Sale" sign pops up. "Good job. Now we'll just have to wait a little while for a customer. You'll find out pretty quick that we aren't exactly Times Square around here."

If that's true, I wonder why she needs an employee. She intuits this question and picks up the heavy book I saw her with yesterday. "I could probably run the place by myself, but I'm working on my psych dissertation. I've been working on it for six years now and I'm just about finished with it. With you watching the place, I can get it done."

"So this is a temp job?"

"Well if you really want to stick around, I can probably sign the whole thing over to you eventually. After I find a job."

"Oh. Wow," I say. I try to imagine myself running a clothes store in the garment district. Is that what I want to do with my life? If it keeps me close to Maddy, then yes.

I hear footsteps upstairs. Then the stairs begin to squeak. I just about faint when I see Maddy come through the doorway. Her pink hair is unbound and mussed while her oversized T-shirt and sweatpants are wrinkled. She looks like she just got up.

Then she kisses Grace on the lips.

***

In none of the scenarios I ran through my head did I ever imagine my daughter is a lesbian. The possibility never entered my mind. But then the last time I'd seen her, she was ten years old, playing Barbies and Pokemon.

I take a couple steps back while Maddy and Grace kiss, until I'm pressed against the wall. My mouth hangs open, but no sound escapes my lips. It's obvious from the duration of the kiss Maddy and Grace are well acquainted with each other and that this is not just a friendly hello. They're a *couple*.

I try to tell myself Maddy is old enough to make these kind of decisions for herself. She's old enough to date whoever she wants. And even if I want to complain, I haven't been around for twelve years and I can hardly butt in now as Stacey Chance.

After they separate, Maddy turns to me; her face lights up with a smile. "I guess Stacey's an early riser," she says.

Grace puts an arm around my shoulder. "I like an employee who's punctual. That's why I didn't hire you."

"You're just afraid I'll steal all the clothes. At least the ones that fit."

"Well you just about cleaned out the swimwear before we went to Atlantic City."

"I needed some bathing suits. I'm supposed to go to the Gap?"

Grace gives my shoulder a squeeze. "The other part of your job, Stacey, is to make sure Madison doesn't use the place like her personal closet."

"Yeah, well, Stacey and I already have an understanding. Don't we?"

"I, uh—"

"I'm sure Stacey was just kidding." Grace turns to me and adds, "You don't want to give anything to this moocher."

"I told you I'll have the rent next week."

"That's what you said. Then you went and got your navel pierced."

"You're the one who suggested it."

I almost laugh at the bizarreness of the situation. My daughter and Grace argue the same way Debbie and I used to when we were married. They're like an old married couple.

Like an old married couple, they make up with a kiss—and probably more later. "I'm sorry," Grace says. "I've just been under a lot of stress lately."

"It's fine. Now that Stacey's here, she'll help take some of the load off your shoulders." Maddy turns to me and says, "Just remember those shoulders belong to me."

I hope she's not serious about that. Though from the look of her, I don't think I want to meet Maddy in a dark alley. Maybe she's a chip off the old block after all. "I won't."

"Well, I'm going to get ready for work. It's good to see you again, Stace. When Mussolini here lets you have a break, come down for a cup of coffee. On the house."

"I will," I say with probably too much enthusiasm.

Maddy goes back upstairs, which leaves Grace and I alone in the store again. "Don't mind her," Grace says. "Maddy can take some getting used to."

"I know the feeling," I say and feel strangely proud.

Chapter 24

Grace and I have the store to ourselves for three hours. She uses that time to show me around the store, which doesn't take long, and to explain how things work. "Some people will want to barter, maybe trade some of their old clothes for our old clothes. If they do, let me know and I'll take a look at them."

"Sure," I say. "Don't you have any men's clothes?"

"We used to, but not many men come in here. Most straight guys aren't that particular where they shop and the gay guys go more upscale. So I phased that out. If a guy does come in here, he's probably a cross-dresser."

I feel my face turn red, though it shouldn't. I'm not a cross-dresser. I'm not a transsexual either. Dr. Palmer made sure of that. I'm a hundred percent real woman. Still, if I ever did tell Maddy what happened to me, she'd probably lump me in with those weirdoes.

"Yeah, I know, we get all kinds in here. Not nearly enough like you."

"What do you mean by that?"

"Nice girls. Most people who come in here are conceited as hell. Myself included."

"And Maddy?"

"Maddy's got other issues."

"She seems normal enough. Except for the hair and rings."

Grace waves a hand at the air. "She's going through a phase. God, listen to me. I sound like my grandma. Next thing you know, I'm going to invite you upstairs for cookies and milk."

I want to press Grace about what kind of issues Maddy has, but the door opens and a fat woman walks in; she wears a tank top and shorts that show me far more of her than I want to see. Grace nudges me in the ribs. "Go get 'em, tiger."

I force myself to take a few deep breaths. I've faced down hundreds of psychopaths in my career; I can handle one fat woman. I fake a smile as I approach her. "Hi. Can I help you find something?"

"I need a dress. A hot dress. I got a date tonight and I need to look good."

My first instinct is to tell her if she wants to look good she should book an appointment for some liposuction. But I need this job so I can stay close to Maddy and so I don't have to keep sponging off Jake and Tess. "Sure. Our dresses are over here."

I show her over to the racks of dresses, where I got my church dress from. I'm not sure if Grace has any plus size dresses. She's taken cover by the register, where she hides behind her psych textbook. The old sink or swim technique.

I give the fat woman a couple of minutes to go through our offerings. "Anything you like?"

"I said hot. These all look like dresses my grandma would wear."

"I can check in the back—"

"Yeah, you do that."

The back room is where Grace leaves all the stuff she hasn't sorted through yet. That will probably be one of my new duties. I get a head start by sticking both hands into a cardboard box nearly as tall as I am. I pull out handfuls of clothes, to look for something that might make the fat woman happy. I can't imagine Grace will fire me if I don't close this first deal, but she probably won't be impressed either.

I manage to find a few things that might fit. When I get back, the fat woman is browsing the undergarments. This unfortunately makes me think of her naked. As unhappy as I am about what FY-1978 did to me, at least it didn't make me look like *that*.

"This is all I could find," I say.

She snatches the dresses away from me. She tosses the first two to the floor without a word. The third one she holds up to her body. It's a short, strapless number that's bright red, guaranteed to draw far too much attention to her. "This might do," she says.

"You're welcome to try it on in the changing room."

I'm not sure if the changing room will be big enough, but I'm pleasantly surprised when she doesn't get stuck in the doorway. I stand back; I hear her grunt and pant a lot. I hope she's just trying on the dress.

It looks as bad on her as I imagined; it exposes more of her than the tank top and shorts. "What do you think?" she asks.

I got plenty of experience in lying to fat women from when Debbie was pregnant with Maddy. I try not to let my smile waver as I say, "That certainly looks hot."

"Yeah, I think I'll wear it out of here. You mind?"

"No, that's fine. I just need to find out the price." I shuffle over to the cash register. The fat woman follows me, which makes it easier to tell Grace which dress the fat woman wants.

"How much you want?" the fat woman asks.

Grace puts down her book to study the dress. "Let's say fifty bucks."

"Fine." The fat woman reaches into her purse for the money.

"Is that all I can get for you today?" I ask.

"I think that'll do it," she says. Grace stands aside so I can ring it up. The woman pays with cash, a crisp hundred-dollar bill. I count back the change while Grace puts the fat woman's tank top and shorts into a bag.

"There you go. Have a nice day," I say.

"Yeah, sure."

I wait until the woman waddles out the front door to sigh. Grace claps me on the shoulder. "You're a natural, kid."

"Thanks."

"I'm not sure I could have handled it so well. I mean, did you see her arms? They looked like two uncooked loaves of bread."

"It was pretty gross." Something about the encounter bothers me. It takes me a moment before I figure it out. "When I came in yesterday, did you just tell me what I wanted to hear? Does this look bad on me?"

"I could answer that, but how do you know I won't be lying?"

"That sounds like a dodge."

"Some people you have to lie to. Some can handle the truth. Now if I'd tried to sell you a dress like that, then I'd have to lie."

"You don't think I'd look hot in a dress like that?"

She puts a hand on my shoulder. "Of course you

would. But would you really want to wear something like that?"

I think for a moment and then shake my head. "No, I guess not."

"Then stop complaining, would you? You did fine. Better than fine. You were great. Now, why don't you take a break? Go fetch us a couple of cappuccinos."

"Sure," I say, grateful to get away. As I reach the door, it occurs to me I'm just as insecure as the fat woman or Debbie when she was pregnant. Women.

***

The Kozee Koffee is empty when I get there. I'm about to call out when I hear the toilet flush in the ladies room. Maddy appears a minute later; she wipes her hands on her apron. "I was wondering when you'd show up," she says with a smile.

"Grace wants a cappuccino."

"Yeah? What about you?"

"I'll have one too."

I reach into my pocket, but Maddy waves at me. "Don't bother with that. It's on the house." While she starts on Grace's cappuccino, she asks, "How's the first day going?"

"I made my first sale."

"That fat girl in the red dress, right?"

"How'd you know?"

"I figured from the way she was strutting around. Some people are so delusional." Maddy passes a cappuccino across the counter. "So now you're not a sales virgin, eh?"

"Yeah, I guess."

"You don't seem too happy about it."

"It's great. Really." I force myself to smile while

inside I kick myself. This isn't how I wanted things to go. I want us to hit it off, to become best friends. The only problem is I don't know how to be friends with Maddy. I don't know her at all. What I do know came from Grace—my daughter's lover.

Maddy picks up the second cappuccino, the one earmarked for Grace, and takes a sip of it. "That's good shit, don't you think?"

"It is pretty good."

"Come on, let's have a seat."

We don't sit inside. Instead we go outside, to one of the tables by the sidewalk. There's not much foot traffic right now. Maddy takes another sip of Grace's cappuccino. "How long ago did you run away?" she asks and I nearly spit out my coffee.

"How did you know?"

"You got the look. It's like one of those wild tigers at the zoo."

"I'm not going to hurt anyone."

"I don't mean that. I mean you keep looking around, like you're waiting for someone to throw a net on you again."

"I am?" I'm not aware I look like that, but then I've always had to keep on my toes to stay alive. "I'm sorry."

"Don't be sorry. I've seen a lot of girls like you around here. So what happened? You get tired of the suburbs? Or were your parents just shitheads?"

"Shitheads," I say. "They didn't treat me very well, so I thought I'd go out on my own."

"And now here you are."

"Here I am." I'm quick to add, "I'm staying with my aunt. She's really nice."

"She's not really your aunt, is she?"

"What makes you think that?"

"Deductive reasoning."

"What are you, Sherlock Holmes or something?"

"No. My dad's a cop."

"He is?"

"Yeah, or he was. He might be retired by now."

"You don't know?"

"I haven't seen him in years. My mom got full custody in the divorce."

"That's too bad."

When Maddy shrugs I almost start to cry again. "He wasn't around much before they got divorced. He was married to his job."

"But I'm sure he cares about you."

"He never even sent a birthday card."

That's true. I never sent her a card. I figured Debbie would just throw them away. Still, I should have at least tried. She is my daughter. "That's pretty bad," I say. "But at least he didn't punch you in the face for your birthday."

"Your father did that?"

"On my sixteenth birthday. I had a black eye for a week."

"No wonder you ran away." Maddy reaches across the table to take my hand. "You don't have to worry about that anymore. You're free now. Grace and I will help you get on your feet. How about you have dinner with us tonight? I'm not much of a cook, but Grace is like fucking Rachel Ray."

"I'd love to. I'll have to call my aunt. She worries about me."

"I can see why."

Someone walks into the coffeehouse. Maddy stands up from the table. She passes the cappuccino to me. "I'll see you tonight."

"Sure." I let out a sigh and smile. Things didn't go quite as I hoped, but we made some progress. It's a start.

Chapter 25

I make two more sales that day. A couple of hipsters who want something to wear ironically. Each sale gets easier as I grow more comfortable lying to them. I remind myself a lot of police work involves deception; you have to make a criminal think you know more than you do so he'll confess. By comparison it's much easier to tell a girl she looks good in a T-shirt two sizes too small.

Grace doesn't have any problem with Maddy's invitation for dinner. "Sounds like a good idea. Can't promise you anything too fancy, though."

"Maddy said you're like Rachel Ray."

"Only in that I can make something edible in thirty minutes or less."

"I'm sure she didn't mean to put you on the spot."

"It'll be fine." Grace sighs. "Sometimes Maddy doesn't think things through."

"That's not always a bad thing."

"No, most of the time it's great. Other times it gets annoying."

"This is one of the annoying times."

"A little, yeah. Less so if you can handle things for an hour while I hit the grocery store."

"No problem."

While I'm alone I use the phone to call Tess. "My boss invited me for dinner," I say.

"Dinner? That seems a little forward."

"She's nice." I don't mention anything about Maddy; I know Tess would not be happy about me having dinner with a couple of lesbians. She's not the most open-minded on that subject. Not that I'm all that open to it, but if that's what Maddy wants to be then I'll support it. "It shouldn't be too long."

There's silence on the phone for a moment. Then Tess says, "I'll send Jacob to pick you up at nine o'clock. I don't want you riding the train alone at night."

I want to protest I can take care of myself, but I know it won't do any good with Tess. She's taken me in as her surrogate daughter and she's going to make sure nothing happens to me. "All right. I'll be ready."

"Good. So how are things going there?"

"Great. I made three sales already. Grace says I'm a natural."

"That's very good to hear," Tess says, though she doesn't sound too enthused about it. A few hours haven't improved her view of my new job yet. "I suppose I should let you get back to it. Goodbye, sweetheart."

"Goodbye—Aunt Tess." I can almost hear her smile before I hang up. She'd probably rather I called her Mom, but this is the next best thing. I lean back against the wall and sigh. Things have become too complicated.

***

Grace closes up at seven o'clock. She's already been upstairs for an hour to get dinner ready while I mind the store. She shows me how to lock the register and then bring down the metal shutters over the windows and doors. "How is Maddy going to get in?" I ask.

"She uses the fire escape."

"Is that safe?"

"Sure, she does it all the time."

I'd like to go out and check the fire escape myself, but that would look too paranoid. Instead I follow Grace upstairs. She's got two big pots on the stove, one filled with pasta and another with tomato sauce. "You like spaghetti?" she asks.

"I love spaghetti."

"Good. This is all organic stuff. Real organic, not the shit they sell at the A&P or Wal-Mart. We're vegetarians, in case you're wondering."

"That's fine."

"But you're a meat-and-potatoes kind of girl, right?"

"I haven't been able to be picky lately."

Grace stirs the sauce while she asks me seemingly off-hand, "You been having to eat out of dumpsters?"

"A few. Is it really that obvious?"

"I talked to Maddy after I got the stuff. She's going to pick up a bottle of wine."

"I'm not old enough to drink."

"We won't tell—"

"My uncle is picking me up at nine. He'll smell it on my breath."

"Sounds like you've got a pretty strict aunt and uncle."

"They're just old-fashioned."

While Grace tends to the pasta, I walk around the rest of the apartment. It's not much bigger than mine was. There are two bedrooms, but I notice the smaller one has a lot of dust in it. No surprise that Maddy and Grace are sharing a bed.

In lieu of a coffee table or end tables in the living

room, someone—I assume it's Grace—has stacked up old books. A few deal with psychology, but others are dictionaries, encyclopedias, and even old phone books. The posters on the walls are for movies in the last decade, probably ones the theater threw away. In all it looks like the kind of place for a couple of modern young women in the city.

I make myself at home on a saggy gray couch that for some reason smells like Thai food. There's no wall between the living room and kitchen, so I can still watch Grace as she works. She picks up a bottle of some kind of spice to shake a little in. Maddy shows up a few minutes later. "Like the couch? We found it on the corner last week. It was a pain in the ass to carry it up."

"It's nice," I say. I hope she can't tell I'm lying. While I know there's nothing wrong with Maddy and Grace's apartment, the father in me wants my daughter to live somewhere nicer, like a palace. She deserves better than a couch fished out of the trash.

"I'm going to take a quick shower and change," Maddy says.

"Dinner will be ready in twenty minutes," Grace says.

"A real quick shower then."

"Every day she does that," Grace says after Maddy's turned on the water in the shower. "I think she hates the smell of coffee."

"Maybe," I say. Or maybe there was something else she hated about the smell of the coffeehouse that bothered her. As confident and happy as she seemed, maybe she wanted more than to be a barista. I wish I could talk to her about that, but I'm still a relative stranger.

Grace has dinner on the table when Maddy steps out of the bedroom. Her hair is still damp, but it seems a little less pink than before. She's changed into an oversized light blue shirt and a pair of dark blue shorts, only the hem visible. I can't help but notice Maddy has very nice legs, long and toned, like her mother's.

"Glad you could join us," Grace teases. At least I hope she's teasing and this isn't a resumption of their earlier hostilities.

"I wouldn't want to miss this," Maddy says. She gives Grace a chaste kiss. Then she turns to me. "Grace's spaghetti is the best. Not like that canned shit my mom makes."

Debbie never was much of a cook. She was the kind of person who could have burned water. Not that I'm any better. That's why I spent most of my dinners at bars or Rosie's or with Jake and Tess.

I dig my fork into the noodles and sauce. I feel them watch me as I taste it. It is a hell of a lot better than any spaghetti I've had before. "This is great. A lot better than the dumpster."

It takes them both a minute to realize I've made a joke. Then they laugh a lot harder than they need to. Grace pats me on the shoulder. "She's starting to come around. We'll have that shell broken in no time."

Maddy sits down next to me. Now that she's showered, she smells like something floral—violets? Did she put perfume on to impress Grace or me? Maybe both of us. She wraps a hearty ball of pasta around her fork in true Italian fashion. I wonder where she learned that from; it certainly wasn't from me.

"So how was your first day?" Maddy asks.

"It was great. A lot of fun."

"You're just saying that because I'm sitting here, aren't you?" Grace asks.

"No, I really enjoyed it." I'm not lying when I say this. When Dr. Palmer suggested I find another line of work, being a cop seemed like the only thing I could do. But there was something nice about Grace's shop. Maybe it was that I didn't have to worry much some punk would put a bullet in me. Or maybe that I didn't have to stare at the underbelly of society. For one day I could pretend everything was good and everyone was happy. "I can come back tomorrow, right?"

"After that first sale I'm ready to hand over the keys to you." Grace turns to Maddy. "You should have seen the hippo who waddled in there."

"I did see her. I can't believe sweet little Stace here talked her into that." When Maddy pats my shoulder I can't help but grin from ear to ear. "You should be selling used cars."

"I'm not that good."

"Don't be so modest," Grace says. "You did a hell of a job. A lot better than my first day. My first customer tried to shiv me with a hanger."

"I said I was sorry," Maddy says and the three of us laugh.

I let them carry most of the conversation through dinner. Like most married couples they talk about their neighbors and small domestic matters like whether they should call someone to look at the leaky sink. There's a lot I'd still like to ask Maddy, but from the sound of it, she's contented enough. She and Grace seem happy together. And she did it without any help from me.

The subject eventually turns back to me. "You should come out with us this weekend," Maddy says. While Grace smiles, I see her mouth twitch for a moment. This is another of those moments where Maddy speaks before she thinks.

"I'm not sure I can," I say. "My aunt doesn't like me being out after dark."

"She's not even really your aunt, so fuck her."

"Maddy—"

"Sorry. I'm sure she's a nice woman. Doesn't mean you have to let her keep such a tight leash on you."

"She just worries about me. After everything that happened, she has reason to."

Maddy sees she's gone too far this time. "I'm sorry. I just meant it might be fun for the three of us to go out. We don't have to go to a club or anything. We could go to a movie. Something G-rated for your aunt."

I smile at the joke. It's hard to imagine Tess with Grace and especially Maddy with her pink hair, piercings, and tattoos. I feel a sad lump in my stomach as I remember how Tess used to play peek-a-boo with Maddy when she was a baby.

"I was just kidding," Maddy says.

"I know. I was thinking of something else." I tell them about Jenny, though I don't use her name. By the time I've finished, all three of us have tears in our eyes.

"That's so sad," Grace says.

"No wonder your aunt worries about you," Maddy adds. She wipes at her eyes and then forces a smile. "It was just a thought."

"I'll talk to her about it," I say. I check the clock over Grace's shoulder: it's fifteen minutes to nine. "I should probably get going."

"You haven't even had dessert yet," Maddy says. It touches me that she doesn't want me to go yet. I don't want to leave her either, but Jake will probably be early and he won't be happy if I make him wait.

"I couldn't eat another bite anyway," I say. That's a lie. I'm still famished despite two plates of pasta. Apparently my stomach hasn't caught up with the rest of me yet.

"I'll wrap something up for you," Grace suggests. She goes into the kitchen to cut a piece of tiramisu for me.

This gives me a chance to say goodbye to Maddy. "This was a lot of fun," I say. "It's been a while since I had a chance to hang out with someone my own age."

"You're welcome to hang out here anytime you want." Maddy gives me a hug I wish would go on a lot longer than it does. I remember when she used to wrap her arms around my neck and press her little cheek against my shirt. How did I ever let things get this way between us?

"I'll see you tomorrow," I say. I hope to escape before I start to bawl.

Grace escorts me down through the store so she can unlock the door; she doesn't want me to try the fire escape in the dark. Her hug is briefer, though still gentle. "You need anything, you let us know, all right?"

"I will. Thanks."

As expected, Jake is out front in the car, smoking a cigarette. He stares at Grace, to size her up the way a cop does. "So that's your boss, eh?" he asks once I'm in the car. Grace waves as we drive away.

"Yeah, that's her."

"Looks like a flake."

"Then maybe I'm a flake too, because I like her."

"You get to see Maddy?"

"She's upstairs." I turn to Jake and study his face as I ask, "Did you know Maddy was a lesbian?"

"No," he says. I can tell from the way his cheek

twitches that he's lying. He knows I know too. "She came over to visit Jenny a few times. One time she was all broken up about something. I thought it was Jenny being sick, but it was some other girl who dumped her."

"So she's been that way for a while? And you never told me?"

"You could have asked her yourself. She wanted you to."

"She say that?"

"She doesn't have to say it. Every time she came over she'd ask about you." Jake flicks his cigarette out the window. He reaches into his jacket for another while I feel like he's punched me in the stomach.

"I should have called her," I say. "Or at least sent a fucking birthday card."

"You aren't going to get an argument from me."

"I was a really shitty father, wasn't I?"

"It was a bad situation with you and Debbie."

"And I made it worse."

"Maybe. There's no way to know for sure. Not even Dr. Nath invented a time machine. Speaking of which, Dr. Palmer sent me some stuff."

"What stuff?"

"Your test results." It's too dark to read through them, so Jake gives me the short version. "She says you're definitely a woman, and the FY-1978 is still in your system."

"She said as much at the hospital."

"Yeah, but now she's sure."

"What about you?"

"If it's good enough for her, it's good enough for me."

"So what's she going to do about it?"

"She wants to see you tomorrow."

"Tomorrow? But—"

"Take a sick day."

I look in the rearview mirror. I don't want to have to call in sick on my second day, but this is too important. Maybe Dr. Palmer can find some way to cure me, so I can see Maddy as myself and make things right.

Chapter 26

I can't sleep that night. I wind up on the couch again and fall asleep to another infomercial. In my dreams it becomes a commercial for FY-1978. A picture of the old me is brought up on the screen. I look hung over, my eyes red and days of gray stubble on my chin. "Look at this broken down old man," the tanned, aging host says. "He's so disgusting he can't even bring himself to talk to his only daughter."

The audience boos theatrically, as if this is really a taping of *The Jerry Springer Show*. "But with FY-1978 we can make even this monster beautiful."

All of the sudden someone gives me a push onto the stage, into blinding lights. I hear the audience gasp. "Look at the difference FY-1978 can make for you!"

My vision clears enough that I can see my female body. Just as when I first woke up as a woman, I'm naked. I try to cover my breasts with my hands, but it's already too late. Behind me I see the split-screen before and after pictures. The host comes to stand next to me and says, "FY-1978, it's like a Fountain of Youth in a syringe!"

I don't realize I've been screaming until Tess shakes me awake. "It's all right, dear," she says. "It was just a nightmare."

I look around and see the living room of Jake's house. There's no audience in the room, just Tess. Thank God I'm clad in a gray T-shirt and sweatpants too. I let Tess wrap me in a hug and pull me close. She strokes my hair and whispers to me that everything is all right. I'm not so sure about that.

***

When I call Grace in the morning, I don't tell her I'm sick. Instead I tell her I have to go down to the police station to fill out some paperwork about a restraining order against my no-good parents. She accepts this without question. It makes me smile when she says, "Do you want any moral support?"

"Thanks, but my aunt and uncle will be there. I'm sorry about the timing."

"It's fine. We probably won't be very busy anyway."

With my flimsy excuse in place, I'm free to head off to the meeting with Dr. Palmer. She's arranged to meet us at Lennox's headquarters downtown. Because it's such a swanky place, I wear my church dress and a pair of formal shoes from Jenny's closet.

Throughout the drive, I try to arrange the skirt so I'm comfortable without my privates visible to anyone. "I don't know how anyone can stand these," I say.

"Just think of it like a shorter bathrobe," Jake says. This advice isn't very helpful. I finally find a somewhat comfortable position and then fiddle with my hair. Tess brushed it out this morning and then used a couple of barrettes to keep it out of my face. I try to smooth it down anyway; I don't want to look like an urchin as Tess says.

The headquarters for Lennox is a sparkling tower of turquoise glass surrounded by a lot of other gleaming towers. We go around to park in the underground garage and circle down three levels before we find a spot.

Before we get out, Jake turns to me. "No matter what happens, I'll help you through it, all right?"

"I know," I say. "Do I look all right?"

Jake shakes his head. "God, you really are becoming a woman. You look fine. Not that Dr. Palmer will care."

"Maybe she doesn't, but there are a lot of people there who might. I don't want security running me out of the place like I'm a bum."

"No one's going to think you're a bum. You're too well-dressed."

"Thanks."

We take the elevator up to the lobby. As soon as the doors open, I can hear the fountain bubbling. It's just as big as I've heard, two stories of marble in the shape of Athena, the Greek goddess of wisdom. At least that's what Dr. Palmer says. She's there to meet us right by the elevators in a dark blue suit. Again I can't help but feel jealous at how much better she looks in formal clothes than I do.

"You look lovely," she says and gives me a brief hug.

"Thanks. So do you."

"This is quite the spread you guys have," Jake says as the bad cop.

"Pharmaceuticals are a big business," Dr. Palmer says. She gives us a tour of the lobby and explains about the fountain of Athena. "It's supposed to be symbolic of something. I'm not sure what."

"It's beautiful. Can I make a wish on it?"

Dr. Palmer shrugs. "You can try. Mostly just little kids do that."

"I'm not a little kid!"

"Yeah, well, it couldn't hurt to try for a little extra

luck," Jake says. He reaches into his pocket for a quarter. He presses it into my hand.

"I guess so." I flip the quarter into the water, my eyes closed as I wish for Dr. Palmer to have a cure for me.

From there she leads us up to the security desk. We have to give them our ID and sign the register. Though like the factory by the waterfront, the guards just carry tasers that can't stop a serious intruder, not someone like Artie Luther.

The elevator is full of people, all of whom look more grown-up and professional than me. There's barely room for the three of us to squeeze inside. Dr. Palmer presses the button for the eighteenth floor.

When the elevator doors open on the fourth floor to let people out, someone's hand brushes against my ass. Did someone just cop a feel? I smile to myself; it's the first time a stranger's ever flirted with me as a woman. It's a lot better than that fat bastard Jefferson when he checked me out.

With a few people gone, I'm able to press against the side of the elevator, next to Dr. Palmer. "Your bruise is gone," she says.

"Yeah, it disappeared the day after your exam."

She nods as if she expected that. "Must be the serum still in your blood."

"That's what I thought. It's kind of like having a superpower, isn't it?"

"Just don't try leaping from any tall buildings."

Dr. Palmer makes it tough for me to stay positive. I want to believe everything will work out. I know better, but I desperately want everything to get back to normal, or what passed as normal before. The first thing I'll do is call Maddy and tell her I love her. Then I'll buy her twelve birthday cards, one for each year I missed.

The doctor leads us to a windowless conference room. There's nothing in there but a white board, a table, and a dozen wheeled vinyl chairs. "Have a seat," she says. She takes the head of the table, where her briefcase sits. She snaps it open and then pulls out a few folders.

"I'm sure Mr. Madigan already went through the test results with you."

"Yes."

"So we definitely know that you are a hundred percent female and that you have FY-1978 still in your blood."

"Is that good or bad?" I ask.

"Both," she says. "The good thing is that gives us a sample of the serum to work with. The bad news is that even if we had a cure, we couldn't risk using it with so much of the original in your system."

"How long will it take?"

"Probably six months at least."

"And is it…doing anything in there?"

"You're not getting any younger. At least not from what I can tell. As you saw, though, it might still repair some serious cell damage you incur."

"That'll be good if I cut myself shaving."

Dr. Palmer doesn't smile at my bad joke. Instead she frowns. "We might as well get down to business. I brought you here because I wanted to tell you this in person—"

"It's bad news?" I say.

"Depends on how you look at things. Like I said, it's good you had some FY-1978 in your blood so we could get a sample. The bad news is that without the formula or Dr. Nath's notes, we have to try reverse engineering the serum. It's a lengthy process, one that might not be successful."

"How long is it going to take?" I ask.

"It depends. But I'm not going to sugarcoat it for you; it could take as long as five years before we've got it."

"Five years?"

"I'm afraid so." Dr. Palmer reaches across the table to take my hand. I can barely feel it. Five years. Five years of being a woman. I remember what Jake said in the car, that I'm already acting like a woman. I've seen the signs myself. In five years is there going to be any of Steve Fischer left? Or will I be entirely Stacey Chance?

She gives my hand a squeeze before she drops the anvil on my head like in one of those old cartoons. "It gets worse. That's five years to recreate the serum. From there we have to study it, figure out exactly how it did what it did to you. Then we have to come up with a cure. We'll have to do trials on animals—"

"How long?"

Dr. Palmer takes a deep breath. "Conservative estimate: twenty years total."

"Twenty years? You expect me to live like this for twenty years?" In twenty years I'll be thirty-eight years old, on my way into middle age for a second time.

And in twenty years Maddy will be forty-two years old. She and Grace will probably have moved out to the suburbs so they can raise a child they create through artificial insemination—my grandchild. A grandchild who will never know his or her grandfather, just Aunt Stacey.

I put my head down on the table and sob at this image. Dr. Palmer pats my back. "I'm sorry, Stacey. I wish I had better news for you. But it might not be that long. I'll be working around the clock on this, to find a way to change you back."

I look up, Dr. Palmer's face blurry through my tears. I laugh. It's a bitter, hateful laugh. The chances of a cure quickly were remote, but there was still that hope. Now there's no hope left at all. "You? You'll find a way? The only one who could is Dr. Nath and she's dead! You said it yourself; she's the only one who knew how to make this shit. You're too fucking stupid to remake it, let alone to cure me!"

I feel a stronger hand on my shoulder. "Come on, don't say something you'll regret," Jake says.

"I won't regret it!" I reach out to sweep the papers and Dr. Palmer's briefcase from the table in a childish gesture that makes me feel slightly better. "You people made this shit! Your stupid drug did this to me and now you're saying you'll need twenty years to fix it? Fuck you! Fuck all of you!"

"Stacey, please—"

"Fuck you!" I storm out of the room while Dr. Palmer and Jake are still reeling from my outburst. I don't bother with the elevator, knowing it'll be too slow. Instead I kick off my silly girl shoes and take the stairs. I'd like to take off this girly dress too, but that will have to wait until later. It's almost impossible to see through my tears, but my feet guide me well enough.

I expect someone to stop me in the lobby, but no one intercepts me as I run crying through the atrium and out of the building.

Chapter 27

My mind is a blank for the next six hours. All I know is I got on a train to the garment district. By the time I wind up at the Kozee Koffee, the bottoms of my feet are black and bleeding. I should have kept the stupid shoes.

"Stacey? Oh my God, what happened to you?" Maddy says. She rushes from behind the counter to wrap me in a hug I can't feel. "Grace said you were at the police station."

"Yeah, sure. The police station," I mumble.

Maddy sits me down at a table. She uses another chair so she can prop my feet up. I don't feel it when she washes them with a damp rag. I don't feel anything at all. I've cried myself out on the way here.

To finish, she rubs at my cheeks as if I'm a child who had played in a mud puddle. "What happened to your shoes? Did someone steal them?"

"No. They were slowing me down."

Maddy looks me in the eye. Despite how different the rest of her might look from me, her eyes are the same blue. They're my eyes. Or rather, Steve Fischer's eyes. That's not me anymore. From now on I'm Stacey Chance. I decided that at some point during my escape. Steve

Fischer is dead.

That's what brought me here. I take Maddy's hand. It's bigger and there are too many rings on it, but it's as soft as when she was a newborn. No, she's not my daughter anymore. She was Steve's daughter. Maddy is just my friend and now I'm going to perform a friend's duty. "Maddy, I need to tell you something."

"What is it?"

"The people I'm staying with, they're Jake and Tess Madigan."

"Really? I know them. Jake is my dad's partner—on the police force. I used to play with their daughter."

"I know."

"You do?"

"I saw some pictures in Jenny's room of you two."

"She used to be my best friend. But she's gone now. I'm sure they told you that."

I nod. "Has anyone said anything about your father?"

"No. Why should they? No one's said anything about him in twelve years."

I take a deep breath. Even as Maddy's friend this is difficult. "He's dead. He died about five nights ago. There was a break-in at Lennox Pharmaceuticals. He responded to the call. The intruders killed him."

Maddy stares at me for a long time with no reaction. She finally asks, "You're sure?"

"I saw some papers on Jake's desk. It was a police report. Whoever did it burned down his apartment too. You can probably find that in the newspaper."

Maddy drops the damp rag to the floor. After a minute she says, "No, that can't be. Someone would have said something by now. They would have told Mom and she would have told me."

"Go and ask Jake Madigan. See what he tells you about it."

Maddy has a cell phone in her pocket. She whips it out and then punches in a few numbers. She doesn't have Jake's cell in there apparently because she says, "Hi, Mrs. Madigan? It's Madison Griffith. It's good to hear your voice too. I, um, I need to talk to Mr. Madigan. It's important. Is he around? Well, could you give me his cell number?" She listens for a moment and then nods. "Thanks, Mrs. Madigan. No, I'm fine. Really. What? No, I haven't seen Stacey. Is she missing? I'll keep an eye out for her."

Maddy gives me a hard stare, one that penetrates my numbness to make my stomach churn. "You'd better be right about this." She punches in another phone number, Jake's cell. I hope he has it with him. Like a lot of older guys he isn't always the most responsible with the new technology. Apparently he does have it with him, probably in case I call.

"Hi Mr. Madigan, it's Madison Griffith. No, Stacey's not here. I'm not sure where she is. What happened? Oh, I see. Well, I'll keep an eye out for her if she comes here." Maddy pauses and her hand shakes. "I heard about a robbery at this place called Lennox Pharmaceuticals. Do you know anything about that? Uh-huh. Was Dad there? He was? Is he OK?" I wish I could hear what Jake is saying so I'd know if he's lying or not. He must not be, because Maddy's eyes fill with tears. "Thanks for telling me. No, I'll be fine. I have to go."

She throws the phone across the room before she melts against me. "Oh God!" she sobs. "He is dead."

"I'm sorry," I say.

I'm not prepared for her to flip out the way I did in the conference room at Lennox's headquarters. "That son of a bitch! He doesn't call me for twelve years and now he's dead? That stupid fucking bastard! I hate him! I'm glad he's dead!"

"You don't mean that," I say.

"Yes I do! He never loved me, just like he never loved Mom. All he cared about was helping strangers. He never cared about his family."

I want to deny this, but how can I? She's right. I always put my job above Debbie and Maddy. Is it any surprise Debbie found greener pastures? Is it any wonder she didn't want Maddy to live in my seedy apartment every other weekend?

I put my arms around Maddy and hold her close. We sob together, to mourn the death of Detective Steve Fischer.

***

After about ten minutes of crying, Maddy gets up. She pulls me up to my tired, dirty, bloody feet. "Come on," she says. "Jake will be here any minute."

"But you said—?"

"He'll show up here anyway. He knows you'll come here sooner or later. That or Grace's. He's probably got someone staking out the shop already."

I follow Maddy out the back, into an alley. She stops to throw her apron against the door. "Won't you get fired for that?"

"So what? I can get another crummy job."

"Where are we going to go?"

"I don't know," she says. We take a few steps; a sharp pain accompanies each one. "Oh shit, your feet. Wait here a minute."

I sit on a crate in the alley and wish I hadn't worn my dress to that meeting. The hem of the skirt and patches of the rest are as black as my feet. I'm not sure how that happened. Tess will kill me when she sees it. I laugh at this. I won't see Tess again. That's too bad because she's the best surrogate mother an eighteen-year-old runaway can hope for.

Maddy returns with a couple of garbage bags. "These won't be as good as shoes, but they might help a little." She wraps the bags around my feet and then uses a piece of string to tie each bag to my feet.

As she said, the result isn't as good as a real pair of shoes. It is slightly better than to walk barefoot, the pain a little less with each step. Maybe by tomorrow the FY-1978 will have taken care of this too. In the meantime I'll have to gut it out.

Maddy leads me through a winding series of alleys. We end up at the back of Grace's shop. "Stay here," she says again. "I'll go up and grab some shoes."

"Could you get me a shirt and pants too?" I say. "I really want out of this dress."

"I'll see what I can do."

I watch as she climbs up the fire escape and disappears through the window on the second floor. Grace is probably in the shop. If Jake or Tess has called her, she might be worried about Maddy and I by now. Maybe I should go in for a minute—

No, Maddy's right. Jake might show up there. Or he might radio for a car to keep an eye on the place in case I turn up. I'll be a lot safer in the alley.

Maddy climbs down a couple minutes later, a bundle of clothes tucked under one arm. There's a pair of shoes, a dark blue shirt, and a pair of jeans. "Hurry up and get dressed," she says. She turns away while I strip off the dress.

The shirt and pants are a little big. So are the shoes. I'm not too picky at the moment. I leave the dress in the nearest dumpster, followed by the barrettes in my hair. Let my hair get wild. I don't care anymore.

"What do we do now?" I ask.

"Let's get a drink," Maddy says.

***

In some kind of cosmic irony, Maddy chooses Squiggy's of all places. There's something appropriate about that, as if we've completed the circle. "My dad came here a lot," she says.

"I'm not old enough to drink," I remind her.

"So? They aren't going to card us."

Maddy goes in first. She takes a seat at the bar. Big Al stares at her for a moment, as if she's a space alien or escaped zoo critter. He doesn't get many girls with pink hair in here. "Give me a shot of bourbon," Maddy says. "And one for my friend."

"How old is she?" Big Al asks.

"Twenty-one," I say.

He stares at me for a moment and then shrugs. He pours two bourbons. Maddy takes some cash from her pocket. "Keep 'em coming," she says.

The alcohol burns down my throat. I cough. After just the one drink I feel lightheaded. Part of that might be the blood loss; the rest of it is that this body is a lot smaller than my old one. No, there was no old body. This is my only body and it's always been my body. I will myself to forget about the last fifty years, but it doesn't take. I'll need a lot more alcohol for that to happen.

"Hey Al," Maddy says. "You hear about my dad?"

"What about him?"

"He sleeps with the fishes," she says and cackles wildly; she doesn't realize how right she almost is.

"You're his little girl, aren't you? I remember you when you weren't even as tall as one of those stools."

"Yeah, Dad would bring me into a place like this."

"It wasn't to drink," Al says. Even through the alcohol, I remember what he's talking about. It happened about eighteen years ago. I'd taken Maddy to a dentist's appointment. We were about to get some ice cream—which defeated the whole point of going to the dentist—when the call came in. Someone had robbed Squiggy's.

A more responsible parent would have taken his four-year-old daughter home first, but I wasn't that responsible. I put the siren on the top of the dash—which delighted Maddy in the backseat—and drove like a bat out of hell to get here. A detective wouldn't usually stoop to investigate a petty bar robbery, but this case was personal.

"Those uniformed punks wouldn't have done anything. Your daddy made sure to track the bastards down. Got all my money back with interest."

"Yeah, he was a real fucking hero," Maddy says. Her voice isn't even slurred yet. My little girl can hold her liquor better than I can. "Give me another, will you?"

"What happened to him?" Big Al asks.

"Some drug company robbery. He tried being a hero again. This time he bought it."

"You shouldn't talk about your dad like that," Big Al says to defend his best customer. "He was a good guy."

"Yeah, as a cop. And a drinker. He was shit for a father."

"I think you two better leave," Big Al says.

"Oh yeah? Or you'll do what? Call the cops?" She

laughs right in his face. "Just wait till they see you're serving an eighteen-year-old, you stupid bastard."

Maddy's gone too far again. Big Al doesn't need to call the cops. He reaches beneath the bar for a double-barreled shotgun. "I said to get out of here."

"You going to kill us? Two sweet, innocent little girls? The press will have a field day with that."

"Maybe I don't have to kill you. Maybe I'll just shoot one of those pretty legs and let you bleed to death."

"You don't have the guts."

"You want to find out?"

I take Maddy's arm. "Come on, Maddy. Let's go."

"Yeah, fine. You water your booze down anyway. Fat bastard."

Maddy hops off the stool. I lean against her for support as we stagger out of Squiggy's.

Chapter 28

As we stagger along for a few blocks, Maddy sings a song about someone named Alejandro. I don't know it, though I pretend I do. Then she decides on a change of plans. She stops at a liquor store, and puts a hand on my shoulder. "You wait here," she says. "I'll go in and get us a couple of bottles. Just remember, don't take candy from strangers."

She laughs as if this is the funniest thing ever and then musses my hair. "I'm just kidding. You're so fucking serious all the time. You need to loosen up."

"Maybe we should go home."

Maddy guffaws. "See what I mean? Stop being so *responsible* all the time. You're eighteen for Christ's sake. Once you get to be an old lady like Grace, then you can be responsible."

"Grace isn't that old."

"Are you kidding? She's going to be thirty next year."

"Thirty? But she said—"

Maddy guffaws again. "That lying little bitch! She always tells people she's younger than she is. When we met, she said she was twenty-two. Really she was twenty-six!"

I force myself to laugh, though this conversation has sobered me up real quick. I can't imagine why Grace would want to lie about her age like that, except maybe people my age wouldn't want to buy clothes from a twenty-nine-year-old. That or run of the mill insecurity. "Maybe we've had enough excitement for one night," I say.

"Don't be such a stick in the mud!" She pinches my cheek until I cry out. "You just stay right here. Mama will be back with your bottle in a few minutes."

She continues to laugh as she goes inside. I take a few steps away from the door and lean against the wall as I wait. I put a hand to my cheek where Maddy pinched it. This whole night has become surreal, more so than everything that's happened so far. All those times I tucked Maddy in and kissed her forehead goodnight, I never imagined someday we'd be on a bender together. Like any father, I wanted more for her.

An old memory surfaces. One of Maddy's first writing assignments in grade school was to write about what she wanted to be when she grew up. I had hoped she would pick a cop like her old dad. But being only seven years old, of course she picked something fanciful: a ballerina. A drawing accompanied the little paragraph she wrote in crayon, with a vaguely human shape dressed in a pink leotard and tutu. That fifteen years later she would be a barista at a rundown coffeehouse, living with a woman seven years older than her, and drinking bourbon straight from the bottle would have come as a shock to both of us.

I feel the tears start to come again. My poor little Maddy. Here she is, trying to drown her sorrows in bourbon when I'm still here. I'm outside waiting for her.

Why can't I tell her? It's not fair. First to have her taken away by Debbie and the lawyers and now taken away forever by Artie Luther.

Sometimes when you think the universe is complete shit, it decides to throw you a bone. Or in this case, a Worm.

***

I rub my eyes a couple of times to make sure it really is the Worm on the other side of the road. Then my heart almost stops when he turns and looks right at me. Does he recognize me? How could he? No one knows who I really am except for Jake and Dr. Palmer.

He starts across the street and hurries as fast as his thin little legs can carry him. The closer he gets, the more I know it's him. If not by sight than by smell: the stench of menthol cigarettes, cheap beer, and sweat that accompanies him everywhere he goes. What do I do? Should I make a break for it? What about Maddy? She'll be back any minute with the booze.

For the first time since I graduated from the academy I don't know what to do. A few days as a girl have rusted my cop instincts. So I don't do anything. I stand against the wall and stare wide-eyed at the Worm.

As he steps onto the sidewalk, I realize we're the same height now. This makes him more intimidating than before. My stomach roils with fear. Fear of the Worm? He'd need help to kill an infant in a crib.

Before I can wet myself, the Worm turns. He doesn't care about me. He's on his way to the liquor store, probably to get some more cigarettes. Maybe he'd already tried the machine at Squiggy's. Or maybe he was still too scared to go back in there after last time.

With that memory, the fear in my stomach turns to

rage. The Worm did this to me. Not directly, but indirectly. If I hadn't seen him at Squiggy's that night, I wouldn't have known about the robbery at Lennox Pharmaceuticals. I wouldn't have gone there and been injected with FY-1978. I'd still be me, a broken-down fifty-year-old police detective. Maddy wouldn't be inside this liquor store, trying to drink her problems away like her old man.

As the Worm is about to open the door, I call out, "Hey mister! You got any spare change?"

He turns and now he looks at me. I know the smile that comes to his face for what it is: he's checked me out and likes what he sees. "Maybe. What would you do to earn it?"

He lets the door go and takes a few steps towards me. I hold on to the rage like a life preserver and let it think for me. "I don't know, what do you want me to do?"

The Worm puts a hand around my shoulder. "How about we go into the alley and do a little *negotiating*?"

It's suicide for a girl like me to let someone like the Worm take her into a dark alley. But I don't care. This scumbag helped take my life from me; now he'll help me make Artie Luther and his goons pay for it.

We go behind a dumpster, where he presses me up against a wall. I let him move his hand down my shirt so he can cop a feel of my breasts. "I bet you're new around here," he says.

"You could say that."

"Just came to the big city from Ma and Pa's farm, right?"

"Maybe."

"Now you realize this big city ain't what it's cracked up to be."

"I'm starting to see that."

"That's only 'cause you hadn't met me yet, baby," he says, his attempt to act suave. That alone is enough to make me want to gag. His hand starts to move down into my jeans. "I bet you never got laid with any of them farm boys, did you?"

"No."

"I thought so." The pervert actually licks his lips. "A ripe little virgin. How's about you come back to my place?"

"And you'll help me out?"

"Sure, baby. I'll help you out in a lot of ways."

He doesn't just want to touch my privates. He wants to get a good whiff of them too. I try not to flinch as he bends down to unzip my jeans. I wait until he's got his head level with my zipper, then I strike.

Thirty years as a cop, a lot of those years spent in bars, taught me a lot about practical hand-to-hand combat. Most of those moves were better used as a six-three, two-hundred-thirty-pound man. So I rely on something much simpler: I knee him in the face. When he's down on the ground, I kick him in the balls as hard as I can.

It hurts like hell given the state of my feet, but I'm rewarded as the Worm writhes in pain. I wait a few seconds before I give him another kick, this one to the midsection. "You cunt!" he shouts.

The Worm doesn't carry a gun. He'd be more likely to shoot himself with it than anyone else. He does carry a knife, in the inside pocket of his jacket. I've taken it off of him a few times already. This time I aim to keep it.

I take his wallet too while I'm at it. I look through it and find fourteen bucks. "You were going to take my virginity for fourteen bucks?" I ask him. I push the button on his knife and out pops the six-inch blade. "I should cut your dick off and make a necklace out of it."

While I should do that, I put the knife to his throat instead. With my other hand I drag him into a sitting position against the wall; the dumpster makes sure no one will see us. That's a good thing, because a few seconds later I hear Maddy call my name.

"Stacey? Where the hell are you?"

I put my free hand to the Worm's mouth before he can say anything. Between that and the knife at his throat, he keeps quiet. If Maddy comes down the alley and sees us like this, I'll have to tell her this perv tried to jump me and I turned the tables on him. Maybe not the most believable story, but in her present state, Maddy probably wouldn't think too hard about it.

"You stuck-up little bitch! Where the hell are you?" Maddy shouts. When I still don't say anything, she adds, "Fine! I didn't want to share this with you anyway!"

With that my little girl staggers off into the night. I hope she doesn't run into anyone like the Worm before she can make it home.

***

Now that we have some privacy, I take my hand off the Worm's mouth. I bend down so we're eye-to-eye. "Who are you?" he asks. "A cop?"

"You tell me. Look in my eyes."

"What? You some kind of hypnotist?"

"Just do it or I'm going to give you a free tracheotomy."

He stares at me for a few moments. Then his face begins to pale. "Fischer? But, you're a—"

"A cunt? Yeah, it's amazing what modern technology can do."

"That ain't possible. They said you dead."

"Who?"

"Everyone! They said you at the bottom of the harbor."

"Maybe I'm just a ghost then. You want to take your chances?" I press the knife closer to his throat, enough so he can feel the blade.

"Why you haunting me? I didn't do nothing to you!"

"You told me about Lennox Pharmaceuticals. Was that an accident? Or did Luther send you to find me?"

"You go stupid or something? Lex didn't want no cops around. Not around that scene."

"Why not?"

"He didn't want nobody messing up his score."

"Like an anti-aging drug called FY-1978?"

"Maybe. I don't know!"

I can smell that the Worm's pissed himself. To think I was about to piss myself when I saw him a few minutes earlier. "I believe you. A little shit like you doesn't know anything about Artie Luther's operation, does he?"

"No! I don't know nothing! I swear!"

"But I bet you do know someone who knows, don't you?"

"I—"

I press the knife tighter to his throat, enough that blood trickles down. He screams like a girl at this. "Don't make me ask again," I hiss. "Who told you about the robbery?"

"Blades, man! It was Bobby Blades!"

This makes sense. Blades was at the robbery, down in the basement. "Where can I find him?"

"The club. He hangs out there all the time."

"Which one?"

"Honey Well Club. Goes there most every night unless he's got a job."

"Good." I pull the knife back and then pat the Worm's cheek. "You better go home and clean yourself up. Then I'd suggest you hide yourself in a deep, dark hole or I'm going to put you under Ma and Pa's farm. Got it?"

"Yeah, I got it," he says. He doesn't need any more incentive to run from the alley. I wipe the knife off with a hamburger wrapper and then tuck it into my pocket.

I promise myself that tomorrow night Bobby Blades will get a visit from the ghost of Steve Fischer.

Chapter 29

I walk around for the better part of four hours to try to catch up to Maddy. The farther I go, the more my buzz wears off. Even the thrill of the Worm's defeat leaves me. All I'm left with is a sick feeling in my gut that I'm going to find my little girl dead in a gutter or her beaten, violated body in an alley.

It's ironic to think of her as my little girl, because now I'm a littler girl than her. Still, I have the same sense of dread as when Maddy had a fever when she was two years old. I had felt so helpless then, as I watched Debbie mop little Maddy's forehead with a washcloth and force water down her throat. As with most everything in Maddy's life I hadn't been directly involved through most of it. Through most of it I had filled out paperwork and talked with Jake about cases we were working on; I popped into Maddy's room every now and then to make sure she hadn't died. That hadn't lessened the dread and fear; if anything it made things worse because I waited for Debbie to run downstairs and tell me our daughter was dead.

I walk down every alley I come across, but see only a few bums. With the Worm's knife in my pocket I feel much safer about them. There are still a few bars open, but I can't get into any of them, not by myself. It's possible Maddy went into one of those for a few more drinks. I ask a couple of liquor store clerks if they've seen Maddy. We go through a vaudeville act where I point to my hair and then something pink before they shake their heads.

By four in the morning my feet are tired and I'm about to collapse on the sidewalk and sob. I find an open diner and go inside. With some of the Worm's money, I get a cup of coffee to steady my nerves and some change for the pay phone.

I decide to start with Grace. Maybe Maddy's gone back there for a little angry, drunk sex. The phone picks up after one ring. I don't get out more than her name before Grace snaps at me, "What the hell were you two doing?"

"Is Maddy there?"

"Yes she's here." The way Grace's voice falters, I know she's crying. Is Maddy hurt? "She's locked herself in the bathroom. She won't come out. She won't even tell me what's going on. I'm scared, Stace. She's never been like this before."

I look out the window and see a street sign. "I'll be there in about a half hour, OK? Just don't do anything crazy before then. Either of you."

"Stace—"

"I'll explain when I get there."

"OK, just hurry."

I do hurry. I'm grateful for this lithe body that lets me gallop thirty blocks in twenty minutes. By the time I reach Grace's shop, sweat drenches my entire body. I don't have time to rest. I haul myself up the fire escape to the second floor.

I've barely got through the window when Grace

grabs me by the shoulder. She throws me against the wall hard enough that it'll probably leave a bruise for a day or two. I deserve it.

"What the hell is going on? What were you and Maddy up to?"

"I found some papers. About her father."

"Her father? What about him?"

"He's dead. I told her and she wanted to go out for a drink. So we went to this bar—"

"*You* went to a bar?"

"Yes. But we got thrown out. We went to this liquor store and I waited outside. This creep hassled me and we got separated. I looked all over for her. Is she all right?"

"I don't know! I was sitting here working on my dissertation when she came in. I only got a glimpse of her before she locked herself in there." Grace lets me go. Then she shakes her head. "How could you let her do that?"

"What was I supposed to do?"

"You should have stopped her. Or at least called me and let me handle it."

I look down at my feet, at what are probably Grace's sneakers. She seems to notice this too. "What happened to your clothes?"

"I got my dress dirty, so Maddy snuck in here to get me something clean."

Grace throws up her hands. I brace for her to punch or slap me or maybe just to give me another push. She doesn't do any of those. Instead she sinks down onto the living room couch and puts her face in her hands.

I sit down next to her and put a hand on her shoulder. "I'm sorry. This is all my fault. I shouldn't have told her."

"It's not your fault. You don't know Maddy like I do."

"What does that mean?"

Grace looks up at me. "You don't know what kind of life she's had. Her parents got divorced when she was a kid. It wasn't an amicable divorce either. She never saw her father again."

"He didn't even send a birthday card," I say.

"Yeah, what a shit. Her mom isn't any better. The way Maddy tells it, her mom went through about half the phone book in the city. Every time poor Maddy thought it'd work out and she'd finally have a 'normal' family."

Grace stops and shakes her head. "What you don't know about her is that the hair, the piercings, the attitude, it's all a dodge. It's a defense mechanism she's created for herself. She pretends to be this tough chick, but really she's that same ten-year-old girl whose parents broke her heart.

"All these years, she's been hoping they'd get back together, that her daddy would come through the door and sweep her up in a hug and they could go out for ice cream and shit like that and then they'd go back home for dinner with Mommy."

"And I ruined that for her."

"Yeah. Now she knows for sure it's not going to happen. Before the odds might have been one-in-a-million, but now they're zero."

I nod and think of my reaction to Dr. Palmer when she told me it'd be twenty years or more before I could hope for a cure. I had always thought I might be stuck this way for a long time—if not forever—but when she told me that had made it final.

I join Grace in crying for Maddy. If Grace is right, then all this time Maddy's waited for me. But I never came for her. I was so stupid I never even tried to see her.

I just crawled away with my tail between my legs.

"I'm such an idiot," I say, which is putting it mildly.

"You did what you thought was best."

I say nothing. I can't tell Grace the truth. She'd never believe me. Neither would Maddy if I went to the door and told her that her new friend Stacey is actually the father she's longed for.

And then the bathroom door opens.

Grace and I spring from the couch at the same time. We hurry over to the bathroom and get there just as Maddy emerges. But it's not the same Maddy who went inside.

Somewhere along the way Maddy must have stopped at a drug store. The pink is gone from her hair. Now it's entirely jet black. She's taken the scissors to it as well to chop off most of it in favor of a patchy, boyish cut.

She looks at me and then Grace. I mentally urge her to come to me, to collapse into her daddy's arms. But she doesn't. She picks Grace, her lover. She toddles forward a step before she melts into Grace's arms.

"Maddy, what did you do?" Grace asks.

"I'm mourning," she says. She slurs her words a little. "For Daddy."

I want to grab her and tell her she doesn't need to mourn for Daddy; Daddy is right here. But I can't. Instead I watch as Grace leads her away to the bedroom. The door closes and I'm alone.

Chapter 30

I spend the rest of the night in the "guest bedroom" that had been Maddy's when she first moved in. The bed is lumpy and smells like cat piss, but I can't sleep anyway. I have far too much on my mind.

Again I think what a fool I've been. Maddy needed me after the divorce and I was never there. Never a visit or a call or even a fucking card. I cut her out of my life entirely, except once a year to mourn her at Squiggy's. She needs me again now, but I still can't be there for her, not in the way I want. The best I can do is to be next door in a dusty bedroom while Maddy cries on another woman's shoulder.

When I can't stare at the ceiling anymore, I roll out of bed. I put my ear to Grace and Maddy's door, but there's only silence. They've probably fallen asleep by now, entangled in each other's arms for comfort. That picture doesn't disgust me; it only makes me jealous again that Grace is the one Maddy went to for support.

There has to be something Stacey Chance can do for Maddy. I see the stove and think breakfast in bed might help Maddy and Grace. There are eggs and such in the refrigerator, but I know I can't cook anything.

Instead I put on a pair of Grace's sneakers and then

slip down the fire escape. It's six in the morning, late enough or early enough depending on your perspective for the creeps to have gone to bed. I'm still glad for the Worm's knife. A girl can't be too safe in a place like this.

I go down to the diner across from the Kozee Koffee, where Tess and I drank horrible coffee the one day. The service isn't any better as I order three vegetarian omelets and toast to go. I skip the coffee; I figure anything I make has to be better than the shit they serve here.

I wait around by the counter for a few minutes until the surly waitress hands me a sack with three foam boxes in it. I use up the rest of the Worm's money with this purchase. At least it went for a good cause.

I'm almost back to Grace's when a pair of headlights snap on. They hit me in the face just like the light in the interrogation room. I put a hand up to shield my eyes, though I already know who's there. I should have realized Jake wouldn't let this go so easily.

I make sure to grip the bag tighter before he approaches. It comes as no surprise when he pushes me into an alley, against a wall. "Why does everyone keep doing that?" I shout at him. "I'm not a fucking rag doll."

"What the hell do you think you're doing?" Jake hisses. "Why did you tell Maddy you're dead?"

"Because it's true. Steve Fischer is dead. You heard Dr. Palmer. Twenty years at a minimum. You don't think Maddy's going to figure it out by then?" Then again since I'd already gone twelve years without a word to her, maybe another twenty could have gone by.

"You should have let me tell her when the time was right."

"When would that be? Six months? A year? It was going to happen eventually. Might as well happen now."

Jake sighs and lets me go. "You're still such a pigheaded son of a bitch," he says. He reaches into his jacket for a cigarette.

That's when Maddy chooses to walk by. Before I can tell her to stop, she throws herself at Jake. "Get away from her, you creep!" she screams.

She punches at Jake for a few seconds before he says, "Maddy, stop it. It's me! It's Mr. Madigan."

That only adds to Maddy's fury. "You son of a bitch! Why didn't you tell me Daddy was dead?"

I let our breakfast drop so I can grab Maddy around the shoulders and haul her back against the wall. I'm careful not to run her into it as hard as everyone has done to me. She still tries to claw at Jake for a few seconds before she goes limp. I finally get my wish when she puts her head on my shoulder.

"I'm sorry, Maddy. Your father's body hasn't turned up yet. I didn't want to tell you or your mom until it did, when we'd know for sure," Jake says.

"I have a right to know what's going on. He's my dad."

"I know that. I just didn't want to worry you guys until I was positive."

Maddy sniffles a few times. It seems the crying jag is over, at least for now. She pulls her head up, a black mascara stain left on my shirt—Grace's shirt. She wipes ineffectually at her eyes for a moment. "Well now I know. And I'm going to tell Mom."

Jake looks ready to say something, but just sighs again. "I'll drive—"

"The hell you will. I'll take the train," Maddy says. She points a finger at him. "Stay the hell away from me. Me and Mom, got it?"

I try to intervene. "Maddy—"

"That goes for you too. Everyone leave me the fuck alone."

Between Jake and I we could overpower her, wrestle her into the car. Maybe we could drive her over to Lennox's headquarters and have a chat with Dr. Palmer. But even if she did believe our crazy story, what then? She'd still be angry at me for lying to her. She'd probably hate me all over again. Even if she did get over that, what kind of relationship could we have?

It's better like this, I tell myself. I let Maddy go. Jake must sense my line of thought; he doesn't do anything to stop her as she stomps away. He catches me before I can collapse to the ground. Now it's me who needs his shoulder to cry on.

"I've made such a mess of things," I say into his shoulder.

"I know," he says and pats my back. "We'll get it all straightened out. Somehow."

I don't say anything. I'm not nearly so optimistic about that. We'd need a miracle to get things back to the way they used to be. I haven't believed in miracles for a long time.

Chapter 31

After I've cried myself out, Jake lets me go. Despite what Maddy said, he's going to swing by Debbie's condo to make sure neither of them does anything crazy. "Then I guess I'll break the news to Tess."

"I'm sorry."

"So am I. It might help if you were there—"

"I don't think so. Not for a little while."

"Steve—"

"Don't call me that. It's Stacey now. It always will be." I seize the bag from the ground. I stomp off in the opposite direction as Maddy went, back to Grace's. Jake doesn't try to stop me this time.

Maddy unlocked the front door on her way out, which makes it easier for me to get the eggs upstairs. I find Grace on the couch, head in her hands while she stares at the floor. She doesn't even look up when I come in.

I leave breakfast on the table and then sit down next to Grace. I put an arm around her shoulders. Usually I've been the one who's needed comfort over the past few days, so it feels a little odd to be on the opposite end. "Maddy'll come back," I say.

"I know," Grace says.

I'm not sure what to say next. Being a woman, Grace probably wants to talk about her feelings, which will end up with a lot of tears. I wish Tess were here; she would be able to handle this a lot better than me. After Jenny died, I comforted Jake with a trip to Squiggy's and made sure he didn't drown in his own vomit after he passed out.

Unable to think of anything to say, I sit in silence with her for a few moments. Then I say, "I bought some breakfast. Are you hungry?"

"No."

"How about some coffee?" Grace only shrugs. I sigh and say, "There has to be something I can do."

She takes my hand that's around her shoulders and gives it a squeeze. "Just sit here," she says.

"OK." I try not to flinch when Grace leans over and rests her head on my chest. I remember Debbie snuggled up against me on the couch or in bed when we were still newlyweds. After Maddy was born and the wheels started to come off our marriage, she didn't bother to cuddle anymore. I didn't realize until now how much I've missed it.

We sit there for a couple of hours; I stroke her hair and she uses my breast as a pillow. From her soft breathing I figure she must have nodded off by now. As much as I enjoy the intimacy, my arm is asleep and my bladder starts to nag at me.

Right on cue, Grace whispers, "I should go down and open the store."

"You don't have to. I can handle it."

She sits up, turns to me, and smiles. "I suppose I have taught you everything I know. Use it well, grasshopper."

"I'll try." I slide off the couch and then go to use the

bathroom and shake some life back into my arm. When I finish, Grace lies on the couch and clutches a throw pillow to her chest as if it were Maddy. I don't say anything; I just take a box of omelet and head downstairs.

***

There's not much to do in the shop except worry about my daughter and my friend/employer. I can see now why Grace usually has a book with her and wants to get out of this business as soon as possible. For the first two hours I pick at my cold omelet; I eat about half before I toss the rest of it out.

When two customers do come in, I try to stay out of their way. I wait until they've gotten a good look at everything before I ask, "Can I help you find anything?" They buy a couple of T-shirts and then leave.

By two o'clock I'm hungry enough that the cold, discarded omelet starts to sound good. I could always call for some takeout, but I don't have any of my own money. I don't want to take anything from the register, not on what's essentially my second day.

I'm still dithering about this when Grace comes downstairs. Her face looks pale and haggard and her eyes are still a bit red, but she smiles at me. "How are things down here?"

"About the same as always."

"That bad, huh?" We both laugh at this. Then she pats my shoulder. "Why don't you go get us some lunch? I can cover for a few minutes."

"If you're sure—"

"I'm sure." She pats her flat stomach. "Some stir-fry would really hit the spot right about now."

"Any place in particular?"

She gives me the address for a Chinese place down

the street and twenty bucks for both of our orders. She probably could have called, but maybe she wants to get me out of the shop for a little while. Just as well for me; the fresh air—as fresh as it gets around here—feels good after a morning in Grace's stuffy shop.

I order vegetable stir-fry for both of us, after I decide it would be best not to use Grace's money on meat products. While I wait for the order, I see a payphone against the wall. I don't know Debbie's number, but I'm sure I could get it from information. Even if I do, what would I say? Maddy doesn't want to talk to me and Debbie doesn't know me.

I decide to call Tess instead. She's probably been worried about me and Jake might have passed along something about Maddy. Tess picks up on the second ring and before I can say anything, she says, "Stacey! I've been worried sick."

"I'm sorry."

"Jake said you spent the night with your new friends."

"Yes," I say and wonder what else Jake has told her.

"I hope you're not reverting to your old ways."

Apparently Jake hasn't mentioned I spent most of the night at a bar with Maddy. "No, I'm still taking care of myself. I'm getting lunch right now."

Tess clucks her tongue when I tell her what I'm getting. "They probably cook those vegetables and rice in MSG. Do you know how bad that is for you?"

"I'm only eighteen. I don't think I'm going to have a heart attack."

"It's important to create good habits."

"OK, I'll stop on the way back and get some milk to balance it out."

"That's a good start."

I tell myself Tess frets over my lunch to cope with the disappointment of me not coming home. "I am really sorry about last night."

"Do you think you'll be home tonight?"

"I'm not sure."

"I can have Jacob bring your things there. At least a suitcase to tide you over."

I press myself flat against the wall. I can't bring myself to say anything for a couple of minutes. On one hand I care about Tess and I want her to be happy. On the other I don't want her constant mothering at the moment. Plus there's Grace. With Maddy gone, someone should look after her, make sure she doesn't do anything stupid.

"A suitcase would be good," I finally say and hate myself a little for it. I try to cover up with a lie. "Grace is feeling a little under the weather. I thought I'd help take care of her. You know, make some chicken noodle soup and whatnot."

"That's very thoughtful of you, dear," Tess says, although from the flatness of her tone I know she doesn't buy it. "I'll put a few things together for you."

"Thanks." I hear someone call out my number. "I'd better go."

I hang up the phone and then go get my food. I feel like the worst person in the world.

***

Grace must see how downcast I look when I walk through the door. "You get mugged or something?" she asks.

"Huh? No. Just been thinking about things."

"That's always dangerous." On the surface it seems that Grace is back to her old self, but I can hear something hollow in her voice, as if she's going through the motions.

We eat in silence and I notice how Grace bolts her food. Despite my earlier hunger, I pick at the stir fry with a pair of chopsticks; I move it around in the carton more than I eat any of it. A pall hangs over us, a pall with Maddy's name on it.

Grace finishes hers before I've eaten half of mine. She looks at her watch. "I should get to work on my dissertation," she says.

"Sure."

"Can you handle all the excitement down here?"

I flash her a fake smile. "I'll try."

With that I'm alone again. At least until a half hour later when two girls walk in, both of them as fat as my first customer. The reason for that becomes clear once one says, "We're looking for something hot. Our friend said you could help us out."

"I'll see what I can do," I say. I set my half-eaten stir-fry aside to help the fat girls find something to wear. When there's nothing up front, I go into the back to search through the box of recent items.

As I do, I hear one on her phone say, "I can't tonight. We're going out to this club. The Honey Well Club."

This piques my interest. I look up from the box, a dress still in my hands. "It's ladies night," she says. She snorts at something the other person said and responds, "You'd never get in there. It's very exclusive."

I continue to eavesdrop until I hear one of the others grumble, "Where did that skinny little bitch go? Christ, let's just get out of here."

I grab a few dresses at random and then hurry back to them. "What about these?"

After I've rung up a couple of "hot" dresses for them,

I think about what the one said. The Honey Well Club is where the Worm said Bobby Blades likes to hang out. Maybe I should pay it a little visit.

Then I think of Grace upstairs. Despite that she said she wanted to work on her dissertation, I imagine her still on the couch with a pillow she wishes were Maddy. I shouldn't leave her alone tonight. She's my friend. She might need my support.

But Bobby Blades is one of Lex's goons who helped put me in this situation. He's one of the people who took me away from Maddy, which in turn has taken her away from Grace. He's partially responsible for this mess. Why should he get to drink and grope women while Maddy, Grace, and I mope around heartbroken?

There's no decision to be made. The bastard will pay. Tonight.

Part 5:
Sweet Revenge

Chapter 32

I prepare for my visit to the Honey Well Club the rest of the afternoon. I've never been in a nightclub except on raids, but I know I can't wear a T-shirt and jeans. I need something "hot" to wear. Luckily the fat women haven't cleaned out Grace's selection yet.

I try on a few dresses before I find one I like. It's black and short almost to the point of indecency. In the dressing room mirror I spend a couple minutes to adjust the bust, to show as much as possible. Maybe I should try to pad my bra or see if Grace has any push-up ones in stock. I remember how much trouble I had with a regular, unpadded bra and decide to skip it and hope for the best.

The real problem comes with the shoes. I can't wear sneakers or flats. I need heels. I look through some boxes in the back, until I find a pair of black shoes with three-inch stiletto heels. They look right, but they sure as hell don't feel right. For one thing my foot feels like it's perfectly vertical. For another the shoes pinch my toes like someone's clamped them in a vise. How are you supposed to walk in these?

I take my first fall three seconds later. I'm lucky I fall into a box of clothes so I don't scrape my knees or break my stupid neck. After I collect myself, I try again. I remember when I first woke up as a woman, how I could hardly walk barefoot. Baby steps, I remind myself.

So for the rest of the afternoon I shuffle around the shop and kick off the shoes on the couple of rare occasions when a customer comes in. That the salesgirl is barefoot and wears an indecent dress doesn't come as a shock to anyone, not in the bohemian garment district.

I'm in the middle of making my way across the floor when Grace comes downstairs. I look at the clock and see it's time to close up for the night. She raises an eyebrow when she sees me. "What are you doing?"

"Practicing," I say. "For Maddy's father's funeral. If she wants me there."

"Of course she'll want you there," Grace says. She puts an arm around me, which also helps to steady me. "You're our friend."

"Thanks." I look down at my feet and my cheeks turn warm. "Can you help me? I haven't worn these before."

"You've never worn heels?"

"No. The only formal occasions I've been to are trials."

"Come on, let's take those off." Grace holds onto my arm as I kick the shoes off. She goes into the back room and I hear her rummage around for a minute. The shoes she comes back with are shorter, with wider heels. Not as drop-dead sexy as the stilettos, but I might not break my neck in them either. "Let's start with something easier."

These shoes are easier to walk in. For one thing my foot isn't quite so vertical and for another the shorter, wider heel is more like a normal shoe. I feel good when I take a few steps and don't fall—until Grace clucks her tongue.

"You walk like a man," she says.

My stomach flutters. Has Grace figured it out? "I do?"

"I guess it's not a surprise, not the way you were brought up. Am I right?"

"Yeah, right," I say, eager to change the subject. "What am I doing wrong?"

"Watch my feet." Grace puts the shoes on and then glides across the floor. "One foot in front of the other. Heel-toe, heel-toe. See?"

"I think so."

"Now you try it."

She gives the shoes back to me. I take a deep breath and then swing my left heel so it's aligned with my right toes. In the process I just about topple myself. Grace reaches out to catch me before I can fall. "You're still trying to walk like a man. Don't be so aggressive with your stride. Just glide, nice and easy. Go with the flow."

"Sorry." I've never done anything gently. I try to use less torque the next time around. It goes a lot easier. I make it to the front of the shop. It's a problem to turn; I brace myself against the wall to keep my balance.

"You're getting it," Grace says. She holds out her arms as if I'm a baby taking her first steps. Like a baby I collapse into Grace's arms. "Now we just need to do something about that dress."

***

The dress Grace picks out for me is a lot more conservative, the kind better suited for a funeral than a nightclub. I tell her I like it and she promises to get it cleaned before my funeral—Steve Fischer's funeral. With that settled we go upstairs, where Grace reheats some spaghetti and the omelets I bought for breakfast.

Through some kind of culinary magic she makes both

edible and able to work together. No wonder Maddy's stayed with her for the last couple of years. A smart, funny woman who can cook like this is quite a catch. And she doesn't look bad either.

My cheeks turn warm and I look down at my plate. Do I have a crush on Grace? She notices something's wrong and asks, "Not hungry?"

"Oh, no. The food is delicious. I was just thinking of Maddy. Do you think she'll be all right?"

"She'll be better once she vents some of the anger and disappointment."

"Is that your psychological analysis?"

"Mostly. A little personal experience too. When my mom died, I went on a real bender. There's not much I can remember about those couple of days, just that somehow I wound up behind the Kozee Koffee. That's how Maddy found me when she went to take out the trash the next morning, curled up on the back step like an orphan, which I guess was appropriate."

"And that's how you met?"

"Yeah. She took me inside and gave me about a gallon of coffee to sober up." Grace stops and sighs wistfully. "That was her first day too. She was a lot different back then. She was, well, I guess she was a lot like you."

"Like me?"

"She was sweet and shy. Her hair was still brown in those days too." We share a laugh about this and then Grace continues, "She was so sweet I didn't want to get too close to her. I didn't want to corrupt her. I guess I did anyway, didn't I?"

"I don't think you corrupted her."

"Maybe it wasn't just me. It was this whole

neighborhood. The whole city, really. It does that to people. Makes them different."

"But Maddy's still sweet," I say and think of how Maddy had melted into Grace's arms after she came out of the bathroom. "Maybe not as shy."

"Maybe you're right," Grace says, though she doesn't look any happier. When she reaches out to take my hand, I suck in a sharp breath. "You're changing too. I can see it. Pretty soon you'll start dyeing your hair blue and getting holes punched in your nose."

I toss my head. "You think blue is my color?"

"Oh yeah, a nice dark blue to match your eyes." The next thing I know, Grace leans across the table; her lips brush against mine. The basic mechanics of kissing a woman as a woman are still the same as when I was a man. When I close my eyes, there's no difference at all, except I'm the one on the receiving end as Grace's tongue darts into my mouth to make itself at home.

Just as abruptly as it begins, the kiss ends. I'm left with my mouth open and eyes shut for a moment; I don't realize Grace is gone. Then I hear her chair scrape. I open my eyes in time to see her disappear into the bedroom she shares with Maddy—my daughter. What have I done?

***

I cry for a good hour before the phone rings. After the fifth ring I decide Grace won't get it, so I pick up the receiver. "Hello?" I say with a sniffle.

"Stacey?" Maddy asks.

"Oh, hi."

"Are you crying?"

"What? Oh, yeah, a little. I was just thinking about you." About how I've betrayed you, I add to myself. About how Grace has betrayed you.

"I've been thinking about you too. I'm sorry I yelled at you in the alley. I was just lashing out, you know?"

"I know." I sniffle into the receiver again. Maddy's voice has brought on a fresh batch of tears. "How are you holding up?"

"I'm feeling a little better. Mom and I did some talking." Maddy stops and sighs into the receiver. "It's the first time we've really talked since Daddy left. I think things are going to be OK now."

"When are you coming back?"

"I'm not sure. Not 'til after the funeral at least."

"When's that?"

"A couple days. There's a lot to work out yet."

"Oh. I suppose there would be."

"I guess I should talk to Grace now. Where is she?"

"She's taking a nap," I lie. "Hang on a minute and I'll see if I can wake her up."

"Sure." I put the phone on the kitchen counter and then go over to Grace's door. I rap on it hard enough to make the door shake.

"Grace? Maddy's on the phone. She wants to talk to you."

The door opens a crack. All I can see is one of Grace's eyes, red from crying. "I don't think I can right now."

"You have to," I plead. "If you don't, she'll know something's going on."

Grace opens the door all the way and yanks me through the opening before I can say anything. She closes the door and plants herself against it. "What happened at the table was a mistake. I've never cheated on Maddy before. I love her."

"So do I."

"You do?"

"As a friend," I add quickly. "I don't want to hurt her either."

"Good." Grace sighs and then takes my hand. She kneads my hand as she says, "I like you too, Stacey. I think you're really special. You're sweet and smart and tough when you need to be. And you're a great friend, to both of us."

"Thanks."

"But we're just friends. That's all we can be. Understand?"

"I know," I say. "I should go home."

"I think that'd be a good idea." I let Grace pull me into a hug that doesn't go on as long as I'd like it to. "I'll see you tomorrow, all right?"

"Sure. Can I use the phone downstairs? I need to call my aunt."

"Of course you can."

She leaves the bedroom first and takes the phone from off the counter. "Maddy? Oh, good, you're still there. No, I was just napping. You know what a heavy sleeper I am." While Grace laughs uneasily, she waves to me. I nod a goodbye and then head downstairs.

But I don't use the phone to call Jake and Tess. Instead, I call for a cab. While I wait for it, I empty out the cash register. Grace will probably notice the missing cash when she comes down to lock the door, but by then I'll be gone.

It turns out that Jake was right. It was a huge mistake to involve myself in Maddy's life. Just not in the way I anticipated. She'll be a lot better off without me in any form.

Chapter 33

The cab drops me off a block away from the Honey Well Club. I change behind a Thai restaurant's dumpster after I make sure no one is around. Not into the dress Grace picked out for me, but the much shorter one I chose. It'll be far more appropriate for the job.

On the way here I considered whether I should go through with it. Given what happened in Grace's apartment, I'm not really prepared for what I need to do now. Then I reminded myself Bobby Blades was one of the bastards who did this to me, who put me in this horrible situation. If I want to get to Lex and make him pay, I can't shy away now.

I leave Grace's old clothes beneath the dumpster, where I'll either fetch them from later or a rat will use them to make a nest. Then I smooth out the wrinkles from the dress and adjust the bust and skirt to fit as well as they can. I've already got the heels on; they aren't as comfortable as my old sneakers, but I'm getting used to them.

There's a line in front of the club that backs up almost to the Thai restaurant. I see the two fat girls I helped earlier, along with the one from my first day. They're pretty hard to miss. I won't look as bad as them no matter how red my eyes are and how mussed my hair is.

The obvious problem is that I'm not old enough to be allowed in the club. If the bouncer asks for my ID, I'm screwed. As the line shuffles forward, I press myself close to a group of girls and hope to get let in with them.

I don't need to worry, as a much better opportunity presents itself. Ahead of me, one of the fat girls roars, "What are you talking about? We're not getting out of line!"

"You're not on the list," the bouncer says.

"Fuck your list! Come on girls," says the fat girl in the red dress I sold to her. She tries to push her way past the bouncer, but he doesn't allow that. He snatches her by one doughy arm to yank her back. "Let me go, you perv!"

The other two fat girls rush to their leader's aid. They batter at the bouncer with their purses and fists. Reinforcements come from inside the club to wrestle the fat girls away from the front door.

I take advantage of the commotion to slip past the fat girls and bouncers, into the club. It's almost as dark as outside, with only some pink neon lights around the ceiling. The techno music is so loud and full of so much bass that my ears ring. How people can stand places like this, I don't know.

I stagger through a crowd of mostly women and wonder how I'll find Blades in a place so dark and crowded. I manage to push my way through to the bar, behind which is a woman who looks like an older version of Maddy before she dyed her hair black. "Get you something, kid?" the bartender shouts over the noise.

"Just a club soda," I shout back. Now is not the time for alcohol. I need to be clearheaded to make this work.

When the bartender gives me a dirty look, I say, "I'm the designated driver!"

After the bartender saunters off to get my drink, I turn around to survey the club. Most of the people on the dance floor are women, with just a few men. From what the fat girls said, it is ladies night. I focus my attention on the men and try to see if any of them are Blades. Most of them are too tall or the wrong shade of brown.

I'm about to give up and slink out of the club when I see him. He's not on the dance floor. Of course not, he's too important for that. He's in the section cordoned off with a velvet rope, probably a VIP section. He's already got a couple of blond floozies with him, girls a hundred times hotter than me.

No, I can't give up now. Not after I came this far. Not after I stole the money out of Grace's cash register. I won't let this bastard slip away now. He'll pay for what he did to me.

The bartender slams my drink down behind me on the counter. Before she can leave I turn and ask, "Where's the bathroom?"

***

In one of the photo albums Debbie got in the divorce, there's a picture of Maddy at eight and Jenny at six, both of them with their faces caked in makeup they'd stolen from Tess. My first attempt to apply makeup goes about as smoothly, with my cheeks bright pink, my eyelids smeared purple, and my teeth stained red with lipstick. It's certainly not the kind of look that will get me into the VIP section.

I should have practiced this instead of making out with my daughter's girlfriend. The girl at the sink next to me snickers and asks, "You learn that from a blind hooker?"

I bolt into the nearest empty stall. I try not to cry; I don't want to add runny mascara to the mess on my face. I sit there for a while to take deep breaths and force myself to relax. This is such a stupid idea, I tell myself. Even if I get to Blades, what will I do? I'm just a dumb little girl who can't do her own makeup, walk in heels, or control her raging hormones. Blades will probably gut me like a fish the second I try anything.

Then Fate or whatever you believe in lays another opportunity at my feet. The bathroom door bangs open. A moment later, I see a blond woman at the mirror through the crack in the stall door. I can't be positive, but she looks like one of the floozies with Blades, at least until she takes off the blond wig and sets it on the counter.

I decide to go in for a closer look. I open the door and then take the sink next to her. She wears a silver dress; it looks like the ones on Bobby Blades's floozies. I run some water to wash some of the crap off my face while she touches up her makeup, the wig between us.

I give her a minute before I ask as casually as possible, "Hey, weren't you in the VIP area with some guy?"

The floozy turns to look at me. Without the wig her hair is as short and dark as Maddy's. Her lip curls in a sneer. "You get lost from the junior high prom?"

"This? It's just a gag. My girlfriends and I are having a bachelorette party. We thought it'd be funny to put on way too much makeup."

"Yeah, it's funny all right," the floozy says. She turns back to her mirror.

"Maybe you could help me fix it?" I suggest.

"Maybe you should go home and ask your mommy," she says.

That's the wrong answer. I reach into my purse and retrieve the Worm's switchblade. I hold it to her throat. "Here I thought we could be friends. Get in the stall."

"What? Are you joking?"

"Do I look like I'm joking?" My makeup might belie this, so I cut her on the right arm. Not enough to do any serious damage, just enough to draw some blood. Before she can scream for help, I put a hand over her mouth. "Get in the fucking stall."

She lets me push her back into the stall. "Strip," I tell her.

"What?"

"Just do it." There's nothing but anger inside me as I watch this floozy strip. Not at all like when I kissed Grace. Maybe I don't love all women, just Grace. I slip out of my dress and toss it to her so she can cover up a little. Her dress is big on me, but not enough to be noticeable.

I don't have anything to use to tie her up, but she's got something even better in her purse: a pair of handcuffs. I force her to put her hands behind her back and then slap the cuffs around her wrists; for the briefest of moments I feel like a cop again. Then I unroll some toilet paper and use a wad of it as a makeshift gag. That should keep her out of my way for a few minutes.

I leave her locked in the stall and then snatch the blond wig. It takes a couple of minutes to wrestle my hair beneath the thing. Even when I do, I still don't look much like the floozy in the stall. I'll just have to hope that the darkness and booze will cloud Blades's mind enough for me to pass as his girl.

Now it's time for some payback.

Chapter 34

The floozy had on silver stilettos, which I didn't bother to take; I know from experience how bad I am with those. Maybe Blades will notice, but he'd be sure to notice me fall on my face. I take a deep breath before I open the bathroom door. Here we go, I tell myself. I can do this.

I make it as far as the bar before the bartender calls out to me. I freeze and wonder if she recognizes me. She might call for one of the bouncers to throw me out, or call the cops to have me arrested. I'm about to run when she says, "Your drinks."

I turn and see a tray with three martini glasses on it. They aren't traditional martinis; they're green instead of clear. "Oh, right," I say. "Silly me."

I take the drink from off the bar, careful not to look the bartender in the eye, so she doesn't recognize my face. The next challenge is to get across the dance floor without someone spilling the drinks. I have to awkwardly sidestep a couple of elbows aimed at my head; the drinks slosh in their glasses, but don't spill. At one point the people are so tightly packed that I can't breathe. I dish out a couple of elbows to clear a little space so I can dart through the opening.

Once on the other side, it's easy enough to get to the VIP area. There's a bouncer there, but I must look enough like the floozy that he lifts the rope to let me by. I let out a sigh of relief; I've passed the first test.

Blades is still at the same table, the other floozy draped over him like a scarf. I have to will myself the last few steps, to sit down beside him. He turns and his eyes narrow at me. I figure the jig is up, but he says, "What took so long?"

I do my best Valley Girl impression as I squeak, "I was just powdering my nose."

"We were going dry here," he says and then chugs one of the drinks. What he's not low on at the moment is cocaine. He's got three fat lines spread out on the table. One for each of us, I suppose. But I'm wrong. All three are for him.

"Aren't you ever going to share with us?" the other girl whines.

"Maybe later. If you're good," he says with a leer.

She pouts for a moment, until Blades grabs her breast. She squeals and then gives him a playful slap. "You're such a bad boy," she says.

It goes against everything I believe in to do what I do next. I stick my hand down his shirt and rub his chest. "What about me?" I say. I use the same whine as the other girl.

"I ain't gonna forget about you, baby," he says. It takes every ounce of my being not to punch him when he squeezes my left breast. He squeezes it a second time and then frowns. "Damn, girl, you get a breast reduction in the can?"

"No, don't be silly," I say. I give him a playful slap. To distract him, I give him a sloppy kiss on the mouth. It's a lot different than the kiss Grace and I shared. My stomach threatens to come up through my throat as I stick my tongue into Blades's mouth. The only thing that keeps me going is the thought I'll soon make this son of a bitch pay for what he did to me.

I'd like to get out of here right away, but of course I can't. For an hour Blades gropes the two of us between lines of coke. When he gets bored of that, he has us grope each other while he watches. The other girl is drunk enough that she feels me up without hesitation. Since I haven't touched a drop of alcohol all night, it's a lot more of a challenge for me. I close my eyes and imagine Grace instead. That only makes me feel worse.

Just about when I'm ready to go crazy from the mixture of rage, embarrassment, and guilt, Blades puts an arm around both of us. "Come on, let's get out of here!" he says.

A bouncer clears a path through the dance floor for us. As we leave, I look back to the bathroom and wonder what happened to the floozy I left in there. She's probably still locked up in the stall. Someone will find her eventually. I hope nothing too bad happens to her, at least nothing worse than what's going to happen to Bobby Blades.

***

A limo waits outside for us, a white stretch one with a fully-stocked bar. The other girl makes full use of that while I pretend to drink a couple of shots. I toss the booze out the window when no one can see.

While Blades knocks back a few as well, he instructs us to fondle each other. Now that we're in the relative privacy of the limo, he tells us to take off our clothes too. I try to remind myself as I take off the stolen silver dress that whatever he makes us do can't be more invasive than what Dr. Palmer's already done.

Before long I'm naked and I rub up against another naked, sweaty girl, all to please someone I despise. There's no excitement or pleasure in it, only revulsion. I would give anything for Jake to show up and put a couple of bullets in Blades. Then we could go home and Tess could tuck me into bed and I could forget this entire nightmare.

But since I didn't tell anyone what I'm doing, no one will save me except myself. I see another lucky break for myself in that my partner's eyes have started to get heavy. After all that booze—and who knows what before I showed up—she's about to pass out. I give her a little help with that as I force a couple more drinks down her throat.

She finally collapses with a sigh and curls up on the floor like a dog. I giggle stupidly and then turn to Blades. "Guess she couldn't handle her liquor, huh?"

"Looks like we have a winner," Blades says. He reaches out to pinch my bare ass. "Come on over here, baby."

"Sure thing. What do you want to play now?"

He has me sit on his lap. While he strokes the blond wig, he says, "You know what I want now, don't you?" If I'm still unclear about this, I see his eyes look down. He wants me to suck his dick. The son of a bitch.

He gives me a little push so I fall off his lap, between his legs. "Well, go on. Ain't going to wait all night."

There's not enough room in the car to kick him like I did with the Worm. I don't think my teeth are strong enough to bite through his member either, though that would serve the bastard right. So while I lean my head in towards his crotch, I grope around for my purse and the knife I took off the Worm.

My hope is Blades will be too distracted to notice me as I reach for the purse. He isn't. Before I can pull the bag over to me, he grabs at my head and yanks the wig off. "What the fuck?" he says. Then he grabs my real hair and wrenches my head back. "You want this bag, huh? Let's see what you got in there."

I flail at him, but for a short guy he's got a lot of muscle, enough to keep me at bay while he empties out the purse. The makeup, compact, and tampons all fall out, along with my identification. Followed by the knife with a thump.

He grabs the knife before I can try to reach it. "That what you want, little bitch?" He pushes the button and the blade springs out of it. He clucks his tongue. "You want to see a real knife, I can show you a real knife."

I hope this isn't an analogy for his dick. Turns out he means it literally. He reaches into a jacket pocket to pull out a twelve-inch knife, one I saw before at Lennox Pharmaceuticals. He holds it close to my face to give me a good look at it. "You like to play with knives, little bitch? Then let's play."

I do the only thing a woman in my position can do: I scream. One of my hands manages to slap the intercom button as I do. The driver slams on the brakes. Before Blades can slice my throat open, the knife slips from his hands.

He slams my head into the door and then lets me drop to the floor. My head spins. While he lunges for his knife, I see the Worm's knife on the seat, against the door, just inches from my hand. I snatch the knife, the blade already out thanks to Blades. I don't aim for any specific part of him, just whatever happens to be closest.

The knife digs into his right thigh. I drag it along while he screams. He writhes in pain, for the moment any thoughts of his knife forgotten. I yank the knife free and then find his.

The screen between the halves of the limo comes down. The driver finally works up the courage to ask, "What's going on back there?"

"Just a little foreplay," I say. "Drop us somewhere private and then take the girl home."

Blades's screams are enough motivation for the driver to do as I order. He stops the limo in the parking lot of an Italian restaurant closed for the night. To make sure Blades can't escape, I slash his left calf with the knife, which prompts him to scream again. Then I kick him out of the limo. While he tries to crawl away, I grab my clothes from the car and gather up the contents of my purse.

Then I jump out and the moment the door is shut, the limo speeds away. Now we're alone.

***

I let him crawl while I slip back into the dress. He can't get too far with a sliced calf and thigh. For a moment I almost feel bad to watch him struggle. Then I remind myself what he took from me and the kind of things he had me doing all night and I run over to kick him in the face.

He spits up some blood and then rolls onto his back to stare up at me. "What the fuck are you? A cop?"

"Do I look like a cop?" I bend down to look him in the eye. "Just think of me as your conscience."

"What do you want?"

"We'll get to that. First I want you to tell me something: how many girls have you done that to? How many have you dragged into your limo and forced to give you a blow job?"

"I don't know!"

"Too many to count? That's what I figured." I stab him in the right side, just above his pelvis. He screams again. Though I'd like to, I don't feel any pleasure about his screams.

"Whatever you want, I'll get it for you: money, drugs, you name it."

I look him in the eye again. "I want Artie Luther dead. That's what I want. You're going to give him to me or you're going to end up in little pieces scattered all over this parking lot for the rats to snack on."

Half-naked, cut, and bleeding, he starts to cry like a woman. "I don't want to die!" he shrieks. "I'm sorry! I'm sorry! Don't kill me!"

"I don't give a shit if you're sorry. All I care about is Artie Luther. Where can I find him?"

"I don't know!"

I stab him in the other side. He's dying the proverbial death of a thousand cuts here in the Italian restaurant parking lot. I wait for his screams to subside and then ask again. "You have to know where he is. You're one of his top dogs. I know it. You were there at Lennox Pharmaceuticals when he knocked over the place. You and his other little buddies, the ones he trusts the most."

"Lennox? What's that got to do with anything?"

"You remember a woman named Gita Nath? Dr. Gita Nath? She had her wrists slit. I bet you helped her with that, didn't you?"

"So what? She a friend of yours or something?"

Tired of games, I stab him in the gut. It'll take him a long time to die from a wound like that. "Now that we've got that settled, tell me where Lex is and maybe I'll go call an ambulance for you."

"I don't know where he is now!" Blades says and braces for another stab.

"But you know where he's going to be?" I ask.

"There's a big deal going down in two days. On the waterfront."

"Where?"

"An old warehouse on Pier 35."

"What time?"

"Midnight." That figures. The Lennox robbery was set for midnight too.

"Thanks."

"Now you'll call for that ambulance?"

"Would you if you were in my position?"

"But—" I silence the rest of it when I slit his throat. I put the knife to his neck, close my eyes, and then pull the knife across as far as I can. When I open my eyes, Blades's are still wide open; they stare back at me, to accuse me. I've never killed anyone in cold blood before, not like Jake on the Mackenzie case. Just like that creep, Blades needed to die. If I let him live, he could go back to Artie Luther.

Now I have to dispose of the body. I wipe the knife clean to drop down the first storm drain I see. Then I cut off Blades's clothes and empty his wallet of cash and credit cards. The clothes I toss into the restaurant's dumpster. I'd throw Blades in there too, but he's too heavy for me. Instead, I drag him behind the dumpster and sit him up to face whoever finds him.

I look around to make sure no one's seen me. Then I run.

Chapter 35

The blood money I take off Blades allows me to live comfortably on my own for the first time as a woman. The first thing I do is get to a train on its way upstate. That's about the last place anyone will look for me—if they look for me. The limo driver is the only one who saw me without the wig and I doubt he'll go to the police. He'd be more likely to snitch to someone on Lex's crew about who killed their boy.

There aren't many people on the train, which makes it easier for me to avoid everyone. I curl up in the back of a car and hug myself to keep warm in the skimpy dress I stole. For once the tears don't come.

I've killed plenty of people in my thirty years as a cop. The first couple I felt bad about even though they were scum bags, one a bank robber and the other a pimp. For months after each one I replayed the incident in my head, even in my dreams. I didn't sleep well back in those days.

Jake sensed my distress and one night took me to Squiggy's. While I was getting plastered, Jake said, "You're a cop, Steve. Killing dirtbags comes with the badge. You can either accept that or sign up to be a crossing guard."

In manly fashion I sucked the emotions down deep, locked them away until they didn't bother me anymore. The more people I killed in the line of duty, the easier it got. Now I can't remember what those first two looked like, only what they did.

This time is different. I'm not a cop anymore. I'm just a girl, little more than a kid. Until about twelve hours ago I was a salesgirl at a bohemian clothes store. Now I've tortured and murdered another human being, even if someone like Bobby Blades barely qualifies as one.

In thirty years as a cop I've heard my share of stories that began with, "He [or she] had it coming." If anyone tracks me down and takes me to a police station it'll be my turn to say it. But I won't end up any better off than those other saps. I'll wind up in prison for the rest of my life with a bunch of other women who thought someone had it coming.

Still I can't cry because he did have it coming. Bobby Blades was scum. He helped Artie Luther break into Lennox Pharmaceuticals and kill the security guards there. He killed Dr. Nath in her own home. The rest of his rap sheet is about as long as this train. And that doesn't include the kinky shit he had that other girl and I do and what he probably would have done to us later on.

What makes it worse is that I know he's just the first. There's still the rest of Lex's henchmen and then the big boy himself. Blades was the tip of the proverbial iceberg. Maybe I am just a stupid kid now, but they still have it coming.

And I'll give it to them.

***

I ride the train upstate to the capital. By then it's started to take on commuters to head into the city for their jobs. I'm one of the few who goes the opposite way. I have to push my way through a bunch of people in business suits to get off.

I've been here a few times for legal hearings, mostly when some punk complains about excessive force to the state cops. The capital's a nice place if you've got money and I happen to have a fat wad of cash in my purse thanks to Bobby Blades. Not just his cash, but also his credit cards. Those will probably be canceled once someone finds the body and alerts the company; until then they're mine to use as I wish.

I get a cab from the station and then head into town. I'm not dressed for the nicer restaurants, so I just hit a McDonald's and nurse a coffee for a little while. I read the morning paper, but of course there's nothing about Blades in it yet. The TV will probably carry the news about him by six o'clock. That would be enough time for the body to be found, identified, and for word to hit the wires.

Blades wouldn't usually draw much attention, but I've inadvertently helped his bid for immortality. The brutal way I killed him and then left him is sure to draw attention as a "gangland killing." The media love those; it gives them a chance to write their own little episode of *The Sopranos* with all the colorful characters. If the limo driver does come forward or the other girl in the car remembers me, I can expect to have an artist's rendering of my face plastered all over the papers and the TV by tomorrow.

Even if they draw me with the blond wig, I'm sure Jake will recognize me. I might as well have left him a trail of breadcrumbs the way I left Grace's store. He's smart enough to pair my sudden disappearance with Blades's murder. I can hear him say, "What the hell have you done?"

What have I done? Scaring the shit out of the Worm was one thing. No jury in the country would put me in jail for what happened in that alley. The department wouldn't bother to press charges.

Murder is something else. High-profile murders get everyone into a tizzy. Woods and Jefferson will beg Captain Archer to get let in on the case so they can be the ones on the TV and in the papers. That was the kind of stuff that got people promoted, not that Jake and I ever gave a shit about that. Neither of us wanted to sit behind a desk and push papers around. Woods or Jefferson would be all too happy to track me down if it meant a cushy job for them.

I finish with my coffee and then look up at the clock. It's ten o'clock, time to do a little shopping.

***

I've never worn designer clothes before. My old suits and other clothes used to come from the clearance racks at low-end department stores. As a woman my clothes had all come from the thrift store or Grace's shop. The closest I've ever come to something fancy was my dress uniform.

So it feels weird to stroll around the department store in an outfit that costs more than all the other clothes I've ever worn put together. The sunglasses perched on the top of my head cost a thousand bucks by themselves. My new purse—genuine Gucci, not like the imitations I've seen on the street—cost another grand. Then there's the black leather jacket, slinky black dress, and the black heels that would have killed me yesterday, before Grace tutored me. All of it thanks to Bobby Blades's platinum AmEx.

The extreme makeover doesn't end there. I also visit the makeup counter, where I let a salesgirl apply all kinds of stuff to my face and squirt me with a number of different fragrances, so that I probably smell like a greenhouse. She's a lot more experienced with all of that stuff, so when she's finished, I look as if I barely have makeup on. I buy everything she suggests and put it on Bobby's gold MasterCard.

And then comes the jewelry! I buy a diamond necklace, earrings even though my ears aren't pierced, and bracelets for my wrists and ankles. I also buy a few men's watches—honest to God Rolexes—that I claim are for my boyfriends. By the time I've finished there I've spent another five grand. I jingle like Santa's sleigh as I leave the jewelry counter.

The last stop is the salon. I might have started there first, but I wanted to look the part of the spoiled rich girl when I went in there. I give the receptionist a shake of my hair and say, "I want to dye it black, like my dress."

No one has any problem with that. I sit in the chair for two hours and let them wash my hair, cut it to shoulder length, wrap it up in tinfoil, and then go through it with a comb until it's even smoother and shinier than Tess ever got it. The end result is that my hair is now the kind of black that looks dark blue in the right light, which reminds me of what Grace said the night before.

When it's all done, I've spent about ten thousand dollars and transformed myself from a grubby tomboy into a glamorous rich girl. On my way out I even start to feel rich; I swagger along on my heels down the aisles, heedless of anyone around me. I know where the money came from, but for the moment I don't care. I look like a million bucks, almost literally.

Maybe it's that I've been a girl long enough or maybe because I've never had such financial freedom or maybe just that I need a distraction from the guilt over Blades's murder, but I can't stop there. I hit another five clothes stores and buy everything from silk lingerie to bikinis to a floor-length ball gown.

When I've sated my appetite for clothes, I stop at the shoe stores. I never understood why Debbie owned so many shoes, but now I do. There are so many shapes and styles, from sandals to pumps. Despite that I couldn't walk on heels a day ago, I scoop up five pairs of them. I try each one on and feel like a princess as I strut around in them. It's hard to believe eight hours ago I had to figure out how to dispose of a dead body.

My last stops are more practical. At a cell phone kiosk I get a phone, a prepaid one that doesn't require a lot of credit or security information to activate it. I pay for the phone in cash, so that when the cops track Blades's credit card purchases they won't be able to get the phone's number. At the bookstore I buy a couple of the latest fashion magazines so I can better look the part. My last stop is to get some luggage, sumptuous leather bags that fit all of my new purchases.

With my new phone I call for a cab. I've got so many bags I'm grateful there's a big strong man there to stuff them all in the trunk for me. He even opens the back door for me and tips his hat as if I'm a celebrity. I feel like a celebrity. For the first time since I became a woman— probably the first time ever—I don't mind if people stare at me. Let them look at Princess Stacey and wish they could be her, if only for a little while.

I smile to myself and then tell the driver to drop me at a hotel.

***

The driver claims it's the nicest hotel in town. It certainly seems like it from the lobby, which is all marble floors and mahogany furniture. It's even nicer than Lennox Pharmaceutical's lobby. I strut up to the counter; a bellhop trails behind with my purchases. I have my shades down so I don't have to look the common desk clerk in the eyes. I'm lucky the clerk is a man; he looks ready to salivate as I stroll up to him.

"I'd like your best room," I say. The expensive clothes, jewelry, and hair give me far more authority in my voice than I've ever had in this body.

"For how long?"

"I'm not sure yet. What is there to do in this dreadful place?"

The clerk goes on to list a bunch of stuff that I tune out. To play the part of the snobby rich girl, I take out my phone and then begin to hit buttons as if I'm texting one of my many rich friends. I look up about thirty seconds after the clerk's finished his spiel. "Whatever. Put it on Daddy's card," I say and then hand over the AmEx card.

"Can I see some ID, Miss—"

"Sharon Blades," I say. I don't offer to shake hands. I pretend to rummage around in my purse for a driver's license. "Oh dear. I must have left it in one of my other bags."

"That's all right," the clerk says. The hotel is the kind that still uses the old-fashioned keys. He hands a set to me. "This is for our presidential suite."

"That will have to do." I do a quick turn and then start fake texting again while the bellhop follows me to the elevator. I let him push the button for me. He takes the room key from me as well to open the door so I don't have to strain myself.

The suite is twice as big as my old apartment and nearly as big as the whole downstairs of where Debbie and

I used to live. From the doorway I can see a living room, a dining room with seating for eight, and a fully-stocked bar. I pout and say, "Is this it?"

"Yes, ma'am," the bellhop says.

"I guess it'll do," I whine. "Take those to the bedroom."

While the bellhop scurries off to the bedroom, I look around the rest of the place. There's a hot tub off the living room that could fit a half-dozen people. There's an equally big tub in the bathroom, along with a separate shower and a toilet with a mahogany seat and a gilded handle. "Wow," I whisper.

The bedroom is no less spacious. The king-size bed could fit me about a dozen times over. I'd need about fifty more bags of clothes to fill up the closet. There's even the standard mint on the pillow.

"Thank you," I tell the bellhop. I give him a hundred bucks for his trouble. It's hard to wait until he's gone to kick off my shoes and then leap onto the bed with a whoop. The mattress is so soft, it's like quicksand. Since I didn't get any sleep last night, I allow myself to drift away.

***

After four hours of sleep, I eat a hot fudge sundae from room service in the hot tub, which turns out to be a messy combination. I don't care. I've never lived in this kind of luxury and I doubt I ever will again. I might as well enjoy it while it lasts. That won't be very long. Tonight I'll have to sneak out of here in one of my other outfits, before the hotel gets wise to the bum credit card I gave them.

Once I've finished the sticky remains of the sundae, I close my eyes again and let the hot tub's jets massage my body. My mind begins to wander; I think of Maddy.

What's she doing? She's probably still upset about me, unaware that her father is in a hot tub a hundred miles away. If only I could call her and invite her here. We could have so much fun, like a slumber party.

But I can't. I have to leave tonight and even if I didn't, how could I explain all of this to Maddy? She'd never believe I won the lottery or anything like that. I'm supposed to be Stacey Chance, runaway street urchin.

Then there's Grace. By now Grace has probably called Maddy and told her I emptied the cash register. They'll both hate me for my betrayal. Maybe they'll even call the cops to report the theft.

Then again, Grace might not say anything. She might figure after our awkward scene I decided to take an advance on my paycheck and hit the road out of embarrassment. Grace might just replace the money and tell Maddy and Jake I snuck off in the night. I already ran away once, why not a second time?

The more I think about Grace, the more I wish she were here, in the tub with me. All that stuff I did with the floozy last night in Blades's limo I'd happily do with Grace. In my mind I can see us in the hot tub; we kiss as we did at her dining room table, only this time we'd be naked, our bodies warm and covered in suds—

I've never masturbated as a woman before. I don't really know how to do it. I try to remember what Debbie had me do with my hand when she wanted to spice up our sex life a little. I remember I stuck my hand between her legs like Dr. Palmer did with the transducer for my vaginal exam. It's a little awkward in the tub, but I manage to get my hand down in there. I feel around for a few moments until I find that perfect spot.

With a moan I sink beneath the water.

Chapter 36

To get out of the hotel is easy enough. I wait until it's dark and then dress in a different outfit: a longer black jacket, a white blouse, and black pants with a sensible pair of flats. There's a different clerk at the desk this time.

I stroll up to him and get the same look as from the previous clerk. "I'll be visiting a friend for a couple of days," I say. "Keep the room closed until then."

"Of course, ma'am."

With that I'm gone; the bellhop drops two of my suitcases into the back of a cab. I've stuffed everything into those bags, unconcerned about any wrinkles. I tell the cab to drop me back at the train station. In the station I drop Blades's credit cards into a trashcan. I figure by the morning they'll be useless.

I feel a lot better on this train ride, now that I'm swaddled in Prada, Gucci, and a bunch of other designer labels. All I have to worry about is some punk might decide a rich girl like me is an easy mark. If someone does, I won't have anything to defend myself with; that will be something to rectify once I'm back in the city. It's easy enough there for even a rich girl to get her hands on a gun or two.

No one hassles me, although I can see one boy try to make eyes with me. I don't give him the satisfaction of my attention. It's amazing how some clothes and a new hairdo can change me so quickly. Just yesterday I would have shied away from someone who looked at me like that; I would have scrunched myself into a protective ball or simply fidgeted nervously in my seat until he looked somewhere else.

The boy never works up the courage to talk to me. I flip through fashion magazines for most of the train ride and pretend to be interested in the articles on who wears what or what colors are popular at the moment. The conceited part of my brain I've created since this morning brags that I'm as pretty as any of the girls featured inside. I could pose for the cameras just as well; it's not like you need any talent to stand around half-naked.

I have to remind myself I'm not a rich girl or a would-be fashion model. I'm a fugitive. Maybe not officially, but I can't take any chances. I've still got Artie Luther and his goons to take care of. This getup is just a disguise, a cover story to let me do the job. It's hard though not to sink into a cover story as great as this one, such a perfect life with no worries. But it is just a cover story. In a couple of days I'll be back to being plain little Stacey Chance, the kind of girl no one pays much attention to, except for a special woman like Grace.

The thought of her reminds me of the hot tub. I'd like to do it again, but this is a commuter train, not a hotel suite. I turn my head to stare out the window, at the trees and power lines that rush past. Before long we'll be in the city and the fairy tale will be over.

***

I take a cab to the Snowden Hotel. It's a mid-sized

hotel downtown, the kind of place whose day has long since come and gone. The lobby doesn't have any marble floors and the wood of the chairs and front desk is chipped and faded. The clerk is an old man who doesn't wake up until I slap the bell inches from his ear.

"Help you?" he asks.

"I want a room."

"What's that?" he reaches to his ear and fiddles with a hearing aid.

"A room. I want a room."

"Any particular kind?"

"Just so it has a bed," I say.

"And how long will you be staying?"

"A couple of days." In lieu of ID, I pass him a couple hundred-dollar bills. "Consider that a down payment."

"Yes, ma'am."

The bellhop is a Mexican kid who barely speaks English. I give him a twenty to take my bags up to the third floor. The room is a lot smaller than the suite in the capital; everything fits into the one room. The bed is a double and not nearly so comfortable. Still, for my purposes, it'll do.

I sleep for a couple of hours before I roll out of bed to start my errands. There's a lot I need to get done today, a different kind of shopping than yesterday. Instead of department stores with designer labels, I have to visit pawnshops.

I didn't buy all that jewelry just to feel like a princess. I knew I'd have to dump Blades's credit cards, so I bought the jewelry to convert into cash. There's a "cash for gold" place about every fifty feet these days, so it's not hard to find a place to sell the jewelry. The clerk barely listens to my sob story about how I have to pawn Mommy and

Daddy's jewelry to pay for little Tommy's dialysis. The clerk just writes me up a receipt for the amount they'll give me, which isn't nearly what I paid for it, but what I get makes up for the cash I've already spent, with a little extra. "That will have to do," I say and then let her count out the money.

With some of that cash I get a cab to take me to the south side. It's not the safest place for a girl dressed in designer clothes, but I know a pawnbroker there. Amos Glendale doubles as a snitch, about who has fenced what. He's supposed to turn over all of those items to the authorities, but he always keeps a little something for himself as a "commission." I could have tried to trade the jewelry to Amos for what I want, but I figured I'd get a better deal from someone without a criminal record.

Amos is about as old as I used to be, but the way he looks at me is just like the boy on the train. His face turns red and sweat forms on his bald head. I start to wonder if he's going to have a heart attack in his own store.

He shoves aside a magazine I'm sure is a *Playboy*. "Hi there," he says and his voice actually cracks like he's fourteen. Amos doesn't get a lot of beautiful women in his line of work. "Can I help you?"

"Yes you can," I say. I strut up to the counter and then lean forward, until my lips brush against his ear. "I need to buy a gun."

"A g-g-gun?"

"Yes," I whisper into his ear. "A couple of them."

"Well, I, um—" He takes a deep breath to collect his nerve. "I have some guns in the case over there. Of course you'll have to wait a couple of days—"

"I want them *now*," I say with a rich girl whine. I reach out with one hand and stick it down his shirt so I can feel his hairy man-boobs. "I heard you were the man to see about that."

Amos wheezes and his face turns purple. Now he will have a heart attack. "I-I-I guess a girl like you isn't going to kill no one."

"That's right. I just want to scare someone."

"Sure." I let him go and leave him to pant for a minute or two. He clears his throat and then walks over to the glass counter with some of his handguns inside. "A little lady like you would probably be best off with this .25."

He takes a small black pistol out of the case. I pout at the sight of it. "It's so *small*."

"You don't want to hurt yourself, do you?"

"Can't you sell me a big gun?"

He takes out a 9mm Beretta. It's better, but still not a lot of stopping power. "Don't you have anything bigger?"

He scratches his head as he debates whether he should pull out the big guns. I lean forward on the counter so he gets a good look down my shirt. Like a trained puppy he does my bidding. "I do have some things in the back for special customers," he says.

He motions for me to follow him into the back room. He unlocks what's supposed to be a janitor's closet. In reality it's an armory, with everything from pistols to an RPG launcher. I pick up an Uzi and point it at him. "This is more like it," I say. The Uzi might not have much more stopping power than the Beretta, but it can fire a lot more bullets in a short amount of time.

I point up to an AK-47 on the wall. "That looks cool. Can I try it?"

"Um, well—" Amos's head starts to turn red again as he debates whether or not to sell me an assault rifle. His dick wins out over his head and he takes down the gun. "You just be careful with that."

"I will." The assault rifle looks ridiculous in my hands. Still, there's nothing like holding a really large weapon to make you feel powerful. "This is great. How much is it?"

He quotes me a price on the AK-47 and the Uzi. Along with the ammo, it'll just about clean me out. Still, it'll be worth it if I can get rid of Artie Luther and his gang. "So, paper or plastic?" he asks.

***

He gives me a duffel bag free of charge to carry the weapons in. I carry them with me into a diner. Maybe it's my recent brush with the good life, but the place looks filthy. The people aren't any better. I laugh to myself at this. In just over a day I've become a snob.

Another consequence of my brush with the good life is that I order a salad and iced tea. While I wait for the waitress to bring it, I read through the paper for anything on Blades's murder. There's nothing much, just the usual crap about an ongoing investigation and a lot of speculation about Blades's ties to organized crime. As I suspected, the press runs it as a "gangland killing." There's nothing about the killer, no artist's conception of my face. I sigh with relief.

More shocking is the back page of the paper. I'm about to fold the paper up and start to pick at the wilted leaves they call a salad when I see a picture of me—the *old* me. It's the obituary for Detective Steven James Fischer.

As befits my life, most of the obit concerns my career. It lists my six commendations for valor and my three medals for bravery. A couple of my big arrests are listed as well. The end of it says, "Detective Fischer was relentless in his pursuit of justice. He is survived by his daughter Madison."

For the first time in a while I start to cry. It doesn't say I was a good father, husband, or even friend. Only that I was a good cop. Madison's name is given as an afterthought, just as she was when I was a man.

"You all right, sweetheart?" the waitress asks.

I wipe at my eyes and sniffle. "I'll be fine," I snap and summon some of that rich girl authority. I shove the salad back at her. "Send this back and bring me a cheeseburger and chili fries."

After the waitress has gone, I stare at my photo in the paper. It's a good picture of me, taken a few years ago in my dress uniform. That's the best way for people to remember Steve Fischer, I suppose. I never was much else, especially not a father.

With a sigh I read the obit again. Beneath the last sentence is a paragraph that gives the funeral arrangements. I'm being put to rest tomorrow at the Memorial Gardens Cemetery. In lieu of flowers, people are encouraged to donate to the Fraternal Order of Police fund for fallen officers. That's probably Maddy's idea. Good girl, I think and then put the paper away.

Chapter 37

There's not much more of a surreal experience than to attend your own funeral. I make sure to get to the cemetery late, after everyone else has taken their seats. With my dyed hair, big sunglasses, and designer dress it's unlikely anyone will recognize me, so long as I keep quiet and out of the way.

I take a seat in the back, next to Jefferson. He immediately tries to look down my dress. I shift my seat over a couple of inches. I'd like to punch him in the throat, but that would draw too much attention to myself.

Most of the people in attendance are cops or the family members of cops. I see Maddy in the front row; she leans on the shoulder of an older woman with red hair who must be Debbie. Jake and Tess sit next to them. I don't see Grace anywhere. Does Debbie know about Grace? Has Maddy come out to her yet? I have no idea what Debbie's stance on that would be. She might take it hard at first, but like me I figure she probably just wants Maddy to be happy.

I hadn't gone to church since my divorce, but there's still a priest there to read some Bible verses for me. He stands next to a coffin that's probably full of bricks since my body—such as it is—is in the back row. I doubt I've ever met the priest, which doesn't discourage him when he talks about how brave and honorable I was. I feel a cold shiver at this and think of how I murdered Bobby Blades. Do any of the cops here know that his killer is right behind them?

I should probably leave, but morbid curiosity keeps me in my seat. Jake of course delivers the eulogy. "There's no one except my wife I ever loved more than Steve. He was the best friend anyone could hope for. Whenever I needed him, he was there. When my daughter was diagnosed with cancer, Steve came to visit her at the hospital every day.

"As a police officer, there was no one with more tenacity, more guts than Steve. It didn't matter if he were outnumbered a hundred-to-one; he wouldn't let anything get in his way. This police force, this city, this whole damned world is going to be a lot worse off without him.

"If Steve were still here, I'm sure he'd want us to continue the work he started, to clean up this city and make it safe for decent folk. I hope all of us here today strive to be as brave, as honorable, as good as Steve Fischer."

Like my obituary, Jake doesn't say anything about me as a husband or father. Why should he? I was a complete failure on both counts. I watch the front row and try to see if Maddy or Debbie are crying. There's no way to tell from back here. I doubt they are. Why should they be? They're both better off without me.

Neither of them says anything at my funeral. After Jake sits down, the honor guard fires a twenty-one-gun salute. They take the flag off my fake coffin and give it to Maddy. I can't see her reaction to this, but she still doesn't seem to be crying. Maybe she's just being strong, like she figures I'd want. It's not what I want. I want her to mourn me, to let out her pain, not keep it inside the way I always did.

The thought occurs to me that I should run up to the coffin and tell everyone the truth, that Steve Fischer is still alive. Jake could back me up, tell them what Dr. Palmer found out. Except that he probably wouldn't. He wouldn't want to go public with this. He'd put an arm around me and then drag me off somewhere private to lecture me for being stupid. Meanwhile, Maddy would hate me for spoiling her father's funeral. That is if she doesn't already hate me for what Grace and I did.

I do get up, but not to crash the funeral. Instead I slink off the way I came in to escape before Jefferson can proposition me. As I do, I notice another woman in a black dress and sunglasses under a tree. I need a moment to realize it's Grace. We face each other and her brow furrows for a moment. "Stacey?"

"Hi," I say. I feel like a shy urchin again in Grace's presence. Since my cover is already blown, I sit down beside her. "Shouldn't you be over there with everyone else?"

"Maddy thought it'd be better if it were just family and her dad's friends."

"Oh. Did you tell her—?"

"About us kissing? No. I chickened out. Pretty lousy, huh?"

"Not as lousy as me. I'm sorry about stealing from the register. I can pay you back."

"It's all right. I'll just deduct it from your paycheck." She looks me up and down. "You look good. What have you been up to?"

"I, uh, came into a little money. You like it?"

She fingers my shorter, darker hair. "You look gorgeous." She smiles at me. "I knew there was a beautiful woman in there, underneath that tomboy."

"I thought you said I was a functional girl."

"That's just what I told you. Salesmanship and all."

"I bet." I smile back at her and resist the urge to kiss her again. "You look good too."

"You think so?"

"I almost didn't recognize you."

She takes my hand and gives it a squeeze. "You want to get out of here?"

***

We take a cab back to Grace's shop. I could have offered to take her to my hotel room, but then she'd know where it was and she might find the duffel bag of weapons I've hidden in the closet. Plus, Grace's shop is a lot closer.

She kisses me in the cab. It's not as long or as deep as our first kiss, just something to set the mood. When she's sure no one will notice, her hand burrows beneath my skirt. Again not enough to set me off, just a little teaser for what's to come.

Once we stop, I toss the driver a twenty and tell him to keep the change. Then Grace pulls me inside the shop, upstairs to the apartment. The front door isn't even closed before she kisses me again. This one is like our first kiss in the kitchen.

"I've missed you so much," she whispers. "Did you miss me?"

I think of the hot tub and on the train. "Yes."

She leads me into the bedroom, the one she and Maddy share. It occurs to me that I should stop, before I hurt Maddy even more, but I can't. Instead I shed my clothes and leave them in a heap on the floor.

I look down at my naked body. My face turns warm. "I don't know what to do," I admit. "I've never done this before."

"Don't worry," she says with a grin, "I'll teach you."

She lays me down on the bed and then starts to work her hands across my body. She demonstrates how as a woman I have a lot more sensitive areas than just between my legs. She massages my breasts, bites a nipple, and even runs her tongue along my midsection. Each time I gasp not from pain, but from the same pleasure as in the hot tub.

I do the same to her as she did to me. My hands are clumsier, but they still seem to get the job done. It takes a little prodding before I can bring myself to touch her with my tongue. Her skin is salty from sweat, but the way she moans makes it worthwhile. "You're a natural," she says.

Eventually we go inside each other. It's a lot different than sex as a man. It's not so violent; I don't thrust to batter down her defenses to make myself come. This is a lot tenderer, even gentle. We're partners in this, not combatants.

Grace has enough experience that she strings me along for a half hour. That's long enough for my clumsy hands to find the rhythm. We come at the same time, a pair of shrieks, followed by identical sighs. We pull our hands out and smear them on our stomachs. Grace licks my stomach again, to clean it up like a dog. I can't bring myself to go that far just yet.

She uses her cleaner hand to stroke my hair as she cuddles up against me. "You're amazing," she says. "It's hard to believe that was your first time."

"Maybe I had a good teacher."

We fall asleep in each other's arms. When I wake up,

I look over at the clock and see it's ten o'clock. I sit up with a start. Grace's hands fumble to grab me and pull me back down. "Don't go," she says. "Maddy won't come back tonight. She's staying with her mom."

"I have to go," I say. I stroke her hair and then kiss her on the cheek. "I'll be back later."

That is if I survive.

Chapter 38

I take a cab back to the hotel to fetch my duffel bag. I pay the driver extra to make sure he takes a few shortcuts. By the time I've changed into something more appropriate for a commando operation and grabbed the duffel bag, it's eleven o'clock. Shit.

The next cab driver I pay even more handsomely to get me near the warehouse Blades indicated. I can't have him drop me off right in front of it. Not only would I risk someone on Lex's crew might spot me, but also after I'm done here the cabbie might figure out I was responsible.

Along the way I sneak a peek in the duffel bag. I can still turn back. I can have the cabbie drop me off at Grace's shop and collapse into her arms. We can fuck and cuddle for the rest of the night. That's certainly a better idea than to murder people in cold blood, isn't it?

Except I might never get another shot at Lex and his goons. To track them down again could take months or even years. Years I'll spend in this body. I've already seen the changes in my personality. Every day I become more Stacey and lose more Steve. In six months or a year there might be nothing left of him, just a sweet young woman in love with her employer—her best friend's lover. By then I won't have the nerve to kill anyone.

It has to be done tonight. If I survive, then I can go back to Grace. We can work something out, find a way to still be together and not hurt Maddy. How? Continue to see Grace behind Maddy's back? Maybe I'm becoming Stacey more and more, but Maddy is still my daughter. I can't betray her like this again.

I take a few deep breaths to focus again on the task at hand. I'm not sure exactly what security Lex will have or what he's even going to be doing, so I'll have to figure out a way to take care of that once I get there.

I could always take out my phone and call the police. Leave an anonymous tip that something big is going down at the warehouse. Except just like the night of the Lennox robbery, if I call my former comrades, one will probably call Lex and pass the word along. I could at least call Jake. Then I'd have a little backup. Look what happened the last time I went against Lex alone!

No, I can't involve Jake in this. It's too dangerous. He's already said his eulogy for me.

The driver makes it to the docks in a half hour. I'm probably a mile away from where I need to be. A mile away and I've got a good eighty pounds of guns and ammo. In my big old body that would be a lot easier. Stacey is fast like a thoroughbred racehorse; she's not a pack mule.

I have to stop twice to catch my breath. Even if I make it in time, I won't be in fighting trim. That can't be helped now. I've got to push ahead and hope for the best.

When I get in sight of the warehouse it's five minutes to midnight. I'm too late; Lex's guys are already on patrol around the building. I had hoped to get in before them, to set up a nest somewhere so I could ambush them. My rendezvous with Grace means it will be a lot harder to get in there now.

I do a zigzag pattern and dive behind one stack of pallets or pile of rope and then zig over to another when I'm sure no one can see me. At least reasonably sure. There could always be someone on the roof with some night vision goggles. I just have to hope Lex isn't that paranoid.

As I get closer, I hear Bruiser Malloy's voice. "The boss says to keep an eye out for whoever iced Blades."

Another minion whines, "Blades probably just pissed off the wrong dude."

"Shut up!" Bruiser roars. "Keep looking."

The minion waits until Bruiser's shambled away before he grumbles under his breath. He stops to light a cigarette. While he does that, I scamper as fast as I can along a row of old crates. I see what I need: a ladder that goes up to the roof of the warehouse. From there I'll probably find a way inside.

The only problem will be to get up the ladder. I try to sling the duffel across my back, but it's too heavy. It'll pull me off the ladder for sure. If it doesn't, it'll take me too long to climb up, so someone will spot me and shoot me.

I open the bag up and then inventory what I've got in there. The Uzi is light enough to keep. The AK-47 is heavier. I throw out the extra clips for it. That lightens the load. As for the little .25 pistol, I stick it in my pocket as a last resort. The duffel is light enough on my back now that I can walk without a problem.

The guard still smokes and mutters to himself. I don't see Bruiser anywhere; he's either on the other side or else he went inside. For the moment that leaves me an opening to scamper over to the ladder. With the duffel on my back, I climb as fast as I can. I expect someone to shout for me to stop or else the sound of a gun firing, but I don't hear anything.

I make it to the roof. There's no one there with any goggles or a sniper rifle. Lex's security isn't as good as I'd feared, at least not outside. The inside might be a different story.

I stay low to the roof as I make my way around it and look for a door or something to let me inside. I hear Bruiser's voice again. I risk a peek down at the ground and see him as he berates another guard. Apparently none of them are very interested in keeping watch. Good help is hard to find, even for the mob.

There's a door on the front side of the warehouse. At one time there was a lock, but it's rusted away, so it's easy enough for me to push the door open. I do it slowly; I don't want to risk a creak that will alert anyone to my presence.

Through the door is a catwalk that also hasn't fared well in recent years. It's a good thing I'm only a hundred ten pounds—with another fifty in weapons—or else I'd fall through the damned thing. Still I move only one step at a time as if on a tightrope.

I make it over to a corner, where the catwalk is a little more secure and where I can hide behind a support pillar. I let out a sigh. I've made it this far at least.

Then I hear metal shriek. I worry it's the catwalk, but it's not. It's the front doors of the warehouse. A car pulls in. It's a Mercedes and before it stops and the door opens, I already know who's inside. Artie Luther has arrived.

Chapter 39

I'm tempted to take the AK-47 out of the bag and open fire. After a week as a woman, after I intimidated the Worm and murdered Blades, I've finally found my prey. All I have to do is line up a shot and pull the trigger. Then my troubles will be over.

My cop's intuition tells me to wait. Luther came here for something big. Something so big he came himself, just like the Lennox robbery. I should wait and see what it is. Then I can take out all the scum in one fell swoop.

In the meantime I should find a better place to hide. Across the building there's a stairway that leads down to the second floor. That will get me closer, more within range for the AK-47. I should have bought a rifle, even a hunting rifle with a scope. Then I could try to pick off Luther and company from up here. Except I remember what happened on the dock. If I couldn't hit Lex then, I don't have much of a chance now from up here.

I look down and see Lex as he talks with Bruiser; he gestures emphatically at the doors. While they argue, I hurry along the catwalk and try not to make any noise. When I hear a creak, I freeze. I look down at the floor of the warehouse, but no one looks my direction. With a sigh of relief, I keep going.

I make it to the stairs. With another look to make sure the coast is clear, I descend the stairs. The second floor catwalk is wider, with more room for me to walk. Of course since it's closer to the floor it's also more dangerous. If I make any creaks this time, someone might hear me.

There's an office on the second floor that might make for a good place to hide. It's at least fifty feet away. I look around again. Bruiser has gone over to work on the doors while Lex stands in the middle of the warehouse, a perfect target. Who's he waiting for? I'll worry about that later.

I scurry towards the office. I've just about made it when I feel something like a bee sting in my right thigh. Pain burns in my right leg. I nearly collapse right then, but I keep going. I bite down on my lip and then limp into the office.

There's not much light in the office, but as I lean against the wall, I can feel the blood trickle down my leg. I've been shot! I didn't hear anything, which means a silencer. A sniper on the second floor or maybe up on the roof.

The Tall Man. It has to be. O'Neill is Lex's best hit man and I haven't seen him yet. A stupid mistake on my part. I wonder what he'll do next. Since I broke his jaw, he can't call for help. He might go down and write a note for Lex. Or he might come after me himself.

Either way I have to be ready. I look around the office, but don't see any other way in or out. This is my last stand, then. Just like the Alamo and Custer I'll go down fighting. If I'm like them then I'll lose, but I'll lose with honor.

As I take the AK-47 off my shoulder and click off the safety, I think of Maddy. I really will have abandoned her now. Before I could at least be her friend—not a good one after what I did with Grace—but soon I won't be anything. Worse yet, she'll mourn for me a second time.

Thoughts of Maddy of course bring Grace to mind as well. I so badly want to make it home to her, to collapse in bed next to her and have her hug me and tell me everything will be all right. I love her. Not as a friend, but in the same way I loved Debbie.

I hear footsteps on the catwalk coming towards me. It's probably the Tall Man to finish me off. I take a deep breath and try to push the pain away. "Here we go," I whisper.

***

There are a couple of different ways to handle the situation. One is to get into a Mexican standoff by leaning out the door to fire at the Tall Man or anyone else. Two is to do like *Scarface* and jump out the doorway with machine gun blazing. They might get me or I might get them first.

Three is to try a clever ruse. I start to sob loudly, loud enough that I'm sure the Tall Man or anyone else on the second floor can hear me. To make my cries more realistic, I stick one finger in the bullet wound. That prompts me to scream and sob for real.

Through my screams and sobs, I can still hear the footsteps approach. I slide the AK-47 over to the side; it would be much too obvious to use in this situation. The Uzi is a lot smaller and I don't need to have much accuracy with it.

I take a couple deep breaths to try to settle myself down as I hear him approach. I'm only going to get one chance at this. The footsteps stop. I look up at the doorway and try to wipe the tears away with one eye. Maybe I did too good of a job with those.

In the doorway I see Will O'Neill's gangly frame. The bottom of his pale horse face glints from the wires that hold it together. There's a similar metallic glint in his hand from the silenced pistol he's got pointed at me. He gestures for me to get up with one hand.

"I can't get up," I whine. "You shot me. It hurts!"

He gestures to me again; he won't take no for an answer. "I told you I can't! It hurts too much!"

This time he lowers the pistol and cocks it. That's the sign for I damned well better find a way to get up. "OK," I say. I use my left foot to try to push myself up. My right leg really does hurt, just not as much as I've told him. At the same time I lever myself up, I keep the Uzi against the wall and use my body to screen it from him.

When I'm about halfway up, I act like I'm slipping. As I fall, I spin around and fire the Uzi wildly. It's set on full auto, which pounds out a couple dozen bullets in seconds. The Tall Man screams through the wires in his mouth.

I've hit him. Not fatally, as I hear him hop backwards so he can keep his gun trained on the door. Shit. We've got another Mexican standoff. Worse because I can't use that ruse again.

It's time for the second option.

'"Say hello to my little friend!"' I say to myself. I drop the Uzi to the floor and trade it for the AK-47. I count to three before I lunge out onto the catwalk as fast as possible with the machine gun at my hip. The moment the muzzle is clear of the door, I squeeze the trigger.

It's a good thing I have both hands on it or else I probably would shoot at the ceiling. Amos was right that the rifle packs a kick for a girl my size. I keep my finger on the trigger to spray the catwalk ahead of me.

The gun finally clicks as it runs out of ammo. I drop the useless weapon to the catwalk. Ahead of me I see the Tall Man pressed against the wall. Is it possible I missed him entirely? He turns towards me. My entire body freezes as it did when the Worm approached me at the liquor store.

When the Tall Man turns around, I see two bloodstains spreading across his white shirt. He still has enough presence of mind to aim the weapon at me. I stare at the end of the silencer and wait for the flash that will end my life. My second life. Maddy. Grace. I have just enough time to think of them again.

The gun doesn't fire. The Tall Man collapses to the catwalk. He's dead.

One down. But then I feel the catwalk shake as if from an earthquake. Bruiser Malloy appears at the top of the stairs. The sight of him snaps me out of my paralysis. I rush back into the office for the Uzi.

Two to go.

Chapter 40

Bruiser Malloy is big, but a couple of clips from the Uzi should stop him. I take an extra clip out of the duffel bag so I can reload this time. I'm not sure what he packs, probably something big.

I stick my head out the doorway. It's big all right. It's an RPG launcher like I saw at Amos's shop. It's the same kind al-Qaeda and the like use in Afghanistan and Iraq. Pretty powerful stuff to carry to a business deal.

It's probably my fault he's got the thing. With Blades dead, Lex must have decided to bring a little extra firepower. That or Bruiser came up with the idea on his own.

I have just enough time to get into the far corner of the office before the rocket-propelled grenade screams down the catwalk. I put the Uzi between my legs so I can put my fingers in my ears.

Not that it does much good. The explosion rocks the entire office. Plaster from the ceiling comes down on my head. Stray papers left on the floor blow into my face. My ears ring from the blast. I cough from the smoke.

I'm still alive. Once the air is free enough of smoke and dust, I can see the front walls of the office are gone. Part of the back of the warehouse is gone too. I can see the harbor through the hole. The water looks about the same as the last time I went up against Bruiser, calm and black. That's probably where I'll wind up before long. This time there won't be any FY-1978 to save me.

Only if I let them catch me. I take the Uzi from my lap. I don't even have to get up; I see Bruiser in the new, larger doorway a second later. I raise the Uzi and aim for his big shaved skull.

Nothing happens. The gun clicks impotently. I check to make sure the safety is off. I even try to slap the thing a couple of times. It's jammed. Maybe from the explosion and all the dust and such. Maybe it's just a piece of shit. If I survive, I'll have to pay Amos another visit. This time I won't flirt with him; I'll just wring his fucking neck.

With no other ideas in mind, I throw the gun at him as hard as I can. I might as well spit on him. He reaches out with one huge, scarred mitt to grab the front of my black sweater. He hefts me into the air without even a grunt of strain.

He could snap my neck like it's a twig. He doesn't. Instead, he says, "Time for you to meet the boss."

***

I've already met Artie Luther more times than I'd have liked. Not that I could tell Bruiser that. He grabs me around the neck and squeezes to the point I can only get a trickle of air in my lungs. That's at least enough to keep me alive as Bruiser carries me downstairs.

He tosses me into a pile of old tarps. I'd scream, but there's not enough air in my lungs to waste with that. Instead I lie there for a few moments and gasp for air.

I feel one of Bruiser's hands grab me by the shoulder. He spins me around into a sitting position. I groan from the pain in my leg and with fresh pain in my shoulder.

"This cunt killed Willy," Bruiser says. He levels a silver .45 at my head. I know this weapon—it used to belong to me. Killed with my own gun—again. Must be the universe's idea of a joke.

To add to the irony, Artie Luther is my savior. He puts a hand on my old gun. "Not yet," Lex says. He stares down at me. "Let's find out who our visitor is first."

"I'm not anyone," I say. "Just a figment of your imagination."

Almost as bad as being shot with my own gun is being pistol-whipped with it. The butt of my old gun opens up a cut across my cheek. Tears come to my eyes. This time it's not part of a ruse.

"That should teach you to have some manners," Lex says. "Now, who are you?"

"Stacey."

I resist the urge to spit in Lex's face when he takes my chin in his meaty fingers and then looks in my eyes. "Why are you here, Stacey?"

"To kill you slimeballs."

"Why would a little girl like you want to do that?"

"Because you fucks killed my father." That's close enough to the truth as far as I'm concerned.

"Is it safe to assume you killed Mr. Blades?"

"He had it coming."

Before they can continue the interrogation, headlights wash over us; the light reflects off Lex's bald dome. He lets me go and turns to face the lights. "Looks like our friends are here. Keep an eye on the girl. We'll continue our discussion later."

The car parks next to Lex's Mercedes. It's a black Cadillac limo. A chauffeur springs out of the vehicle to open the back doors. I expect to see a bunch of Russians or

Italians or some other European-born gangsters. Instead a half-dozen Asian guys in suits pile out. Four of them carry weapons similar to the Uzi I had. One of the other two carries a silver briefcase. That must be the payment for whatever Lex plans to sell.

Lex heads towards them and holds out one arm to the unarmed one without the briefcase. "Mr. Ling! It's good to see you again."

The man with the briefcase whispers into Ling's ear. Ling says something in a foreign language. Chinese? Japanese? Korean? I've heard bits of all three before, but nothing he says jogs my memory. The guy with the briefcase translates, "We have the money. Where is the product?"

"A direct man. I like that."

Ling says something translated as, "He does not wish to spend any more time in this filthy hovel than necessary."

"I apologize for the state of our meeting place, but one can't be too careful in this city." Lex turns and motions to Bruiser. He hoists me up by the back collar of my sweater. "As you can see, we've already had one party crasher."

"Mr. Ling does not care about squatters. He wishes for you to deliver the formula."

"Of course." Lex reaches into his suit jacket. From the inside pocket he takes out a slim metal case. "It's all in here gentlemen: the formula plus Dr. Nath's notes, at least those we could recover from her apartment after her untimely death."

I go slack in Bruiser's grasp. Formula, Dr. Nath's notes. That can mean only one thing: Lex plans to sell FY-1978 to these people. Are they another pharmaceutical company? That's my guess from what I've seen of Mr. Ling so far. He doesn't seem like a gangster to me.

Everything starts to fall into place. These must be the people Lex stole the formula for. They might have employed him to do the job for them or else he might have heard they wanted it and then broke in to steal it first. The latter sounds more like Lex's style.

"Now, let's see the payment," Luther says.

The translator opens the silver briefcase. There's a bunch of thousand-dollar bills in it. Without being asked, the translator flips through some of the stacks to show there aren't a bunch of blank pieces of paper inside. He probably saw that in a movie. "Very good," Luther says.

I can't let them make the exchange. Forget about killing Bruiser and Luther; I need that case with the formula and notes. If I give that to Dr. Palmer, it could cut years off the estimate to make a cure for me.

"Hey assholes!" I shout. "You really think a son of a bitch like Luther is going to give you the real formula? What he's giving you is probably the formula for dandruff shampoo. Then after he gets your money, he'll turn around and sell it back to Lennox to screw you over even more."

Lex glares at me. "I think we've heard enough from the peanut gallery," he snaps. "Dispose of her, Thomas."

"Sure thing, boss."

"Wait!" Mr. Ling says. Apparently he knows a little English after all. "How do we know what she says isn't true?"

Lex turns and gives the Asians his best salesman grin. "Now gentlemen, why would I lie to you? We've made an agreement—"

"We will alter agreement!" Ling says. He barks

something to his translator.

The translator says, "Mr. Ling has decided we must verify the information you give us is accurate before payment is made."

"That's absurd! We don't have time for a scientific analysis," Lex says. He glares at the translator. "Tell him if he doesn't take this deal I'm giving the formula back to Lennox. They'll pay me quite a handsome price for it."

Ling says something to the translator, who says, "Mr. Ling does not appreciate being blackmailed." For emphasis the translator gestures to the armed thugs behind him.

Now we've got a real Mexican standoff—or maybe Chinese standoff would be more appropriate. Lex doesn't want to give the formula to the Asians or as sure as the sun rises in the east they'll take it and kill him, Bruiser, and me. At the same time, the Asians don't want to pay for something without being sure of what it is.

But Lex has a trump card. He whistles shrilly. A moment later, the windows on the Mercedes come down. Two machine gun muzzles stick out. They start to fire a second later. They're a lot better shots than me and their weapons don't jam. Mr. Ling's guards topple like dominos. The translator takes a bullet in the throat, more universal irony.

Throughout the gunfire Luther just stands there with arms crossed. Also during the gunfire, I reach into the waist of my pants. Bruiser forgot to search me before he dragged me down here. I take out the .25 I tucked down there. Bruiser is focused on the slaughter instead of me.

The tiny pops of the .25 are barely audible against the noise of the machine guns. I put three bullets into Bruiser's head. He's still alive enough to roar like a bull and then hurl me a good hundred feet, as if I'm a human Frisbee. Somehow I keep the pistol in my hand as I land. I roll over and aim the gun at the vast expanse of Bruiser's chest. I empty the rest of the clip into him.

He wobbles for a moment on his feet. Just like at the end of one of his fights, he pitches forward. Only this time it's not a dive. He hits the canvas one last time.

I scramble to my feet and toss the pistol away. By now Lex has seen what's happened to his enforcer. He reaches into his jacket for a pistol. I lunge towards Bruiser. My old pistol is still clamped in his right fist. I tug at his hand to no avail. I am able to move his arm; I bend it back towards Luther. I pull the trigger.

I fire six times and never hit the bastard. On the plus side, it forces him to dive for cover. Behind him, I see the two goons from the Mercedes get out. I'm outnumbered and outgunned now. As much as I want the formula, I want to live a bit more.

I turn and make for the back door of the warehouse.

Chapter 41

Adrenaline gets me the first ten blocks, until I'm away from the docks. I look over my shoulder along the way and expect to see a Mercedes with Luther's thugs in it. When I see headlights, I dive behind a garbage can. But it's not Lex's goons, just a white cargo van with the logo of a fish company on it.

As I lie there, my leg begins to throb, to remind me I've been shot. I've been shot before—you can't be a cop in this city for long and not take some lead. I still have to bite down on my lip so I don't scream at the pain as the adrenaline wears off.

I struggle out of my sweater; some snobby part of my brain laments it's cashmere as I tear off a sleeve to use as a bandage. The rest of it I toss on the ground. Even if Lex would find it, there's nothing it would tell him, except that I have expensive tastes.

I lever myself up to my feet and groan from the effort. When I start out again, my pace is much slower. Each step becomes an ordeal; pain shoots through my right leg. I want to collapse to the ground, curl up into a ball, and sleep. I know I can't or I might never wake up again. This wound isn't fatal, but it would be easy enough for Luther's thugs—or someone just as bad—to find me and nothing good happens to an innocent girl in the middle of the night on these streets.

It takes me an hour to limp another five blocks. By then my body is coated in sweat and I shiver. I shouldn't have got rid of the sweater, not that it would have done me much good. Don't be a wimp, I tell myself. It's hard not to give in when I see my reflection in the glass. I'm not a hardened cop anymore, just a scared little girl out way past her bedtime. I should be home in bed, with Grace.

With a sob I collapse onto a bus stop bench. I need to get this damned bullet out of my leg. But I can't go to a hospital. They would ask some inconvenient questions and Lex will probably check the hospital records in case I turn up there. Even if I could use an alias, there aren't a lot of little white girls getting shot in this neighborhood at this time of night.

What I could use almost as bad as the bullet out of me is a drink. A couple shots of whiskey right now would really take some of the edge off. The thought of booze brings me a solution to both of my problems. I reach into my pocket and take out my cell phone to call for a cab. I hope I'm not too late.

***

Big Al is closing down for the night when the cab drops me off at Squiggy's. By the time we arrive, my head swims and the slightest movement prompts everything to spin. I'm not sure how much money I give the driver, but it must be enough because he drives away without a word.

Al is locking the front door as I stagger towards him. "We're closed," he says. "Go find one of them after hour clubs." He turns and gives me a harder look. "Wait, I remember you. You're that kid who was in here with Maddy the other night."

I stumble forward and trip on the concrete. Al catches me before I can fall. He brushes sweaty hair out of my face to look me in the eye. "What's wrong with you? You OD-ing?"

"I've been shot," I say. I wave my hand towards the bullet wound. "Help me."

He sets me down on the sidewalk so he can unwrap the makeshift bandage from around my wound. "Jesus," he says. "We have to get you to a hospital."

"No! No hospitals. They'll find me."

"Who?"

"The bad guys," I say. I reach out towards Al and grab a handful of his shirt. "You can fix me."

"What? I'm not a surgeon, kid."

Despite the pain and blood loss, I still have the wherewithal to keep to my cover story. "Maddy said you fished a bullet out of her father."

"What? Oh, right. That was years ago." Ten years ago. It started down the road in an apartment building. Jake and I were on the trail of some jewel thieves who'd killed a security guard. A routine case. At least it should have been.

We tracked them to the apartment building, where Steve Fischer charged into the apartment where he thought they would be. I found one of them on the couch with a girl, pants down around their ankles. I was careless; I let myself get distracted by the scene on the couch to let one of the guy's buddies get the drop on me. I'm lucky he only shot me in the left shoulder.

Before Jake or I could take him down, he hopped onto the fire escape and headed down for the streets. I wouldn't let a little bullet wound slow me down; I followed him down the fire escape. I ran after the bastard until we were almost to Squiggy's. Then I started to get tired. So I reached for my gun and fired.

My aim wasn't very good; I hit the sign for the bar. The thief would have gotten away, except Al charged out with his shotgun at the ready to see who'd broken his sign. He didn't shoot the kid, just clobbered him in the face with the butt of the shotgun. I staggered up, blood oozing from the wound in my shoulder.

"Christ, Steve, what happened to you?"

"Punk shot me," I said. I kicked the bastard in the ribs, though he couldn't feel it.

Jake had caught up with us by then. We let him take care of the perp while I went inside. Al took me upstairs to his apartment over the bar. From the closet he took out a black bag. "I didn't know you were a doctor," I said.

"I was an army medic," Al explained. He was in Vietnam in the last days of the war, not long enough to see much action. I was only his third patient. He gave me a couple of drinks to ease the pain and then took the bullet out of my shoulder. The hospital cleaned it up later, but he'd done good work.

Now I need him to do it again. "Let's go inside, kid," he says. He scoops me up in his arms and then carries me upstairs. It looks about the same as ten years ago. I use my hands to sweep some old magazines and bills off of his dining room table so he can set me on top of it. The last time my legs dangled over the edge, but now there's enough room for my entire body. Al finds a throw pillow to set beneath my head. Then he gets to work.

***

The hardest part, even worse than the pain, is to stay awake. While Al washes his hands and sterilizes his instruments, he gives me a fifth of vodka. I drink just about the whole thing by the time he's ready to operate. The alcohol along with the pain and blood loss make my eyelids heavy. He must notice this, because he says, "It's OK, honey. You can sleep."

I shake my head. "No. You'll take me to the hospital and then they'll find me."

"No one's going to find you. You'll be safe. I promise."

While I know Al would never lie to a girl in trouble, I still force myself to stay awake. The fresh pain from when Al starts to cut around the wound helps to keep me awake. I'd like some more vodka—or something stronger—but then I might fall asleep. Instead I stare up at the ceiling and try to count the number of holes in the tiles while I try not to whimper too loud.

After a couple of minutes, he pats my hand and says, "This isn't too bad. Looks like it didn't hit any of your arteries or anything."

"Good."

"I need you to be very still, honey. I have to pull the bullet out now. If you move, I could wind up doing some damage and you might lose this pretty leg."

I smile a little as I think of his threat to Maddy a couple days ago. "I'll be fine," I say. "Just get it out of me."

I hold onto the edges of the table to make sure I don't flinch too much as Al starts to pull out the bullet. I can't bear to look, so I keep my eyes squeezed shut. When I open them again, I'm on Al's bed. I try to sit up, but pain shoots up from my leg at the effort. I sink back against his pillows.

I see a bandage spotted with blood around my right leg. There's no sign of Al until I hear the toilet flush.

Before I can pretend I'm asleep, he sticks his head into the room. "How are you feeling?" he asks.

"It hurts," I whine.

"It will for a little while," he says.

I nod and wonder how long it will take the FY-1978 to kick in, if it kicks in. A couple of days maybe that I'll be laid up. Will Lex have worked out a deal for the formula by then? I try to sit up again, but sink back down from the pain.

"Hey, it's all right," he says. "I'm not going to hurt you. Or turn you in."

"Thanks. For everything."

"Anything for a friend of Maddy," he says. "You want to call her?"

"No!" I say too quickly. I force myself to smile. "I don't want to worry her."

When I think of Maddy, I think of Grace and what Grace and I did. I start to sob, which triggers more pain in my leg; this prompts me to cry harder in a vicious cycle. Al is pretty much a stranger to Stacey Chance, but he's a good-hearted man. He leans over to wrap me in a hug until I've cried myself out. "It's all right, sweetheart," he whispers again and again.

"Thanks," I say again once I've gotten myself under control. With a sniffle I ask, "Can I use your phone? I want to call my uncle."

"Not a problem." Al hands the phone to me. It's an old rotary model; I need three tries before I can get Jake's cell phone number right.

He answers on the first ring. "Al?"

"No, it's me."

"Stacey? What are you doing at Al's?"

"I needed him to take a bullet out of me."

"A bullet? Jesus Christ! How bad is it?"

"I'll be fine. It's just a flesh wound."

"Thank God. Do you have any idea how worried we all are? That friend of yours—"

"Grace?"

"Yeah, her. She called and said you disappeared. Tess had me out beating the bushes. Where have you been?"

"I'll tell you later. Can you just come and pick me up?"

"All right, but stay right there. Got it?"

"I couldn't go anywhere if I wanted to," I say with a yawn. "I'd better go before I pass out."

"I'll be there soon as I can."

"OK." I hang up the phone. I'm sure Jake will be here in about ten minutes. That should give me enough time to make another call. My clumsy fingers need a couple more tries before I can get Grace's number right.

Like Jake, she answers on the first ring. "Stacey?"

"It's me."

"Thank God! Where are you?"

"A friend's house."

"A friend? You mean Maddy? Is that why you left? You didn't tell her, did you?"

"No, not Maddy. Someone else."

"Tell me where you are, Stace and I'll be right there."

"Don't worry, my uncle is coming to get me."

"Oh. I see." I can hear Grace start to cry. "I should have expected it. You care about Maddy. She's your friend."

"She's your girlfriend," I say.

"I know. What a mess." Grace sniffles into the phone. "Can't I come over and talk to you in person? We need to work this out."

"I don't think that's a good idea. My uncle will be here soon."

"Stace, don't you understand? I love you. Don't you love me?"

"Yes," I say and mean it. The pain of that hurts almost as much as the bullet wound. "Maddy loves you too. I don't want to come between you two."

"Stace, please—"

"No. What we did was a mistake. It can't happen again."

"But we love each other. We can't just break it off." I hear Grace sob. "God, I've been thinking about you all night. After a couple of hours when you didn't come back I started to freak out. I thought you might be dead. I didn't want to lose you, not so soon."

"Grace, please—"

"No, you have to hear this. Stacey, you're the most wonderful person I've ever met. What happened tonight was so magical. It was like nothing I ever experienced before."

"Me either."

"Then why are you trying to keep us apart?"

"Because I love Madison—as a friend," I say. I tack on the last part before I can slip up and admit she's my daughter.

"We can figure out a way to break it to Maddy. Please, Stace, I love you. I want to be with you."

"I'm sorry," I say and heave a sigh into the receiver. "There's a lot you don't know about me, Grace. I'm not who you think I am. I'm not sweet or smart or any of that. I'm a monster."

"I know you feel guilty Stace, so do I—"

"It's not that. I've done some bad things." I stop, thinking of what I did to Blades, how I butchered him like a pig. Then I remember what I did so I could get to him. "I've done terrible things. If you knew, you'd never want to see me again."

"That's not true. Whatever it is, no matter how bad it is, I'll still love you."

"I killed a man. Three men, really."

"I'm sure you had a good reason—"

"I had reasons. Maybe they weren't so good. I've whored myself out. I've lied, I've stole, I've hurt everyone I care about."

"It doesn't matter. We can work through it. I'll help you."

From Grace's voice I'm sure she does want to help me through the pain. I'm tempted to let her try. I think of the night we spent together, how perfect it was until I had to go. I can see her as she welcomes me back; I fall into her arms—

It's no good. I've hurt Madison so much already. I was a lousy father to her. I won't hurt her anymore. "I'm sorry, Grace. I can't see you anymore."

"Stacey—"

"My name isn't Stacey," I say.

"What?"

"My birth name was Steven."

"Stace, please, don't joke."

"I'm not joking. I was born a man."

"But you don't look—"

"I had a really good surgeon. That's why I ran away from home. My parents didn't want to have a daughter." I hate to lie to Grace like this, but it has to be this way. I can't come between her and Maddy. The only way to make sure is to push Grace away, to horrify her so much she'll never want to see me again.

Grace whispers, "But I've been *inside* you. I didn't feel anything different."

"I told you I had a good surgeon. It's an experimental procedure. They use this stuff called FY-1978 to alter my DNA. I agreed to be a guinea pig and they did the operation for free."

"No way," Grace says. "That's not possible."

"It is possible. It's from Lennox Pharmaceuticals. There was a Dr. Nath there who came up with it."

"Why are you saying this? I thought you loved me!"

"That's why I have to tell you. You shouldn't be with me. Go back to Maddy. She's the one you deserve. She's everything you said about me, only for real."

Grace doesn't say anything. From the sound of her sobs, I don't think she can muster any words at the moment. The phone disconnects. I put it down. Then I hear footsteps pound upstairs, two sets of them. Al with Jake, to take me home.

Chapter 42

Jake carries me downstairs and sets me on the backseat. In the glow of a streetlamp he studies my wound. "We should have a real doctor take care of it."

"It'll be fine," I say. "He got the bullet out. The drug will take care of the rest."

Jake grunts and then closes the door on me. I manage to ignore the pain as I prop myself up to see Jake and Al talking. I wonder how much Al heard of my conversation with Grace? Not too much, I hope. When I think of Grace, I collapse onto the backseat with a sigh.

Jake doesn't say anything when he gets into the car. Not for a couple of blocks. Then he says, "There was a call on the radio. Fire at a warehouse. You'll never guess who they pulled out of there."

"The Tall Man and Bruiser Malloy."

"Bingo. Some Chinese guys too. I suppose that's your handiwork?"

"I didn't kill the Chinese guys. Lex did."

"What'd he want with them?"

"He was going to sell the formula for FY-1978 to them. I planted a seed of doubt in their heads. Lex decided to pull the plug on the deal—and them."

"Great. So now what?"

"He's going to sell it back to Lennox. It's his only move."

"Wonderful. So what's our move?"

"Talk to Palmer. The higher-ups are going to want someone to verify what they're getting. Palmer is the best choice. They'll want her at the meet. As soon as she knows, she can tell us. We swoop in and finish Lex off."

"I swoop in and arrest Lex, you mean," Jake says.

"Jake—"

"No. No more fucking games. You got to stop this Rambo shit. Next time it's not going to be your leg that gets shot."

"So what? I'm already dead. You delivered my eulogy, remember?"

"Shit. I thought that was you in the back row." Jake shakes his head and then lights a cigarette. "I like the hair."

"Thanks."

"I bet you got it done at that department store upstate, didn't you?"

"Yeah. You guys trace the card?"

"Of course. But you already knew that. That's why you doubled back here. Where've you been staying?"

"The Snowden. I've still got some clothes there. Really nice ones."

"Bought with blood money."

"Blades had it coming."

"You realize I could arrest you? It might do you good to sit in the cooler for a few days."

"I didn't want to kill him," I whine. "He would've talked."

"You sound like one of them."

"Well I'm not a cop anymore in case you haven't

noticed."

"You're not a thug either."

"What was I supposed to do? Sit around playing house with you and Tess?"

"You should have let us handle it."

"You guys have done such a bang-up job. I did more in a week than the whole department has done in twenty years."

"You really aren't Steve anymore. He would never talk like that."

I cup my breasts and give them a jiggle. "Look what he did to me! He ruined my life. And you want me to go by the book?"

"I know what he did was terrible, but you can't let it change you inside. You can't let it make you a monster."

I think of what I told Grace. "It's too late for that."

***

Jake carries me into the house, which I'm grateful for. Tess just about knocks both of us down. "Oh my goodness! What happened to you?"

"I got shot," I say.

"Shot? By whom?"

"A mugger."

"What were you doing out by yourself at night?"

"I—"

Jake intervenes to save me. "We can interrogate her later. Right now she needs to get some rest."

"Yes, of course," Tess says. She brushes hair away from my face. "Everything will be all right, dear. We'll take good care of you."

"All right. Here we go, kid," Jake says. He groans theatrically as he starts up the stairs. "You're lucky I don't drop you on your head. Not that it'd do any good."

"I'm sorry about what I said earlier," I say. "I shouldn't have tried to go this alone."

"Well you don't have to worry about that anymore."

He's careful when he sets me down on the bed. He pulls the blankets up over me, just as gentle as Tess. The way he looks at me, I'm sure he'd like to give me a kiss on the forehead like he used to do with Jenny. Instead, he musses my hair. "Try to get some rest. I'll call Palmer and let her know."

"Thanks." Before Jake can go, I call for him to stop. "If Maddy calls, tell her I'm not here."

"Steve—"

"I don't want to see her right now," I say. I know I wouldn't be able to hide the truth about Grace and I from her.

He mulls this for a few moments. Then he musses my hair again. "All right, kid. I'll tell Tess to hold all calls."

"Thanks." By the time Jake reaches the door, I'm asleep.

***

I'm asleep for twelve hours. When I wake, my stomach rumbles to remind me I've missed breakfast and lunch. When I sit up, pain courses through my leg. I guess the FY-1978 hasn't worked its magic yet. Of course it might take a little while on something this serious. My leg could hurt for days.

I don't want to get out of bed just yet. Tess's motherly instincts are still well-honed, though. She turns on the light a couple minutes later. When she does, I notice something I didn't before I went to sleep: Tess has redecorated the room. Or rather she's undecorated it. All of Jenny's posters are gone from the walls. Her school ribbons and athletic trophies have disappeared. Even her clothes have vanished from the closet.

"You're looking better," Tess says. She puts a hand on my forehead. "Got some color in your cheeks."

"Oh, that's good." I motion to the walls. "What happened?"

"That day you disappeared, I thought I would surprise you by putting Jennifer's things away. I was hoping to take you shopping for some new decorations."

More color returns to my cheeks as I blush. "I messed that up, didn't I?"

"Don't worry about it."

"No, I should worry about it. You've been so nice to me and I've been such a shit." Tess clucks her tongue and I apologize. "When I came here I didn't have anything but the clothes on my back. You and Jake took me in, cleaned me up. You helped me through…you know, my time of the month."

"I know, dear. I was happy to do it."

"And then I took off without even saying thank you."

"It doesn't matter. You're here now, that's the important thing." Tess gives me a hug that only makes me feel worse. It seems all I've done in the last twenty-four hours is make people's lives miserable, especially my own. "I bet you're hungry. I've got some lasagna in the fridge. I can heat it up in a jiff."

"That sounds good." Before Tess can leave, I give her a hug. "Thanks."

I lean back in bed after she's gone. Maybe this is where I belong, with Jake and Tess as my surrogate parents. I could do as Dr. Palmer suggested and go back to school. Get a college degree, maybe a nice job. Then my own place, until I can find someone else, someone who isn't involved with my daughter.

With a sigh I shake my head. Maybe later. For now I need to rest and then figure out how to finish my business with Artie Luther.

***

Jake brings in the TV from his bedroom for me to watch while I recuperate. As I watch a rerun of *Friends* that's new to me and eat a bowl of chocolate ice cream, Jake shows up with my luggage. "Hey, kid," he says. "How you feeling?"

"Better." I heft the ice cream spoon. "Tess is fattening me up."

"You could use it." He drops the bags over by the closet. "I got everything from the Snowden. Paid the bill too."

"I'll pay you back—"

"Don't worry about it." He sits down at the end of the bed. He pats the blankets where my left foot sticks out. "I talked to Dr. Palmer."

"She in?"

"Yeah, she's in. She'll give us a call as soon as she hears something."

"Then we just have to hope Lex doesn't find another buyer."

"I doubt he will. Not on short notice. And he's going to have to do it quick. He knows you got away. Does he know who you are?"

"No. I just gave him my first name."

"Then he probably won't be able to find you. Might want to dye your hair again, just in case. Maybe let Tess cut it even shorter."

"It'll be fine. He won't find me out here."

"Let's hope not. Anyway, he has to figure you'll come to us about it. Or you'll try tracking him down on your own again. Either way, with Blades, Tall Man, and Bruiser gone, he's got to be running scared. He'll try to dump the goods first chance he gets."

"That sounds right. Then we move in."

"We being the police. No more Charles Bronson shit."

"I thought it was Rambo shit."

"Both."

"Fine. I'll sit this one out. Just be sure to get the formula back. Dr. Palmer needs it if I'm ever going to be me again."

"She'll get it," he says. He pats my foot again and then gets up. He unzips my bags and takes out my expensive clothes. "You have good taste. I have to give you that."

"Thanks. Maybe you should see if any of that would fit Tess."

"I don't think this is her speed," he says. He holds up a silk teddy. "Why the hell did you buy this?"

"I got a little nuts. Girl with a credit card, you know."

"Yeah, that's why I'm glad Jenny never got one." He grimaces and then tosses the teddy away. "I should let Tess put these away. She knows how to take care of stuff like this."

"I can do it later."

"You just lie there and rest. A bullet wound is nothing to sneeze at."

"Yeah, I guess you're right." Jake leaves me to the TV again. I can't imagine all of these people being friends, not even in New York. But it does make me think of my friends Maddy and Grace. I wish I could call them, but I can't. Our series has been canceled.

Chapter 43

Two days later, the bullet wound is gone, only a pink spot left behind. Tess looks beneath the bandage and frowns. "That's very strange," she says. "It shouldn't be healed for weeks."

"I told you I'm a quick healer," I say, though I know it's the FY-1978 at work again.

That morning I'm able to get out of bed and use the bathroom for the first time in three days without crutches. I can't watch TV and stuff myself with ice cream all day. Now I have to get back to work.

That's what I think until I hear Tess call from downstairs, "Stacey, breakfast is ready!"

As usual it's a balanced breakfast with eggs, toast, and oatmeal. Tess has even cut pieces of bananas to form a smiley face in the oatmeal. She pats me on the back. "Dig in, sweetheart."

I take a cautious bite of the oatmeal. I've never really liked the stuff. I always thought it looks like someone ate a bowl of cereal and then spewed it back up. Still, I know Tess's feelings will be hurt if I don't eat everything. I've hurt her enough in the last week.

I've eaten the eggs and toast and am halfway through the oatmeal when I hear someone tap on the patio door.

Through the glass, I hear Maddy's voice call my name. My first instinct is to dive beneath the table and hope she goes away. Except then I'd have to explain to her and Tess why I'm so jittery. So I smile and wave as Tess opens the door to let her in.

Maddy doesn't waste any time to give me a hug, which just about causes me to choke on my oatmeal. "Mr. Madigan said you were here," she says. "He said a mugger shot you?"

"Oh, yeah. It was just a flesh wound." I wiggle my leg for her. "See, no problem."

"That's a relief." Maddy opens her purse. She rummages around for a minute before she takes out an envelope. "I got you a card."

"Do they make 'Sorry You Got Shot' cards?" I ask.

Maddy stares a moment, still not used to my sense of humor. Then she laughs uproariously. "No, silly. It's just a 'Get Well' card."

I open it and see Snoopy with an ice pack on his head and a thermometer in his mouth. Does Maddy think I'm seven years old? I look inside and chuckle anyway. "Thanks," I say. "This is really sweet."

There's an awkward pause and then Maddy touches my hair. "This looks really cute. Maybe I'll let mine grow out like that. Then people will think we're twins."

I force myself to laugh, but she's right. Now that our hair is the same color, there is a much stronger resemblance between us. Too bad I can't tell her the reason for that.

Tess pats Maddy on the shoulder. "I still have some oatmeal left if you'd like some."

"Oh, no, that's fine," Maddy says. She was never a big oatmeal fan either. "I already ate."

"Well at least let me get you a cup of coffee. You look bushed." Tess is right; there are dark circles around Maddy's eyes. I thought it was makeup, but her eyes are puffy too. Maybe she had grieved for her father all night.

"That would be nice," Maddy says. While Tess goes into the kitchen for that, Maddy explains why she looks so tired. "Grace kicked me out."

"What?"

"Well, she actually said she thought it'd be best if I stayed with Mom a little longer. She's almost done with her dissertation and she doesn't need me distracting her."

"She said that?"

"Yeah." Maddy's eyes start to water. "I mean, she actually went on with all this psychological mumbo jumbo. Something about staying with Mom will help me focus on my grief and get closure or whatever. It's just her way of saying she doesn't want me around crying on her shoulder while she's working."

I take Maddy's hand and give it a squeeze. At the same time I feel a cold lump in my stomach that isn't Tess's balanced breakfast. This is my fault. Grace broke up with Maddy because of me. I've come between them. "I'm so sorry," I say.

"It's not your fault."

I want to tell her it is my fault. I betrayed her when I fucked Grace. I don't say that. If I do, Maddy will hate me—again. I lost her once already; I don't want to lose her again. There has to be something I can do to make things right. "Hey, I have an idea. How about I go talk to her?"

"You don't have to do that. I mean, you got shot—"

"I'm fine now. Like I said, it was just a flesh wound. No big deal."

Maddy smiles. "You sound like my dad."

"I do?"

"Yeah. When I fell off my bike and scraped my knee, he looked at it and said, 'Stop crying. It's just a flesh wound.'"

I remember that now. Maddy was six years old. It was her first time without the training wheels. We were on the street in front of our house. I gave her a push to get her started. Then I let go so she could pedal on her own. She made it about twenty feet before the bike toppled over. She had on a helmet, but not any knee pads—something Debbie would complain about later—so the leg of her overalls tore open and blood oozed out.

The second Maddy saw the blood she began to wail. I scooped her up in my arms. I ran her inside the house as fast as I could. In the bathroom, I moistened a washcloth and used it to wipe at the wound. It wasn't too deep, but that doesn't matter when you're six years old. "Don't cry, sweetheart," I said. "It's just a flesh wound."

"But it hurts!" she wailed.

I kissed the scrape and tasted blood. "How's that?"

Maddy sniffled. Then she shouted, "I want Mommy!" That pretty much sums up Maddy and I in a nutshell.

"I'm guessing he wasn't Father of the Year," I say.

Maddy smiles and then shrugs. "I guess not. But when I think about it now, he wasn't so bad. He was trying to make me feel better in his way. Dad was from that old school, like John Wayne and Humphrey Bogart and all that. He wasn't real good at talking about feelings."

"That sucks," I say, unable to think of anything else to say. Even as a woman it's still tough for me to talk about feelings.

"Yeah, sometimes it did. But when I thought about it the last couple of days, I realized he was doing what he thought was right. He thought his job was to be strong for Mom and me. That's why he worked so hard, so he could protect us." Maddy wipes at her eyes. "I wish I'd gotten a chance to tell him he didn't need to do that. All Mom and I wanted was for him to be around, you know?"

I take her hand and give it a squeeze. "Yeah, I know."

Tess returns with the coffee. I wonder if it really took her this long or if she stood in the doorway for a while to give us some alone time. "Here you go, dear," she says. She pats Maddy on the shoulder. Then she gives me a glare of disapproval. "Your breakfast is going to get cold, young lady."

"Sorry," I say and dig in.

Tess bustles off again. After Tess is gone, Maddy giggles and says, "She really smothers you, doesn't she?"

"I guess." I smile a little. "It's nice."

"I know what you mean." I eat my oatmeal and Maddy sips at her coffee for a minute. Then she asks, "Do you think I could stay here tonight? Mom and I have worked out a lot of things, but after too long we start to get on each other's nerves, you know?"

As much as I'd like to spend the night with Maddy, there's a chance tonight will be the night Lex tries to move the FY-1978 formula. If it is, then I need to be at the meeting. Still, when I see the hopeful look on her face, I know I can't say no. She's already been dumped by Grace; if I turn her away too, it might destroy her. "Sure," I say. "As long as Aunt Tess agrees."

"You leave that to me," Maddy says with a sly grin.

Chapter 44

I leave Maddy at the Kozee Koffee later so she can get her paycheck and talk with her manager about her schedule. This gives me the chance to go over to Grace's shop. I just hope Grace is there and not at the library or somewhere else.

The front door to the shop is open. I don't see her inside. "Grace? It's Stacey. Are you here?"

She appears from the back room, a load of mismatched clothes still in her arms. Her face brightens with a smile. She dumps the clothes on the floor. "Oh my God, there you are! I thought you got shot?"

"I'm feeling a lot better," I say.

She tries to hug me, but I put out a hand to stop her. "What's wrong? If it's about what you said before, don't worry about it. You were probably just hopped up on painkillers."

"That's not it," I say. "How could you kick Maddy out?"

"I didn't kick her out. We're just taking a little break. So we can get our heads right."

"Don't bullshit me. You're breaking up with her. Because of me."

"Not just because of you." Grace sighs and then

continues, "I'm only twenty-seven—"

"Twenty-nine."

"Fine, twenty-nine. The point is I'm not an old woman yet. I don't want to get married. Maybe Maddy and I aren't trying on wedding dresses yet, but we're like an old married couple. There's no secrets between us anymore."

"Until I came along."

"Well, yeah, until you came along." Grace tries to put an arm around me, but I push it away. "It's not your fault, Stace. It was going to happen eventually. You just gave us a push."

"No, that's not true. Maddy loves you."

"She does, but it's like I said, Maddy is still a little kid. Like any kid, she wants something safe and secure."

"And you're too sophisticated for that?"

"It's not like that." Grace sighs. "When Maddy and I met, I was a scared little kid too. Mom had just died and I wasn't sure what I was going to do and along came Maddy. She was so *effervescent*, you know?"

"No, I don't know."

"She was so full of life. She was young and sweet and inexperienced."

"She still is," I snap.

"Well, the first two," Grace says and the father in me wants to punch her. "The point is, we each had something the other wanted. She wanted someone to take care of her and I needed someone to take care of."

"And now she doesn't?"

"Not as much, but I don't want to take care of her anymore."

"You'd rather take care of me."

"Is that what you want?"

"Don't start talking like a shrink now."

"I'm not." She tries to touch me again and again I bat her hand away. "Look, Stace, you're a lot like Maddy was in some ways, but in other ways you're not. I mean, Maddy would never have emptied out the register and gone off on her own."

"You're probably right about that. Maddy isn't that stupid," I say and tap my leg for emphasis.

"Maybe, but the point is, you don't need me like she does. You're a lot stronger than she is. I mean, you got shot a couple days ago and you're walking around. Maddy would still be in bed whimpering."

The father in me finally snaps. I grab Grace by the throat and shove her back against the wall, out of sight of anyone who might pass by. She tries to say something, but I choke the words from her the way Bruiser Malloy did to me in the warehouse. I growl, "Don't you ever talk about Maddy like that again or I'll snap your fucking neck. She's a good girl. She's got a good heart." The kind of heart that can forgive even a shitty father like me, I add to myself. "For whatever reason that heart loves you. So you're going to cut this bullshit and you're going to make things up to her. Got it?"

Grace nods slightly. Her face starts to turn purple around the edges. I let her go and she sags to the floor. She lies there for a couple of minutes. When she's recovered a little, she looks up at me and says, "You psycho! What's the matter with you?"

I bend down so I can look her in the eye. There's still a part of me that loves Grace, but the much larger part of me loves Maddy far more. "Maddy is staying with me at Jake and Tess Madigan's tonight. I want you to show up there about eleven-thirty. Then you're going to apologize to Maddy. You're going to say you were wrong and that you want her back. You can't live without her."

"You can't make us stay together forever."

"No, just until she wises up and realizes what a shit you are." Out of spite I kick her in the ribs. She grunts and gasps for air again. "Consider that my resignation."

I'm tempted to light the store on fire on my way out, but I can't. That would probably burn down the apartment too and then Maddy wouldn't have anywhere to go back to. Maybe it's stupid to get Maddy back together with someone who doesn't really love her, but it's all I can think to do right now.

Maddy waits for me outside the Kozee Koffee. "How did it go?" she asks.

"I think we got everything out in the open," I say. I put a hand on her shoulder. "Come on, let's do a little shopping. It'll make us feel better."

I signal for a cab and soon we're on our way out of the garment district.

***

We end up on the south side, in a department store. Maddy stops us at the perfume counter to try on a few fragrances. With each one she holds her wrist out to me so I can sniff it. "What do you think?" she asks.

"It's nice," I say with each one. They all seem about the same to me; maybe my nose hasn't acclimated to being a woman yet.

We stop at the jewelry counter next. Maddy tries on a slim gold watch. "Isn't this nice?" she asks.

"It is," I say, though it clashes with the black Ramones T-shirt, ripped blue jeans, and combat boots she wears.

Then she points out a pair of diamond studs. "I wish I could get something like that."

"To put in your nose?"

She laughs until she realizes it wasn't a joke. "No, silly. In my ears." It seems to me she has enough earrings already, but I don't say anything.

I start to see the pattern once she starts to pick out clothes. They're all plain and sensible: button-down blouses, floral print skirts, and drab slacks, the kind of stuff Tess would wear. She finds a salmon-colored suit and insists on trying it on. When she comes out of the changing room, my jaw nearly drops to the floor. For the first time I see my little girl as a grown woman, so long as I ignore the haircut and piercings.

"You like it?" she asks.

"It's really…different," I stammer.

She touches her shorn hair. "I know, it looks kind of weird with my hair and stuff. But from the neck down, don't I look like a real power broker? Like a lawyer or CEO or something?"

"Yeah, you do."

I wait for her to laugh and say that this is all a joke. Instead she turns to the mirror and adjusts the knee-length skirt. "I was thinking about going back to school. I mean, I can't work at the Krappy Koffee forever, can I?"

"No, I guess not." I start to feel the same jealousy I've felt around Dr. Palmer. Here my daughter looks so grown up and I'm still dressed like a kid. Makes me wish I'd worn one of my expensive outfits. "What are you going to major in?"

"Well, at Daddy's funeral I got thinking about how proud everyone was of him for being a cop, all his commendations and stuff."

"You want to be a cop?" I ask. A cold lump forms in my stomach as I try to imagine my daughter going up against the likes of Artie Luther.

"No!" she says in a way that makes me relieved, though a little sad she's so adamant not to follow in my footsteps. "But I was thinking I should go into something where I can help people too. I thought maybe journalism."

"You want to be a reporter?"

"I think so. Not one of those dumb anchorwomen either, a real investigative reporter." She turns to me again. "You can't see it, can you? Me as Lois Lane?"

"It's not that. I didn't know you liked that sort of thing."

"I know, you think I'm just some scatterbrained barista who writes bad poetry."

"No—"

"It's all right. That's what I have been since I dropped out of school. But in high school I used to write for the paper. I did a whole exposé on teachers fixing grades for the football team. Didn't make me very popular around school, but I felt really good about it. Like I was doing something. You know, making the world a better place." She looks down sadly at her boots. "I don't know what happened. I guess I stopped caring."

I put a hand on her shoulder. "I think you'll be a great reporter. I'll buy out every newsstand in the city when you get on the front page."

"Thanks, but then no one else would be able to read it." We laugh at this. Then Maddy turns back to the mirror. "I guess I'd better go take it off before some salesgirl starts hassling me. Do you think they have a layaway?"

"I don't think so." I wish I could buy it for her, but my spending spree at Amos's shop has used up most of the money I took from Blades. "It'll probably be on sale in a couple months. Black Friday, you know?"

"Yeah. Maybe I should try to hide it until then." Maddy doesn't go that far, but as we leave, I see her look back at the suit.

We walk through the rest of the store without trying anything on. As we pass an aisle full of pink Barbie doll boxes, Maddy asks, "What do you want to do? You can't work at Grace's forever, can you?"

"Actually I quit."

"You did? Why?"

"It wasn't really for me."

"Yeah, that makes sense. I don't see you as a salesgirl."

"You don't?"

"No. I think you're like me. The do-gooder type."

"I'm not sure about that."

"Well come on, when I said Grace kicked me out, you volunteered right away to help."

"Sure, but you're my…friend," I say. I almost make things awkward and say she's my daughter.

"You're a good person. Don't try to deny it."

"You think I should be a reporter?"

"What do you think?"

The only thing I've ever written are police reports and Captain Archer constantly harassed me for my poor spelling and grammar. "I'm not sure that's for me either."

Maddy motions to a couple of little girls squeezing the stuffed animals. "How about a social worker? You could help kids who had it rough like you did."

As a cop I met a few social workers. Most of them seemed to have given up long ago. I suppose Maddy's kind of idealism is only for the young. To let her down easy I say, "I'll have to think about it."

"Sure, nobody's saying you have to do anything today. Maybe you just need to work as a barista for a couple of years first."

"Maybe I should dye my hair pink too, right?"

"I think blue is more your color."

I smile as I remember Grace said the same thing. Then I remember what happened after that. But Maddy doesn't kiss me. She just gives me a friendly pat on the back and then we continue to explore the store.

***

We have lunch at a deli about three blocks from Amos's shop. While Maddy nibbles on a pastrami sandwich, I get up to use the bathroom. "I've got to powder my nose," I say and give her a wink. I hate to lie to her, but there's no way I can tell her I need to go to a pawnshop to buy a gun. After all her idealistic talk about helping people, I know she'd never accept her friend is a brutal vigilante.

I hurry as fast as I can, given the number of people on the sidewalks. It still takes about ten minutes to reach the pawnshop. I stop at the door and catch my reflection in the glass. I wonder if Amos will recognize me like this?

He doesn't recognize me, not at first. "Can I help you, sweetheart?" he asks.

"I want to buy a gun," I say.

He stares at me in my T-shirt and jeans; I look about fifteen years old. "We can't sell guns to minors, honey. Come back when you're eighteen."

"I am eighteen, dipshit," I say. "And that Uzi you sold me was a piece of shit. Fucking thing jammed on the first clip."

He blinks as he matches my appearance with that of the spoiled rich kid who came in for assault weapons.

"That was you?"

"Yeah, it was me. Now I need something else. Preferably something that won't jam."

"Oh, well, let's see what we can do."

He shows me his wares again. It's largely the same as last time. I pick up the 9mm Beretta. It probably won't jam on me. "This one," I say. "And give me three extra clips."

"All right. If that's what you want. I have some other—"

"No thanks. Do you have a silencer for this?"

"I think so."

"I'll take that too."

I wander around the store while Amos tries to find the silencer I want. My phone rings as I examine some knives. I drop the phone when I hear Maddy's voice. How did she get my number? Maybe Tess gave it to her.

I scoop up the phone and hear Maddy say my name. "I'm here," I stammer.

"Where the hell are you? And don't say the bathroom because that's where I am. Why are you ditching me?"

"I'm not ditching you."

"Then what would you call it?"

Shit, I say to myself. I'm such an idiot. Maddy and I had just connected and I threw it away so I could buy a gun for my stupid vendetta. No, it's not just a vendetta. It's important. I need the FY-1978 formula so Dr. Palmer can find a way to cure me, so I can be Maddy's father again instead of her friend.

"If you don't want to hang out with me that's fine, but just say so. Don't pretend like you're my friend and then ditch me," Maddy says. Her voice becomes almost as menacing as mine when I threatened Grace.

"I'm sorry, Maddy. I—I wanted to surprise you. Tonight."

"What?"

"I wanted to buy you something special. For being such a good friend."

"Are you lying?"

"No, I'm serious. I couldn't do it with you standing right there, could I?"

"No, I guess not."

"Right, so just stay there and I'll be back in a half hour or so. All right?"

"OK." Before she hangs up, she says, "And thanks."

I feel even shittier that I lied to her and got away with it. I'm not much better at being her friend than I ever was as her father. Maddy deserves better. She deserves someone who will be true to her, to not lie and betray her.

I walk past the jewelry case. Something sparkles at me. I turn and see a pair of diamond studs like those Maddy saw in the department store. I'm still looking at them when Amos returns. "I found it," he says. "Anything else I can help you with?"

"Yeah, these earrings," I say.

"Those are nice. They're—"

"How about we call them compensation for that busted Uzi, eh?" He still has my gun, but I have a foot-long hunting knife in my hand and won't hesitate to use it on someone as scummy as him.

"Sure," he says. "Then we'll be square, right?"

"Right." As he takes the earrings out, I add, "Can you gift wrap those? They're for my daughter."

Chapter 45

Jake gets home just as Maddy and I are setting the table for dinner. I see him frown for a moment when he sees Maddy. She waves to him and says, "Hi, Mr. Madigan! I hope you don't mind me staying over tonight."

"No, of course not," he says. I can see from the vein on his forehead that he does mind. "Would you mind if I talk to Stacey in the study for a minute?"

"No problem." Before I can leave, she elbows me gently in the ribs. "Looks like you're in trouble."

"It's your fault," I say and we giggle like a couple of schoolgirls.

I follow Jake into the study, where he sits down with a weary sigh. "What's Maddy doing here?" he asks without preamble.

"Her and Grace are having a rough time. She asked if she could stay here tonight. How could I say no?"

"No. See how easy that is?"

"Don't be a smart-ass."

"You know how creepy it is to see you two together? And the way you were laughing together—"

"Like a couple of schoolgirls?"

"Yeah."

"Well, we are a couple of girls if you haven't noticed."

"Now who's being a smart-ass?"

"Look, it freaks me out a little too, but I've never been this close to Maddy before. Did you know she wants to be a reporter?"

"She does? Since when?"

"I don't know. She told me today when we were shopping. She thinks I should be a social worker. Work with abused kids or something."

"Yeah, that sounds up your alley. They can tell you their problems and then you'll go rough up their parents, right?"

"I'm not a thug."

"That's not what Amos says. He called me up and said some girl was hassling him. Pretty little thing in a blue T-shirt and jeans. I wonder who that could be?"

"Amos said I'm pretty?"

"Not in so many words. He called you a nice little cunt."

"That sounds more like him."

"What the hell are you up to now, Steve? I thought we decided no more of this Dirty Harry bullshit?"

"You said Charles Bronson bullshit."

"It's the same fucking thing!" He pounds the desk so I'll know he's serious. The way he winces, he's done more harm to himself than me or the desk. "Whatever happens, you're staying out of it."

"I just want to be prepared," I say. "If Lex figures out who I am, he might come after me—and anyone around me."

"Let me worry about my wife."

"And I'll worry about my daughter."

"Do you know how silly it looks when you say that? She's older than you now for Christ's sake."

"I know that. But it doesn't change anything."

He throws up his hands. "Fine. Go have your slumber party or whatever. Maybe it'll keep you out of my hair."

At that moment the phone on his desk rings. He picks it up. "Yeah? You're sure?" Jake reaches out for a pad of paper. He scribbles down a few notes. It's hard to read them upside-down, but I figure out he's written down "Nath's Lab" and "midnight." That can only mean Lex is ready to deal with Lennox Pharmaceuticals. "OK, Doctor. I'll be there. What? No, *she* is going to stay put, no matter if I have to handcuff her to the bed. Right. Stay safe, Doctor."

"Nath's lab, eh? Lex is a sucker for irony, I guess."

"Symmetry is more like it," Jake says. He pushes the notepad back towards him. "I suppose you already figured it all out. They want the deal to go down in her old lab at midnight. Dr. Palmer will be there to verify a copy of the formula. If they try to screw Lex over, he'll sell the original to the competition."

"Sounds like he's learning."

"That was my thought."

"Are you really going to handcuff me to the bed?"

"Will I need to?"

I think for a moment. I should put up a fight about it, but Jake will carry through with his threat. "No. I'll stay here with the women folk."

"Good. This is going to be tricky enough without some little hothead interfering."

Someone taps on the door. "Jacob, Stacey, dinner is ready," Tess says.

"Well, I could eat," I say.

***

The only movies I ever watched with Maddy were Disney ones like *The Little Mermaid* and *Beauty and the Beast*. I remember when she fell asleep in my arms on the couch. Then I would carry her back to bed and tuck her in. "G'night, Daddy," she would whisper.

It's a little different this time. For one thing we both wear nightgowns and lie on the floor of Jake's living room. For another, instead of a Disney movie we watch something called *Twilight*. I've never heard of it before, but Maddy says it's her favorite movie. When did it replace *Beauty and the Beast* in her heart?

Maddy crunches down a handful of popcorn and then sighs. "Do you think I could be as gorgeous as Kristen Stewart?"

"Who?"

She gestures to a pale brunette on the screen. "I mean, if I let my hair grow out and stuff. Don't you think I'd be as cute as her?"

I squirm a little at this question. I remember what Jake said about how creepy my relationship with Maddy is. Right now I have to agree with him. "I suppose so. You might have to stay out of the sun for a couple of months."

She slaps me on the arm and says, "Me-ow. I didn't know you were such a little bitch."

"Well—"

"I'm joking." She throws a handful of popcorn at me. "Come on, loosen up."

"I'm sorry. This is kind of new to me."

"Yeah, it's been a while since I did something like this. You know, just hang out with a friend, watching a movie and stuff."

"How long?"

Maddy thinks about it for at least a minute. "About five years."

"That long?"

"Yeah, that long. Believe it or not, I wasn't that popular in high school. I never really had many friends. Not any I'd want to hang out with like this."

"Oh. That's too bad," I say, though inside I feel a surge of pride that Maddy considers me a good enough friend to hang out with. That or she's just desperate to be away from her mother.

"Jenny was always my best friend. When we were real little we'd sleep over at each other's houses all the time. Then Mom and I moved into the city and I couldn't see Jenny as much. And then, Jenny, you know—"

"I know," I say. I think back again to Jenny's last days in the hospital. I never saw Maddy at the hospital, which was probably Debbie's doing. "Tess said she was really nice."

"Yeah. She was like my little sister." Maddy sighs and then gestures to the screen. "Wouldn't it be great if you could live forever?"

"But then you'd have to drink blood and stuff."

"So? I've drunk blood." She stares at me for a moment before she laughs. "OK, it was Clamato juice at this Halloween party. We were all decked out in black and with the little plastic fangs. You should have seen what Grace was wearing. She had on these fishnet stockings—"

Maddy stops and sighs. It seems we can't shake the dark clouds hanging over us. I look at the clock and see it's eleven o'clock. A half-hour until I told Grace to be here. And an hour until Artie Luther will meet with Dr. Palmer.

I pat Maddy's arm and say, "Grace will come to her

senses. She just needs some time."

"Maybe I don't want her to."

"What do you mean by that?"

"If she's going to be so flaky, then maybe I don't want her around. I got enough bullshit in my life, you know?"

"Yeah, maybe, but when you guys are together it's like—" I struggle to find words for how to phrase it. "You two just seem so *right* for each other."

"Well obviously we're not that right. Not if she kicks me out when I need her the most. I mean, my dad *dies* and all she can think about is herself and her stupid thesis."

When Maddy puts it like that, I wonder if I should have told Grace to come over here. "That's true, but maybe it was because your father died. Maybe it reminded her of her mother dying."

"If that's true then she should know how much it hurts. She should know I need her support." Maddy shakes her head sadly. "I thought she loved me."

"I'm sure she does. It's not always easy for people to express their feelings. Look at my parents. The only way they knew how to express their feelings was to get drunk and beat each other up—or beat me up. Maybe Grace just doesn't know how to express what she's feeling."

Maddy stares at me for a moment. "Wow," she says. "That's really deep. I think I was wrong. You shouldn't be a social worker; you should be a shrink."

"I'm not sure that's for me. I've got a lot of my own baggage, you know?"

"So does Grace."

"Yeah, I guess."

We don't say anything for a little while; we silently munch on popcorn as we watch the movie. It doesn't seem like I've really helped Maddy get out of her funk. If anything she's spread her funk to me. The movie is turned down low enough so I can hear something rattle against the window.

"What was that?"

"I'll go check it out," I say. I pretend like I'm looking out the window, but I already know what's going on. I see Grace by the bushes. I motion her towards the front door.

"What's going on?" Maddy asks.

"I think it's a cat," I say. It's a stupid excuse, but the best I can think of. I go over to the door and open it as quietly as possible so I don't alert Tess.

Before Grace can say anything, I put a finger to my lips. Then I reach into a pocket of my nightgown for a little red box—the earrings I got from Amos. "These are for Maddy," I say. "You're so thoughtful, aren't you?"

Grace gives me a dirty look to indicate she's doing this under duress. I take her arm and lead her to the living room. We just about run into Maddy, who's saying, "Stacey, what's—?" She and Grace stare at each other. "Grace? What are you doing here?"

Grace looks down at her feet. "Stacey came to see me. She convinced me what a selfish bitch I was being. I'm sorry." I nudge Grace in the ribs, not hard enough for Maddy to notice. "This is for you. Stace said you'd like it."

Maddy looks from Grace to me as she takes the gift. She rips the red paper off the box to reveal a gray velvet box underneath. She opens this and her eyes go wide. "Are these diamonds?"

"Yep," Grace says.

"They're beautiful." She gives Grace a long, passionate kiss. Though at first Grace is unresponsive, she eventually gives in. When they finish, Maddy leans over to kiss me on one cheek. "Thanks, Stace."

"That's what friends are for."

Maddy takes Grace by the hand to lead her into the living room. They face each other on the couch and hold hands. I listen at the doorway for a moment as they reaffirm their love. Despite what she said earlier, I think Grace means it. She just needed a good kick in the teeth to realize how much she loves Maddy. And despite what Maddy said earlier, I think she just needed Grace to do something unselfish, even under duress.

I slip upstairs to give them some privacy. There's no more time to play Cupid; I've got work to do.

Chapter 46

Tess is the kind of organized woman who keeps a spare set of car keys on a pegboard in the kitchen. I snatch the keys off the board and then sneak into the garage. Tess is asleep upstairs; I poked my head in to make sure. Maddy and Grace are making out on the couch, all difficulties resolved at least for the moment.

I get behind the wheel of the station wagon and then set the shoebox Amos gave me on the passenger's side. The pistol is inside, along with the spare clips and silencer. I figure I'll keep them in the box until I get to Lennox Pharmaceuticals just to make it more comfortable when I drive.

The clock on the dash says I have fifteen minutes to get to Lennox Pharmaceuticals. I'll have to drive like a NASCAR driver to make it. But the station wagon is up to the challenge with its big V8 engine. I roar out of the driveway and floor the accelerator as soon as I put it into drive.

I don't bother to stop or even slow down for stoplights or stop signs. I'm lucky that in Jake's neighborhood not many people walk their dogs at midnight. There's not much traffic either, so it's easy to swerve around anyone who gets in my way.

Once I'm into the city, the traffic gets heavier. I see a line of cars up ahead. I flash my high beams and hold down on my horn. One stalwart car refuses to get out of my way. I swerve onto the sidewalk and give him the finger as I race by.

Someone else fancies himself a hero and tries to weave back and forth to keep me from getting by. Lucky for me this brave soul drives a Hyundai Sonata. I tap his rear bumper with the front bumper of the station wagon. Just like in NASCAR, he careens off the road, into a shoe store that's closed for the night. I take a moment to look in the rearview mirror. There's no sign of a fire; he'll probably be fine.

I'm lucky no cops see me. Maybe Jake cleared them away from the area so Lex wouldn't be scared off. It's two minutes until midnight when I yank the wheel hard to the left, onto the maze of service drives that run around the waterfront. There's no traffic to speak of; I just have to be careful not to run into the forklifts and shipping containers left lying around for the night.

I see the Lennox building ahead. I'm sure Lex and his crew are already there. Jake's probably there too. And Dr. Palmer and her associates. I'm the late one to the party. I turn off the headlights as I approach so they won't see me. No one fires at me as I skid to a stop beside the fence for the building.

I turn off the engine and then roll down the window to listen. Silence. I guess no one's seen me. That might make things easier. I open the shoebox. I haven't ever used a silencer, but from the movies I know you're supposed to screw it on. This is easier said than done. It takes a bit more torque than I expect to get the silencer on tight. I check the ammo load and hope Amos didn't screw me on this deal.

Then I stuff the spare clips into the waistband of my black pants. I open the door just enough to slide out. I shut it as gently as possible; I don't want to let anyone know I'm here. Here we go.

***

I follow the fence the way I did last time. I'm svelte enough now that I could try to squeeze beneath it. I think about it for a minute before I decide I'm not *that* svelte. Instead, I go to the end of the fence.

I'm glad I didn't wear one of my expensive pairs of shoes, just an old pair of work boots, as I sink into the water. Since I've lost about nine inches in height, the water comes up higher on me, up to my breasts. That makes it harder to wade through. The smell brings tears to my eyes and I start to wonder if I can really do this. I run through what I've already done to Lex's henchmen—and Grace earlier—and decide I'm tough enough to handle a little muddy water.

With the water higher on me and my arms not as strong, it's a bit more difficult to lever myself onto the pier. I grunt as I free one leg from the water. I swing it up onto the pier and then with another groan bring my other leg out to join it. I take a few precious seconds to gather myself.

I'm still on the pier when a flashlight blinds me. I scramble to find the pistol, but I'm too late. Someone grabs me by my ponytail and yanks my head back. I squeal with pain. Something cold and metal presses against my cheek. A gun, no doubt.

"I figured you'd be here," Jake says. He pushes me back onto the pier. "What the hell do you think you're doing?"

"Making sure Lex gets what's coming to him," I say.

He blinds me again with the flashlight. "Yeah, well, I'm no babysitter."

I fumble around until I find the pistol. Though most of my vision is just green blotches, I hold the pistol up to where I think Jake is. "Not many little kids have one of these."

"Right," Jake says. He takes my arm. "Come on, let's go."

"I'm not leaving."

"I didn't say that, did I? You just stay behind me. If something happens to you, Tess is going to cut off my balls."

"She doesn't seem like the type for that."

"You'd be surprised."

I shiver at the image this brings up. "Let's get moving," I say.

***

I follow Jake along the edge of the water. Lex doesn't have any guards posted here, nor does Lennox. We stay low to the ground anyway, to minimize our profiles. I hear Jake grumble under his breath about his back, not to mention the annoyance of having some punk kid with him.

"You can stay out here if you want," I whisper. "I can handle him."

"I've seen how you handle things," he says. "We're going to do this the smart way for once."

He stops at the edge of the building. Like the warehouse farther along the waterfront, there's a ladder that runs up the side of the building. A fire escape maybe. Jake ignores the old adage of ladies first and starts up. He continues to grumble as he climbs.

"How'd you know this was here?" I ask.

"I've been here for three hours," he says. "I had plenty of time to scope the place out."

This I know is another jab at my tendency to rush into things. If I had called Jake the night of the robbery maybe we would have put an end to Luther then and I wouldn't be wearing a bra and panties right now. Then again, we might both be dead. Who can say for sure?

The ladder ends at a metal door. As I suspected, there's a sign to indicate it's a fire exit. Thank God for OSHA. From my position beneath the door, I watch Jake take out his knife to slice through some wiring. "You scope that out too?" I ask.

"No. Just common sense that a fire door has a fire alarm."

My cheeks turn warm at this. I really have gotten soft. I hope we end this tonight, before I don't have any cop instincts left.

Jake opens the door. No alarms go off. Jake peeks his head over the edge, just enough to see down the hallway. When he's sure it's safe, he climbs inside. He holds the door open for me like a proper gentleman.

"Where are we?" I ask.

"Third floor, I think," he says.

"You don't know? I thought you scoped it out?"

"Smart-ass," he grumbles. He takes his pistol from its holster and then flattens himself against the wall. I do the same and then edge down the corridor in time with him. At the corner, he stops and then winds his pistol around, followed by his head. Again, once he's determined it's safe, he motions for me to follow.

When we walk past Dr. Nath's office, I realize Jake is right; we're on the third floor. Dr. Nath's lab is two floors up. We start up the stairs. There's no one on the fourth floor stairs. But halfway up to the fifth floor, Jake motions for me to stop. We hear a rough Eastern European voice grumble above us, no doubt someone on Luther's payroll.

We head back down to the fourth floor. "What's the play?" I ask.

Jake thinks about it for a minute and rubs his chin. "I got an idea, so long as you're not opposed to humiliating yourself a little."

"If it means getting Lex I'll get on all fours and squeal like a pig."

"You might have to before we're done." Then he tells me the plan.

***

I creep up the stairs to listen for any noises. About halfway up, I hear a rough Eastern European voice again. A hiss of static accompanies it. Probably telling Lex no one is here.

Jake might pat himself on the back for his cunning, but his plan is really the one I used on the Tall Man. Before I reach the landing, I work up some tears.

I come around the corner, onto the landing. There's a guard almost as big as Bruiser Malloy up there. He's got a flak vest on, but his bald head is uncovered. When he sees me, he says in English, "Who you?"

"Have you seen my mommy?" I whine. "She was working late and I fell asleep and now she's gone." The story doesn't make sense, but he probably understands only every other word. The point is that I focus his attention on me.

The silencer is as good as advertised. I hear a faint hiss of air and then a slug appears in the guard's head. He pitches forward; I run up the stairs to grab him before he can tumble down, which would make a hell of a lot of noise. He's too heavy for me to stop, but I manage to cushion his fall a little.

I don't wait for Jake to get up here; I open the door a crack and then peek out. There's no one in this part of the corridor. They're probably closer to the meeting place. I feel Jake tap me on the shoulder. He presses my pistol into my hand. "Nice weapon," he says.

"Yeah, Amos was due."

I open the door wider, so Jake can slip out. He motions for me to follow. We do the same shuffle along the corridor, down to the turn. I can hear voices nearby. More Eastern European ones of Lex's hired muscle. They're coming from the right.

I don't wait for Jake here either. I throw myself against the opposite side of the corridor and then spin around. There are two more guards down the corridor; they jabber to each other in Russian or Albanian or whatever it is. Even with the silencer the Beretta packs a wallop. It bucks in my hand and threatens to slip out. I steady my grip as they take their machine guns off their shoulders. It's a Wild West showdown.

I win the draw. I put one bullet in the throat of a guard. My second shot hits the other guard in the left eye. He has just enough time to scream before I put another bullet in his head. Pretty good shooting for me, but not good enough for Jake.

"You idiot," he hisses. "They probably heard that."

"Maybe—" I start to say until I hear footsteps rushing down the hallway. I barely have time to get the pistol back up before the three guards come around the corner. These ones aren't nearly so casual. They have their weapons on their hips, ready for business.

I fire without aiming. By some miracle the shot hits one guard in his gun arm. The weapon falls to the floor and fires a shot into the ceiling. Since any attempt at subtlety is screwed now, Jake opens up with his .45. He bullseyes one guard in the head. The other we hit at the same time: me in the right thigh and Jake in the throat.

The one I winged in the arm reaches with his good hand for a pistol. Jake calmly puts a bullet in the man's face. This battle is over. We wait a moment and listen. There aren't any more footsteps. Did Lex only bring a half-dozen?

We hurry around the corner; Jake goes in double-time now that our cover is blown. I recognize this corridor from the last time. Dr. Nath's lab is just ahead. There's no one to welcome us. I don't hear any voices either. Did Lex already bug out? Did we miss him?

No. Jake scurries across the doorway; a shot accompanies him. The bullet hits the wall. I take the closer side of the door. I peer around the corner—

Lex faces the doorway. Just like before he has his gun pressed against a woman's temple.

This time it's Dr. Palmer. "Throw your guns down or I kill the girl," he says. Dr. Palmer gives him the same look to indicate she doesn't like to be called a girl.

I hear a man's voice from inside the room say, "You kill her and the deal's off."

"Is that so?" Lex says but doesn't turn. "I doubt that. I'm the only one with the formula. You can always get another scientist."

"Give it up, Luther," Jake says. "The only ways out of here are in handcuffs or a body bag. It's your choice."

"Then it appears we have a standoff," Lex says. Then he does something odd: he bobs his head. It's just a slight movement, more like a twitch—

There's the boom of a pistol. This time when I'm shot, it's not like a bee sting; it's like someone ran a railroad spike through my left thigh. I drop to the floor, but manage to keep hold of my pistol.

Jake stands over me, his gun pointed at my head. "Sorry, kid. It's past your bedtime."

Chapter 47

I look up at Jake with disbelief. I study his face, to see if there's some kind of ruse at work here. There's a secret language partners develop over twenty-five years. Just a twitch of the cheek or the blink of an eye can communicate volumes.

There's nothing written on Jake's face. He just looks hopelessly sad and suddenly a lot older. "Why?" I say.

"I didn't have a choice. Jenny's treatments cost hundreds of thousands of dollars. We were going to lose everything."

"So you took a bribe."

"Yeah, I did."

"And what did you do to earn it?"

"What anyone in his employ does. I made sure we busted the guys he wanted busted. I tipped him off on any raids."

"And you played me for a sap."

"I'm sorry, Steve. I knew you wouldn't go along with it. You'd already lost everything after Debbie divorced you. You didn't have any reason to go bad."

"But you did."

"Don't act so high and mighty. If it had been Maddy, you would have done the same thing as me."

"I would never have taken money from a shithead like Artie Luther."

Jake gives me a nasty smile. "You think your hands are clean? You butchered Bobby Blades like a fucking hog. Then you stole his money and credit cards to treat yourself to a little vacation."

"You think that's the same thing? Blades was dirtier than a convention of hobos."

"I did what I had to do to save my daughter!" I wait for him to pull the trigger, but he doesn't. With his free hand he rips the Beretta out of my hand. He stuffs it into his pants. Then he motions to me with his gun. "Go on and get up, cupcake."

I do as he says. I don't have any choice now. Maybe I could have tried to shoot him, but Jake is my partner. *Was* my partner. Now he's just another of Lex's thugs. Unbidden, tears come to my eyes. "You knew about the robbery," I say. "You knew and you didn't say anything. You let him do this to me!"

"I'm sorry, Steve. I thought you would be too shit-faced at Squiggy's to interfere. I didn't know that fucking Worm would show up there."

"Now you're going to let him keep me like this."

"Stop being so fucking dramatic." He shoves me into the lab. I stumble and land at Dr. Palmer's feet. Now that he's safe, Lex has let her go. She takes me into her arms to press me close to her and stroke my hair. Jake motions to me with the gun. "Stop bawling, kid. Lennox is still going to get the formula. Palmer can still use it to try to find a way to make you normal again. The only difference is that Lex goes free. You can either accept that or end up in the harbor again."

"You son of a bitch!" I shout at him. There's nothing I

can do though but sob in Dr. Palmer's arms like a child. Through my tears I watch as an older white man—the one I heard earlier—hands Lex a briefcase. Lex opens it to verify his payment. Then he takes out the silver case from his jacket.

"Here you are, Dr. Lennox, as promised."

"And you don't have any more copies of the formula?"

"Of course I do. Should you try to cross me, I'll send them to all of your competitors." Lex motions to Jake. "Not that it matters. As you can see, I already own the police."

He snaps the briefcase shut and then tosses Lennox a mock salute. "Now, to attend to one final loose end." Lex yanks me out of Dr. Palmer's arms. She looks ready to leap after him, but Jake aims his pistol at her head. Lex drags me through the doorway by the arm. I could try to resist, but there's no point, not with Jake behind him, his pistol at the ready.

As we start down the stairs, Lex looks down at me. He smiles and asks, "Tell me, darling, can you swim?"

***

Soon I'll go full circle. I lie on the rotten dock with Lex and his new pal Jake over me. Lex grins evilly again. "She's your partner. I'll let you dispose of her," he says to Jake.

"You said you weren't going to kill her."

Lex reaches down to pinch my cheek and then pat it. "We can't leave our sweet little detective alive. She'd find a way to finish what she started eventually. Wouldn't you, sweetheart?"

"Go fuck yourself."

He hits me across the face with the butt of his pistol. I

keep the tears at bay; they'll only amuse a scumbag like Lex. I won't give him the satisfaction of crying, not anymore. "Such language for a young girl."

"I'm eighteen, asshole."

"Not for much longer." Lex stands back; he motions to Jake. "Dispose of her."

Jake stares at me for a moment. There's nothing in that look but sadness. Then he puts his pistol away. He picks up a cinder block that lies near the base of the dock. He wraps a length of rope around the block. It'll be more than enough to anchor me to the bottom of the harbor.

"You son of a bitch!" I shout again. I spit in Jake's face. He raises one hand as if to slap me, but he doesn't.

"Sorry, kid," he says instead. When he turns his back to Lex, I finally get the look I've hoped for. It's nothing much, just a glance down. But after so many years as partners, I know what he means.

He wraps the rope around my right leg and starts to tie it. It might not be the sturdiest bond, but it only needs to last a few minutes, until I've drowned. "It didn't have to be this way," he says. "You should have just stuck to your dollies."

"You saw what he did to me! I couldn't let him get away with it."

"But I got away anyway," Lex says, never one to miss a chance to gloat. "Any last requests?"

"I already made it: go fuck yourself."

"Very well then. Off you go." He gives me the same mock salute as Dr. Lennox. Jake scoops me up in his arms and uses one hand to secure me to his chest and the other to hold the weight that will seal my fate.

"Goodnight, sweetheart," he says and then tosses me in.

***

This time I'm awake and in my body as I sink to the bottom of the harbor. I do what I can to take a breath before I hit the water. I won't have a lot of time to get out of this.

That look Jake gave me? It meant he didn't tighten the rope to my leg. That was why he kept hold of the weight, so Lex wouldn't see how loose it is on my ankle. It's tight enough that I'm still sinking, but it should be loose enough for me to shake out of it.

I can't do that right away. Lex has to think I'm at the bottom of the harbor. He'll watch for me, at least for a couple of minutes. If I pop right up to the surface, he'll put a couple of bullets in me to make sure. He should have to start with, but he must have figured it'd be more fun to drown me. That way I struggle and gasp desperately for air to prolong my suffering. After what a pain in the ass I've been, I can't blame him.

The harbor isn't deep enough here for the descent to take very long. About a minute by my reckoning. My lungs start to burn and I can see spots in my vision. The anchor hits the bottom first. The impact isn't enough to spring me. I shake my leg frantically and ignore the pain from where Jake shot me.

I start to panic. In that panic I open my mouth to scream. Now I don't have any air left. Shit. My vision darkens. I think of Maddy. She's lost me as Steve and now she'll lose me as Stacey. At least she and Grace made up. They're such a good couple, whether Grace appreciates that or not. Maybe she's a lesbian, but my daughter will have a much happier marriage than I ever did.

I'm still shaking my leg as I think my goodbyes. As I

regret that I'll never get to see my grandchildren, the rope slips off my ankle. I start to swim; my arms and legs flail faster than they ever have before. My vision continues to dim. I'm not going to make it—

I pop up beneath the pier. I'm tempted to sucking in air with loud gasps, but I resist that urge. I take smaller gulps, just enough to keep me going. My vision is clear enough that I can see two sets of feet above me.

"That should do it," Lex says. "It's too bad. She was a pretty little thing. Deadly too. It's a rare combination in a woman."

"That's my partner you're talking about."

"Yes, it is." I hear the telltale click of a pistol being cocked. "But don't worry, you're going to join her soon enough."

"What? I did what you wanted—"

"I know, but as they say in the spy movies, you know too much."

"Who am I going to tell? You already own the police."

"It doesn't pay to take chances."

I don't have time for anything fancy. From the click of the gun I drift over to the edge of the pier. With Lex's last words, I'm in position. I reach over and grab his leg with both hands. In my old body I could have tossed him into the water, but as a girl all I can do is stagger him.

That's enough. His shot goes over Jake's head. Jake's shot goes *into* Lex's head. I watch from the water as blood trickles down Artie Luther's big, bald head. He looks at Jake in disbelief for a moment. Then he totters for a few seconds before he splashes into the water.

With his last spiteful ounce of strength, he seizes me by the hair. He's a lot heavier than any cement anchor.

Once again I'm being pulled down into the harbor. I ignore the pain in my scalp and kick at him with my right leg. His eyes glare at me and his mouth is locked in a feral snarl. If he's going to die, he's going to take me with him.

There's still enough life in him that when my foot hits him between the legs, he lets go of my hair. Again I paddle for all it's worth, away from Lex as he sinks to the bottom. Unlike his many victims he'll probably surface again later, but I don't care. All that matters is he's dead.

Jake seizes my wrist as I break through the water. He swings me onto the pier, where I flop around like a fish for a moment; I suck in air for the second time in five minutes. He slaps at my back to try in some vague way to help me.

"Stop it," I snap at him.

"Sorry."

I roll into a sitting position. I fumble with the elastic band that ties back my wet hair and then shake it out. I smooth a soggy tress away from my face. "You son of a bitch."

I hear the click of a pistol again. I look up, but Jake doesn't have it pointed at me—it's pointed at his own temple. "I'm sorry, Steve. I never wanted this."

"What are you doing?"

"I won't go to prison. They'd eat me alive."

I stare at him for a moment. Part of me wants him to pull the trigger. It's his fault I'm stuck as an eighteen-year-old girl. He helped Lex set up the Lennox robbery. He played me for years, to help his benefactor.

The other part of me—the larger part—sees my best friend. I see the friend who helped me after Debbie left me and took Maddy with her. I see the partner who saved my ass numerous times, not just from bullets or knives, but also from inquiry hearings and Internal Affairs. He stuck up for me when I needed him to, covered for me when I crossed the line.

"You won't go to prison."

"I have to, Steve. We can't cover this up."

"Why not? Lex is dead."

"Palmer and Lennox—"

"They aren't going to talk. Then they'd have to reveal how they bought their formula back from a known criminal."

"What about you?"

"I won't say anything. It'll be just like the Mackenzie case." I reach out to pat him on the knee. "You killed the most wanted man in the city. You're a hero."

"I'm a fucking traitor." He presses the gun tighter to his head. "I don't want to live with it anymore. I'm tired of the guilt."

"Don't do it, Jake. Think of Tess. She loves you."

"She hates me. It should have been me who died, not Jenny. That's what she thinks."

"No she doesn't. If she blames anyone, she blames herself. Instead of blaming yourselves, you two need to just sit down and talk it out. Get a fucking therapist."

Jake smiles slightly, which I consider progress. "What about you? How am I supposed to go on, knowing what I did to you?"

"I'll be fine," I say. "You were right back there. If it had been Maddy, I would have taken the money from Luther. I would have done anything to try to save her, just like you did."

"You're just saying that. The great Steve Fischer would never go bad."

"You said it yourself: I got plenty of blood on my hands. All those people I killed." I can't stop myself from crying now.

And that turns out to be a good thing. Jake's fatherly instincts take over. He puts down the gun and wraps me in his arms. "It's not your fault. It's my fault. All of it. Any blood on your hands is mine. You understand?"

"Don't kill yourself, Jake. I need you. Tess needs you. We've both lost enough. We can't lose anything else. Understand?"

He strokes my hair and whispers, "I understand."

After a while, he picks me up to carry me home.

Epilogue

I turn in the mirror and see the gold sparkle in my earlobe. I touch the gold stud and wince. "Is it going to keep hurting like that?" I ask.

"It'll be fine in a few hours," the middle-aged woman who put the holes in my ears says. She gives me some instructions on how to care for my newly pierced ears. Just in case I forget, she gives me a sheet of paper.

Maddy is the first to pat me on the back. "They look great," she says.

"So do yours," I say. I gesture to the diamond studs in her ears. She's gotten rid of the others. For the first time in who knows how long, her hair is back to its natural brown. Over the last three weeks it's grown out a little, so it doesn't look as patchy.

"Our little girl is growing up," Grace says. She gives me a hug to congratulate me. It's not a lover's hug, just a friend's hug. That's all we are now, friends.

We hashed out our differences a few days after Grace and Maddy's reconciliation. Grace called me up and thanked me for helping her see the error of her ways. She invited me to come back to work at the shop. Without any other job offers, I agreed on one condition: from now on we're only friends.

Sometimes, like when Grace hugs me, I still think of our night together. At times like that, I force myself to remember Maddy. She comes first in my life from now on, even before the woman I love. Our hug ends much quicker than that selfish part of me that remembers Grace's love would like.

Maybe it's not a big deal to get my ears pierced—there are babies with pierced ears these days—but it feels like one to me. It's another threshold I've crossed on my way to womanhood. A month ago that prospect would have scared the shit out of me, but with every day it seems less scary.

"Now, when are you going to get your first tattoo?" Maddy asks. "I think you should get a little butterfly on your chest. Something simple to start with."

"Not for a couple of weeks," I say. "One thing at a time."

"Aw, don't be a baby," Maddy says. "I know a great place. They do real good work." She lifts up the hem of her shirt so I can see the Chinese character on her back. "That didn't even hurt."

Grace gives Maddy that old look to signal she's crossed the line. "We can't force Stace to get one if she doesn't want it."

"Spoilsport," Maddy says. She pouts as long as it takes us to go through the front doors of the nearest clothes store. Then she's got all sorts of things she wants me to try on: blouses, pants, skirts. I politely decline most of her suggestions.

What I don't want, Maddy takes for herself. We go into changing rooms next to each other, where Maddy talks through the wall. "I think I like the pink one better. Do you think the pink one is better?"

"They're both fine," I say. I mean it too. I think Maddy looks good in any color.

I try on a dark purple blouse. Maybe pink would look good on me, but I'm not ready to go there yet. Purple seems like a good place to start in that direction. I turn in the mirror and put a hand on my stomach. I've gained ten pounds since I moved back in with Tess. A couple more months and I'll be fat.

I snort at this. I'm definitely becoming a woman. "Something wrong?" Maddy asks.

"No, nothing's wrong. Everything's fine."

***

We get lunch in the food court. We don't usually come out here to the mall, but this is a special occasion. Maddy and I are going back to school. Different schools. Maddy's going to the state university to work on her journalism degree. I'm going to community college to decide whether college is what I want. If it is, then I can transfer to a four-year school later.

"We're going to be the best-dressed kids on campus," Maddy says. Her enthusiasm is infectious; Grace and I smile in time with her.

"I don't think that's hard at community college," I say.

"Don't start running yourself down," Maddy says. "A lot of people have started with community college and gone on to something big."

"Name one," I say.

She waves the question away. "You need to think positively. This is a chance to find yourself."

"She's right," Grace says. "You got to learn to walk before you can run."

"I guess so," I say. I know they're right. I need to

find some direction in my life. Grace's shop isn't much of a career. The way things have been going, she'll probably shut it down in a few months when she's finished with her dissertation. Then I'll be on my ass with no money and no prospects. I pat Maddy's hand. "I wouldn't be doing it if it weren't for you. Thanks for giving me the push."

"You're welcome, sweetie," she says. I feel funny when she kisses me on the cheek. It's not the way she used to when she was little. That was a loving kiss; this is just a kiss between good friends.

The phone in my purse rings. I fumble around until I find it. "Hello?"

"Hi, Stacey," Dr. Palmer says.

"Hi." I put one hand to my ear to filter out some of the noise from the food court. "I didn't expect to hear from you for a while."

Maddy and Grace look at me. I signal it's OK. Then I get up. I hurry outside, to stand opposite a couple of smokers by the front doors. "Does this mean you have good news?"

"Not as good as I'd like," Dr. Palmer says. "I've looked over the formula Luther gave us and Dr. Nath's notes."

"They're good?"

"The formula matches what we took from your blood. It's definitely FY-1978."

"That's a good thing, isn't it?"

"It is. And Dr. Nath's notes seem to be legitimate."

"Are they helpful?"

"They should be. Gita was nothing if not thorough. A lot of what she did, she documented in these files." Dr. Palmer sighs. "Maybe she knew they were coming after her."

"Maybe," I say. "Maybe she's just thorough, like you said."

The doctor sighs again. "Anyway, I think we'll have our first batch ready to test in a couple of months."

"That's great. Isn't it?" When it comes to this biology stuff I still don't understand most of what Dr. Palmer says. I figure I'll take a couple of college classes in that area.

"Yes. But there's still a long way to go before we can try it on humans. Years of testing on animals."

It's my turn to sigh. Though I've been a woman for a month now, I still check the mirror every morning to make sure there's no change. I'll have to do that for years to come. "I guess we already knew that, didn't we?"

"Right, but look on the bright side: it shouldn't take us as long now."

"Fifteen years instead of twenty?"

"Maybe. Don't lose hope, Stacey. We can beat this thing."

"I know." I smile a little and think of how many times the doctors said that to Jenny. She did beat it for three years, but eventually the disease won. Maybe that's how this will be. Maybe by the time Dr. Palmer finds a cure there won't be anything left to cure.

Then I look inside. Through the doors of the mall I can see Maddy and Grace at our table. Maddy sees me and waves. I wave back to her. Things could be a lot worse. This isn't the end for me; it's a new beginning. Like Dr. Palmer said, it's a chance to start over again. Maybe this time I'll get it right.

"Thanks for letting me know, Doctor," I say. "And good luck."

"You too."

I hang up the phone. Then I go to rejoin my friends.

Also From P.T. Dilloway:

Second Chance (Chances Are #2): When Stacey Chance and her friend Madison are kidnapped by a Chinese scientist, they're given a dose of an experimental drug, one that causes them to revert back to children. As they search for a cure, Stacey and Madison get a second chance at childhood.

Last Chance (Chances Are #3): Five years after she first became a young woman thanks to an experimental drug, Stacey Chance has come to enjoy her new life. That life gets even better when the man she loves pops the question. But when that experimental drug starts to wear off and an old enemy from Detective Steve Fischer's past resurfaces, Stacey's wonderful new life is thrown into chaos.

A Hero's Journey (Tales of the Scarlet Knight, Volume 1): Dr. Emma Earl never wanted to be a hero. But when she finds a magic suit of armor that can deflect bullets and turn her invisible, she becomes part of an ancient war between good and evil. It's up to Emma as the latest incarnation of the heroic Scarlet Knight to save Rampart City from the fiendish Black Dragoon and his plan to rule first the city and then the whole world.

Acknowledgements:

I'd like to thank Jean Seiler-Bonifacio for beta reading this and helping to lend a female perspective to the story. You rock!

About the Author

P.T. Dilloway has been a writer for most of his life. He completed his first story in third grade and received an 'A' for the assignment. Around that time, he was also placed in a local writing contest for a television station, receiving an action figure in lieu of a trophy, thus securing his love with the written word. Since then, he's continued to spend most of his free time writing and editing. In the last twenty years, he's completed nearly forty novels.

In 2012, Solistice Publishing published P.T.'s superhero novel *A Hero's Journey, Tales of the Scarlet Knight #1*. That same year, December House Publishing included P.T.'s flash fiction stories as part of the collection *We Are Now*. Also in 2012, P.T. created the imprint Planet 99 Publishing to publish the remainder of the Tales of the Scarlet Knight series as well as a variety of other novels, all of which can be found at http://www.planet99publishing.com.

When not writing, P.T. enjoys reading and photographing Michigan's many lighthouses. In order to pay the bills, he earned an accounting degree from Saginaw Valley State University in 2000 and for the past ten years has worked as a payroll accountant in Detroit. Visit his website: http://www.ptdilloway.com

Made in the USA
Charleston, SC
23 August 2013